ILLUSIONS OF WARSAW

David Bradwell

ABOUT THE AUTHOR

David Bradwell grew up in the north east of England but now lives in Hitchin in Hertfordshire. He has written for publications as diverse as Smash Hits and the Sunday Times and is a former winner of the PPA British Magazine Writer of the Year Award. Aside from writing, he runs a hosiery company with web sites at www.stockingshq.com and www.tightsandmore.com.

Get in touch at:
www.davidbradwell.com

ILLUSIONS OF WARSAW

A suspicious suicide. A vengeful girl. Connecting the dots could send a group of friends to the morgue...

Warsaw, 1997. Fugitive journalist Clare Woodbrook refuses to ignore a colleague's questionable death. Teaming up with a fellow reporter, she uncovers a trail of corruption that could expose the killer. But when they get too close to the truth, they're framed for a series of bloody crimes.

London. Secretive, bright-eyed Louise arrives on Anna Burgin's doorstep, claiming to be Clare's long-lost niece. But her true agenda is simple and deadly: revenge for her father's murder. And her ill-conceived plan to infiltrate a crew of con artists puts both Anna and her in a vicious gangster's crosshairs.

As Clare discovers shadowy links between Poland and Britain, she races against time to clear her name and reveal the culprit before more body bags fill. But with Louise and Anna caught up in the mess in England, it might be too late to save everyone...

Can the unlikely team catch a sinister mastermind before they're ruthlessly erased?

Illusions of Warsaw is the fifth book in the twisty Anna Burgin mystery-thriller series.

ILLUSIONS OF WARSAW

A Gripping British Mystery Thriller - Anna Burgin Book 5

ISBN: 978-1-9993394-6-3

Illusions Of Warsaw was first published in 2020 by Pure Fiction
Copyright © David Bradwell, 2020
www.davidbradwell.com

For Ray and Gwen, with love.

Chapter 1

Monday, January 6th, 1997

THE alarm sounded, but he ignored it, as he'd been paid to do. A glance at the CCTV screen showed that everything was in order. In the corridor, at least. He reached out to mute the siren before anyone came running, asking awkward questions. Because that was all part of the deal.

And when they opened the cell and found the body the next morning? Well, then there'd be more questions still. He'd be called in front of his superiors, given a dressing-down. He might even lose his job. But again, it wasn't a problem. They'd made provisions for that.

They'd promised him a generous monthly allowance, for as long as he needed it. No rush, they'd said. Take your time. Treat it as a paid holiday, and only return to work when you feel like it. When you find something better, with higher pay and more time to spend with your family. We'll look after you. All you need to do is ignore the alarm.

They hadn't mentioned that they'd change their minds as

soon as the furore died down, or that his body would be discovered weeks later, on the outskirts of Warsaw, naked, in a shallow grave.

Chapter 2

Sunday, January 19th, 1997

GEORGE Brandrick slammed down the phone.

"Useless prick."

"Has he still not fixed it?"

Brandrick scowled at the man opposite.

"What do you think?"

"I think it's not my problem, George. In fact, I think it's none of my concern whatsoever."

"Yeah? Well you can piss off as well." George stood up, rubbed his face with both hands, running his fingers through his close-cropped beard, then turned back to the man. "You still here?"

"I'm not going anywhere."

"Really?"

"Not until you tell me how I explain this to Mr Devlin."

"Jason!" George called out to his bodyguard, who came into the room, all muscle and testosterone. "Would you please escort our friend off the premises?"

"Not wise, George," said the man, as the bodyguard moved alongside him.

Brandrick took a step forward, and poked a finger in his visitor's face.

"Hamish, I don't give a flying fuck what you tell Mr Devlin. He's going to have to wait. We're all going to have to wait. And until then, he can spend all day, and all night, shagging your mother, for all I care. Understood?"

Hamish laughed.

"Is that the best you can do? You're letting yourself down, big man."

George moved closer still, then lowered his voice to little above a whisper.

"Piss. Off."

"Okay." Hamish sighed, louder than necessary, then headed to the door, brushing against the bulk of the bodyguard, who was still standing silently, menacingly, watching the drama unfold. "I'll be in touch, George. I'll let you know what Mr Devlin says. Enjoy your Sunday. I'll be going to church later. I'll put in a good word for you." He opened the door, but turned back before finally leaving. "Oh, and George? You are aware Mr Devlin is not a patient man?"

But he didn't get a response, apart from a shove in the chest from the bodyguard, who then slammed the door behind him.

Brandrick exhaled, returned to his desk and started tapping his fingers absent-mindedly on the surface. A trickle of sweat made its way past the starched collar of his Thomas Pink shirt.

"Problem?" asked Jason, taking a chair opposite.

There were always problems. But some were bigger than others.

"Not as much as I expect there'll be for Hamish, when he goes back empty-handed."

"What does he want? Money?"

George shook his head and smiled, in spite of the pounding

headache that was beginning to seriously grate. He liked Jason. The man had his uses. He could be intimidating when he had to be, but sadly, he wasn't always the brightest. Still, he'd proven to be a loyal servant over the last eighteen months. Better to have him on the payroll than in the employ of a rival. George was well aware of how Jason liked to deal with conflict.

"No, not money," said George. "Money would be easy. I'd have still told him to piss off, though. Devlin needs to learn that he can't send his lackey with a list of demands and expect me to bend over and take it, however he chooses."

"What then?"

"Information." George turned off his computer, and stood up. He had better things to be doing on a Sunday.

"What sort of information?"

He stopped and fixed his bodyguard with an irritated stare.

"You ask a lot of questions."

Jason raised his hands.

"I'm just curious, boss."

"Yeah, well, to paraphrase the proverb, curiosity killed the twa-" He stopped himself just in time, aware that he was losing his temper. It wasn't Jason's fault, but Tony Devlin's messenger had got under his skin. He sat down again, and turned to face the younger man. "I'm sorry, son. It's nothing. Devlin's daughter is in a bit of trouble, that's all. She's got herself arrested for possession, and she's been paying for her habit the hard way, on her back."

"Shit."

"Exactly. He's not happy. He thinks I might know who her dealer is. And he thinks the same guy's her pimp. And while we're on, the father of her unborn child."

Jason exhaled.

"That's quite the hat-trick. I wouldn't want to be in his shoes."

"Exactly. But I'm not going to give up one of our own, am I?"

"He thinks it's one of ours?"

"He knows it's one of ours. He just doesn't know which one. So I have to pretend I'm doing my best to find out."

"And if you don't?"

George shrugged.

"He's threatening to turn informant. Could cause me a bit of trouble if it gets out of hand."

"You want me to sort it?"

George paused for a moment. He didn't know what he wanted, but he knew something would have to give, sooner or later. Hamish would be back, cocky as ever. Perhaps it was time to put him in his place, and sort Devlin once and for all. But sending Jason would stoke a feud that had been brewing for years, and he really didn't want to think about the repercussions of that.

"Leave it with me," he said. "That might become necessary. You're a good lad. Let me think about things this afternoon and I'll let you know." He collected his coat and keys, and headed towards the door. "Don't go too far. I'll call you if I need you."

But he hoped it wouldn't come to that. There was one other person he could call.

Harry Rushton gestured for the young woman to follow him through the hotel lobby, then ushered her to the lift without saying a word. He'd recognised her from the picture, although her hair looked darker and less bottle-blonde than he'd expected. The navy trouser suit and red scarf were perfect. Exactly as he'd suggested. When the doors closed, removing the threat of being overheard, he finally introduced himself.

"I hope you're Louise," he said, with a coy smile, once he'd confirmed his own name. "Clare has extolled your virtues in a most enthusiastic manner."

"I am, and thank you." She returned the smile. She'd been

warned that he was an old-fashioned charmer, but immediately felt drawn to him, and was impressed by his immaculate old-English dress sense. "I've heard lots about you, too."

"I am deeply flattered," he said, with a sparkle in his grey, all-knowing eyes. "I hope some of it was agreeable, although I fear for the fruits of her dark and elaborate imagination." He chuckled. "But tell me, my dear, your accent? It is quite delightful, but I venture to suggest it is not native to any of the London boroughs?"

It wasn't the first time she'd had the query, but she'd never heard it expressed in that way before.

"I'm Polish. I grew up near Kielce, although I've been living in Warsaw. To study."

"Ah, very good." He took a moment to look her up and down, clearly admiring the lithe figure, and the understated elegance of her outfit. "I'm afraid my experience of your motherland extends no further than Gdansk. I always wanted to venture inland, but alas, the opportunity has been denied, and now I fear my travelling days are largely behind me. But I should love to learn about your upbringing. It's been a tumultuous time."

"It has."

The lift doors pinged open. Harry stood aside so his companion could exit, although he extended an arm to indicate which way to turn.

"Before we cross the threshold," he continued, once the doors had closed, "I ought to ask how much you know about the others? I assume you've had a thorough briefing, but one feels it is pertinent to check."

"I've only really heard the basics. Adam's the boss, Abby is a technical genius, and when it comes to Toby, I should be on my guard."

Harry nodded.

"Very good. And yes, I concur with that assessment of young Toby. He is enthusiastic with a good heart, but is prone to a certain impetuosity. And he will doubtless fall in love with you, my dear, the moment he registers your fine Slavic beauty." He leaned in closer to whisper, bending slightly. "Clare has asked me to look after you, but I think you will flourish if your reputation bears scrutiny. And she is a very dear friend, so you must never fear you are troubling me, if anything ever causes concern."

"Thank you." She smiled again, and offered him a handshake. "I look forward to hopefully working with you."

Louise took one last look around. It was about to begin.

And with that, Harry opened the door.

Chapter 3

Sunday, January 19th, 1997

I MUST admit, I love a slap-up Sunday lunch, but it's a superhuman effort to be up in time to cook one, especially - ironically - on a weekend. And even more so when you live on your own, and there's nobody to help with the kitchen chaos that follows in its aftermath.

So, when the call came, I was easily persuaded. I was promised the full works, washed down with a bottle of gorgeous wine, all in the company of one of my oldest and dearest friends. And then she insisted that it would be her treat, which immediately made me nervous, because when she's up to something, there's always a risk of carnage.

The problem with a friend like Clare Woodbrook is that her frame of reference is different to everyone else's. It's not only that she's super intelligent, independent and self-assured, but more that she gave up her career as an investigative journalist to mastermind an art fraud, and it's increasingly difficult to keep count of the people she's killed. Even if she insists she's a reformed character now.

Yet despite knowing that she's seen, and done, some horrendous things, I have, for a long time, been in awe of her. I feel privileged to be in her company. She makes me feel safe, which is ironic, given that she's previously pointed a gun at me, and several times nearly had me murdered. No matter how well I get to know her, and how many secrets she's shared, I've never come close to really understanding what goes on behind those beautiful hazel eyes. She can be as funny as she is infuriating, and sometimes as warm as she can be brutal. I am proud to consider her one of my very closest friends, but I'm sure the gingerbread man once also thought that about the fox.

I saw her approach through the maze of crowded tables and stood to greet her. We hugged in lieu of the usual double cheek kiss.

"Anna, it's wonderful to see you," she said.

"Fantastic hair," I replied, admiring the back-combed work of art that would have been the height of fashion a decade ago.

"It's a tribute to your goth phase." She winked. She'd gone heavy on the eyeliner too. Part of me thought she was taking the piss, but most of all, I was delighted to see her. I couldn't place her perfume, but it smelled expensive.

"I love your coat, too," I said, as she eased herself out of it, and passed it to the waiter.

"Thank you. And you look as gorgeous as ever."

I didn't feel gorgeous. I'd tried to make an effort, but next to Clare and her effortless chic, I would always feel underdressed. I'd tried to be clever, mind you, and gone for a slightly rebellious and yet still-sophisticated biker look, with a leather jacket, black skirt and my new knee-length boots. But I'd rather ruined the no-nonsense appearance by banging my knee on the underside of the table as I'd stood up to greet her, and now there was a ladder in my tights that I was doing my best to hide. It was a shame because I really, really liked the boots, and I'd have been very happy for her to notice those.

We took our seats opposite each other, and she reached out across the small marble table to squeeze my hand. There was never any hint of awkwardness, despite our shared past. And although her appearance changed regularly, in an effort to preserve her liberty, there was a warm familiarity that I found deeply reassuring.

"It's been too long," she said. "Tell me everything."

I laughed. There wasn't much to tell.

"The flat's good, work is interesting. I'm just battling on, really. How are you? Are you in London long?"

"Just for a few days."

The waiter returned with menus, and asked if we wanted to order drinks. Clare glanced at me, then scanned the wine list and made a suggestion. I nodded.

"So what exactly are you doing now?" she asked.

"The job title is content producer, but it's an Internet start-up so a bit of everything. Lots of meetings. It's an exciting industry."

"But quite a change from photography."

"It is, but it pays the bills."

She nodded.

"I do worry about you," she said. "My offer is always there, if you'd like to get your studio back up and running."

The memory of my studio being ransacked was still vivid. There was no way I could afford to replace everything, especially when my insurance was declared invalid, but I have always valued my independence.

"I know, and I'm grateful, but life moves on. Sometimes I think things happen for a reason."

The waiter reappeared with a bottle of wine, and offered me a taste. It was exceptional.

"Did they give you stock options?" Clare asked, once the glasses were poured.

"They did."

"Hold on to those. They might be worth something."

"Hopefully. We'll see. Anyway, more importantly, what are you up to?"

She shrugged, as noncommittal as ever.

"Oh, you know. Trying to be a good person and keep out of mischief."

I laughed again. I could believe she was *trying* to be a good person, but mischief and mayhem were never far away. But I wasn't going to get any more detail - especially surrounded by diners in a busy Camden restaurant.

"And how's the new flat?" she asked.

"It's good. I'm settled now, I think. It took a bit of adjustment, but I'm used to being on my own. I'll take you back for coffee if you like, and give you the guided tour."

"I'd love that. So, still no sign of a boyfriend?"

"It's the great dating paradox. Anyone attractive enough for me to fancy could, by definition, do so much better."

She laughed, and so the conversation flowed. Our roast beef arrived, and I couldn't help but be impressed by the presentation, despite the nagging doubt that artistic flair made up for smaller-than-average portions. The wine flowed too, and I began to lose track of time. We shared stories, and discussed current affairs, Princess Diana's campaign against landmines, the chances of Tony Blair winning the forthcoming election, and Brian Harvey being sacked from East 17. I doubted Clare could name an East 17 record, but she didn't let it show.

And yet, all the while, I was aware that she was building up to something. It came just as we were considering the dessert menu.

"I do actually have a favour to ask," she said, appearing bashful all of a sudden.

Here we go, I thought. I noticed that she was refilling my glass as she said it, which kind of hinted at the scale of the thing.

"Fire away," I said. "Anything to help."

"It's a bit of an imposition, so I absolutely understand if you want to say no, but I will make it worth your while."

"You don't need to do that. I'd be happy to help you. Depending on what it is, and as long as it's not illegal."

She glanced to the table closest to us, as though checking that we weren't being overheard, and I made a mental note to try to speak more quietly, despite the wine.

"Of course it's not illegal. What do you take me for?" she continued. "I don't even know if it'd be possible, but I'm looking for a room for my niece. It's just for a few days because she's new in London, until she finds a place of her own. And I hate to ask really, but I wondered if you had space and would be willing to put her up for a bit? Maybe up to a week?"

"Wow." I hadn't been expecting that.

"I'll pay towards the rent, obviously. But seriously, it's not a problem if you want to say no. She could stay at my flat but I won't be there, and it would be nice to know she was with somebody."

It took me a moment to process.

"Sorry, I shouldn't have asked, really," Clare continued, but I waved her apology away.

"No, I'm sure that could be done," I said. "It would be nice to have somebody there and honestly, it'll be no problem. But who is she? How old is she?"

"She's called Louise. She's nineteen, and she's had a bit of trouble at home, so she's moving to London to make a fresh start. I offered to help but I'm only here for a couple of days."

"When you say trouble at home, do you mean she fell out with her parents?" If she was having trouble with her mother, I empathised. I knew all about that. "Is she some kind of a wild child?"

"No, far from it. It's a bit complicated but that's all in the past. Honestly, she's lovely. You'll like her."

"I'm sure I will."

"So you'll help me?" She looked so touched and humble. "Only if you're absolutely sure."

"Of course I am and of course I will."

"Thank you." She reached out and squeezed my hand again. I noticed she wasn't wearing her Ceylon sapphire ring, which was unusual. And then I thought she'd probably left it at home deliberately so that I'd notice and be distracted, and wouldn't then ask the obvious question. One nil to me for rumbling the plan. All the more reason to ask it. I took a deep breath and frowned, in an effort to stop myself laughing. Nothing was ever straightforward with Clare.

"Who is she really?" I asked.

She looked taken aback by the question, which was encouraging. I wasn't going to give up.

"It's just - correct me if I'm wrong on this," I continued, "but technically in order to have a niece, you'd need to be her aunt. And in order for that to be the case, you'd need to have a brother or sister. Which, in all the years I've known you, you've thus far neglected to mention. In fact, you're famously an only child."

"Your point?"

"My point, without wanting to sound anything less than completely subservient, is that you struggle to qualify for the basic criteria of having a niece. I may be wrong."

She folded her arms, fixing her eyes on me with a hurt expression. I found it very difficult to suppress a giggle.

"So which is it?" I continued.

"Which is it, what?"

"Your secret sibling. Brother or sister? Possibly both. Names? Where do they live? What do they do? Why have you kept them secret all this time?"

"Louise was adopted."

I laughed.

"*Louise* was adopted? That still doesn't actually change anything. It's not Louise that's the issue here. It's her non-existent parents."

She frowned, then made a show of lighting a cigarette, with exaggerated nonchalance.

"Do you want to meet her or not?"

"Ooh, touchy."

"Which is not an acceptable answer to a simple yes or no question."

"Neither is changing the subject."

"I'm pretty sure I haven't changed the subject. The subject is my niece. If anything, I've got us back onto the subject."

"Except if she isn't your niece then the subject is rather a moot point."

Clare sighed.

"Why would I lie about having a niece?"

"I don't know. You tell me."

"I wouldn't."

"A normal person wouldn't. No disrespect." I raised my eyebrows.

"How's Danny?" she asked.

"See? Now you are changing the subject."

"I got bored of waiting for you to answer a simple yes or no question. Is he still with Lisa?"

"And now you're trying to provoke me. I'm wise to your methods, Ms W."

"Well, is he?"

I tried to imitate a hurt and slightly confused expression.

"Should we pour another glass of wine and start again?" I asked eventually.

"Excellent idea," she said. I was thoroughly enjoying myself, although deep down I knew the alcohol was inhibiting my ability to be alert to the warning signs.

Chapter 4

HARRY stood aside so that Louise could enter the room ahead of him.

The hotel suite was impressive, and was clearly costing a fortune, but if the stories she'd heard about Adam were true, he wouldn't blink at the cost.

"You must be Louise," said the man walking towards her with his hand outstretched. "Adam Kirwin." She was as impressed by the firm grip as she'd expected to be, and used both of her own hands to return it. Adam introduced the two people rising from the sofa. "This is Abby McDowell, and Toby Morgan."

"Pleased to meet you," said Louise, shaking Abby's hand. But then she winked at Toby, and instead of a handshake, gave him a hug.

"Coffee?" asked Adam.

"Yes, please, white no sugar," said Louise.

"I'll get them, babe," said Abby, while Toby re-took his place on the sofa, and Harry sat alongside him.

"I love the picture," said Louise, moving to the fireplace and admiring the canvas that dominated the wall above. "Is it an original?"

"It's a copy I'm afraid, but quite beautifully done," said Adam. "You appreciate art, do you?"

"I do. I'm not an expert, but I know what I like."

Adam indicated to an armchair, and then perched himself on the edge of the desk while Louise sat down, placing her clutch bag on the arm of the chair. It was considered unlucky in Poland to place a bag on the floor. She smiled at Abby when the coffee was delivered. There was an expectant silence in the room.

"So, Harry said you come highly recommended," said Adam, at last. He was younger than she'd expected, but dressed in an immaculate suit, and clearly looked after himself, with dark hair and a tanned, clean-shaven face. She guessed at mid-thirties. Abby was younger still, and black, with blonde streaks in her hair. Toby's suit was less well-fitted than Adam's, and his demeanour much more casual, but she was impressed by his piercing blue eyes.

"As do you," she said, turning back to Adam. "You have quite a formidable reputation. Thank you for agreeing to see me."

"Well, let's see if we can think of a way of working together. How much, exactly, do you know about what we do?"

Louise took a sip of the coffee before responding.

"The basics," she said, "are that you run an impressive crew." She nodded in the direction of the others. "You specialise in the long con. You're the boss. Abby is the computer genius. Toby is the newest arrival, while Harry is the old hand with years of experience, and a fearsome record at the poker table."

"That's a good start," said Adam, warmly. "And what do you know about our projects?"

"I know that you choose the marks carefully. They're generally not nice people and deserve everything that comes to them." She paused, then smiled. "And obviously it helps if they're extremely rich."

"Quite." Adam stood up, then walked round to the other side

of his desk, and picked up a folder. He crossed back to the chair and passed it to Louise.

"Here's some of our press coverage," he said.

She glanced at the contents, leafing through the first few photocopied pages.

"I think I've already read most of it," she said. "I've done my research. And I know you've taken a leap of faith just to invite me here."

"Believe me, this is a very rare occurrence, for obvious reasons. Harry vouches for you and I'm always looking at ways to develop. But no disrespect, you appear to be very young. How old are you?"

"Nineteen."

"Hmmm."

She waited for him to continue.

"We already have one *trainee*, for want of a better word," he said, looking at Toby. "I'm all for youthful vigour, but this is a tough business. You need to be brave. Believable. Creative. Adaptable. And experience plays a very big part. I can't risk fucking up an operation because I've employed some underdeveloped grifter who doesn't have strong natural instincts. If you excuse the language. So what is your experience?"

Louise shifted slightly in her chair.

"Well," she began, "obviously you know I'm from Poland, yes?" Adam nodded. "So let's just say I was raised on the black market. It's changing now, but when I was younger, if you wanted anything you had to come up with creative ways to get it. Whether it was getting hard currency, or extra rations, or anything really. We didn't have the choice we have today. If you wanted a new pair of jeans, you couldn't just walk into a shopping mall. So we learned to survive by playing the system."

"Which is all very laudable, but how does that help us?"

"Most of my experience is in the short con. And yes, I admit I don't have much experience at this kind of level, but I don't think you'd be disappointed. I *am* willing to learn. But more than that, I'm a very fast learner."

Adam nodded but didn't look convinced. He looked towards Harry.

"What do you think?" he asked.

The older man took a moment to consider his response.

"I have been in this profession, in one form or another, for most of my three score years and ten," he said at last. "And I have seen many come and many go. But the essence of everything is trust, and I trust the source of her referral. Obviously time will be the judge, but I think she would fit in well."

"Okay." Adam pinched his chin between his thumb and forefinger. He perched back on the edge of the desk. "I think before we take this any further, and before we discuss this internally, we need to see you in action."

"Okay." Louise straightened in her chair, crossing her legs. "What sort of thing did you have in mind?"

"I'm going to set you a challenge. I need you to go now, and return this afternoon, with four objects. You have five hours, so that's an hour each, plus an hour for travelling. The only rules are that they can't belong to you or anyone you know, and you can't pay for them."

"You want me to steal them?"

"Or negotiate. But you can't just borrow them. They will be specific items and each must be authentic. We will not be able to return them, so yes, steal them if necessary."

"I don't think we can ask her to do that," said Harry, from the sofa.

"No, no, I am happy to go along with it," said Louise. "And if I'm successful?"

"Then I will speak to my colleagues, and we will assess the situation. But I can't make any promises. And obviously, if you fail, then it was nice to meet you, but I'd suggest learning your trade elsewhere before coming back to me again."

"That's understandable. But I won't fail."

She glanced at Toby, who seemed to be impressed, although whether by her confidence or her appearance was open to debate. Abby's expression was harder to read, but maybe she felt a challenge to her status as the group's alpha female.

"Any questions?" asked Adam.

"No, I don't think so. Just the list of items."

"I still don't think ... " Harry began, but Adam interrupted him.

"Four things." He paused in thought. "A wallet. That's basic. A Breitling watch. Men's or women's. A pair of Christian Louboutin shoes, size six ..."

"Six? What is that in European sizes?"

"I don't know, but I'm sure you'll work it out."

"Okay."

"And a first edition novel by either Charles Dickens or Agatha Christie."

"In five hours?"

"Do you have a problem with that?"

Louise uncrossed her legs and leaned forward.

"In one sense, no. But I have to go to a meeting soon, to sort out accommodation."

Adam shrugged.

"It's a test of resourcefulness. Imagination. If you want to work with us, you'll need to prove you've got lots of both."

"Okay. I take that on board."

She reached into her bag.

"Here's the wallet," she said, turning to Toby. "This is yours, I believe."

"What the fuck?" Shocked, he patted down his jacket pockets, but found them empty.

"Thanks for the loan. And the hug." She winked again, and then stood up and handed the wallet back. "And given that this is partly a test of my negotiation skills, I have a suggestion to make."

"I'm listening," said Adam, who clearly didn't quite know what to make of what he'd witnessed.

"I'm down to three already, but I still have time constraints this afternoon, so I'm going to suggest one item in lieu of the others."

"One?"

"Yes. But it'll be a good one."

She stood patiently waiting for his response.

"Okay. I have to ask. What one item?"

"A cufflink."

Immediately all three men in the room looked at the cuffs on their shirtsleeves. Harry laughed, but Adam looked confused.

"Here you go," said Louise, walking towards him, with his missing cufflink on the open palm of her hand. But before Adam could reclaim it, she closed her fist, and then blew on her fingers.

"Ooopsadaisy, gone again," she said, then opened her hand to reveal nothing inside. She shrugged and sat back down, crossing her legs again. All eyes were upon her.

"Very good," said Adam. "But the idea was to bring me something, not make it vanish."

"I know," said Louise. "And that's the flaw, because I'm better at making things disappear. I'm still learning how to get them back. Sorry." She could sense Harry's smile from the sofa.

Adam frowned, looking perplexed. Toby and Abby sat silently, enthralled by the theatre in front of them.

"You could check on the mantlepiece, though, just in case," Louise continued, then sat back while Adam crossed the room. A moment later, he turned back with the cufflink in his hand and a smile on his face.

"Very good," he said.

"Deal?" she said.

Adam thought for a moment and then nodded with a new-found respect.

"Thank you."

She stood up.

"I will leave you to have a conversation, but look forward to speaking to you soon. And when I come back I'll bring details of a mark for you, and a plan. It's slightly unconventional but I think you'll like it."

She shook Adam's hand, then nodded at Abby and Toby. Toby seemed less keen to have a second hug. Harry stood up, and escorted her back to the lift.

"We'll be in touch, my dear," he said. Then leaned in close again before continuing in a whisper. "But, between you and me, I think he was impressed."

Louise smiled and shook his hand as the lift doors opened. And then she headed to her second meeting of the day.

Chapter 5

AT some point it occurred to me that Clare had started refilling her own glass from a bottle of mineral water, and mine from the bottle of wine. Again, I was proud that I'd spotted her plan, but it was too late to stop it working.

We opted against desserts, but as the restaurant was beginning to empty, there was no rush to vacate our table. The waiter turned up with the bill, and Clare paid, as good as her word. Obviously, I made a token attempt to contribute, but she wasn't having any of it. In fairness, she's got vastly more money than me.

"I like what you've done with your hair," she said, once she'd returned from what my American employers would describe as a comfort break.

"It's exactly the same as it's been for ages," I said, wondering where she was going with this. "In ten years' time I expect you'll have something similar." I failed to stifle a giggle.

"I know, but seriously. It suits you. It's soft and wavy and I just want to run my fingers through it." She leaned forward and reached out her hand, but I managed to intercept it.

"So, going back to Louise," I said, fighting hard to keep a degree of seriousness in my voice.

"Yes, Louise." She frowned. "Are you sure that'll be okay? She'll be no bother, I promise you. And as for rent, would a couple of hundred be enough?"

"Yes, it'll be okay and I don't want your money," I said. "But I would like to know more about her. What she does, who her parents are, that kind of thing."

She snapped her fingers.

"Exactly. So what I've done is asked her to join us, to say hello, so you can meet each other." She looked very pleased with herself. I glanced around the rapidly emptying restaurant but there wasn't anyone who looked even vaguely like a candidate. There was a family with two young children, and several couples who didn't seem to be paying us any attention. "She should be here in a moment."

As if on cue, a young woman in a navy trouser suit and red scarf came in from the street, spotted us, and started heading over. Clare followed my eyeline, and then quickly put her cigarettes in her bag, before standing up to greet the new arrival. She made the introductions. My first impressions were entirely positive. Louise had an instantly engaging demeanour, and I couldn't visualise her smashing my place up.

She grabbed a chair from an empty table, and pulled it up to ours.

"Glass of wine?" I asked, looking at the bottle, and deciding it wouldn't be a bad thing if somebody else finished it instead of me. I'm not normally that mature.

"No, I'm driving," she said, in an unusual accent that threw me slightly. "I'll order a Diet Coke if I can catch the waiter, although I can't stop long."

"Leave it to me," said Clare, and she headed to the bar, leaving the two of us together.

"So, Louise, lovely to meet you," I said. "Clare's told me absolutely nothing about you."

She laughed.

"She's told me a lot about you. What should I call you? Miss Burgin? Auntie Anna?" I could tell she thought the charade was as ridiculous as I did.

"Just Anna is fine. Do you call Clare Auntie Clare?"

"No."

"Thought not." I did a secret internal head shake. "What do you actually do? You're new to London, apparently."

"Yes, well, kind of. I'm hoping to get into acting, so I thought this would be the place to be. There are a couple of part-time courses that I'd like to take, but I need to find a place and get myself sorted." She paused. "Clare said she was going to ask you if it would be possible to stay for a few days. I hope you don't mind."

"She did, and I don't."

"Oh, thank you." Her smile was beautiful. She looked so young and innocent, I immediately wanted to take her home and protect her from the influence of her non-aunt. Clare returned with the drink.

"Thank you," said Louise, and a look passed between them that I couldn't decipher.

"How are you getting on?" asked Clare.

"All good," I said, and I meant it. She seemed nice. It could be fun. I'd lived on my own since leaving my former flatmate, Danny, in a fit of jealous pique.

We made small talk for a few minutes. I asked Louise about her first impressions of London, but Clare kept interrupting, presumably paranoid in case I asked how they'd met and how long they'd known each other. By the time Louise said she had to be leaving, I was looking forward to getting her on my own.

I gave her my address and arranged for her to visit my flat

later that afternoon. Then she disappeared as abruptly as she'd arrived.

"So what did you think?" Clare asked me, once we were back on our own.

"She seems nice," I said. "But I couldn't help noticing the accent."

"What accent?"

"Louise's accent." I expect she caught the eye-roll. "It wasn't quite as, how should I say, cut-glass English as I was expecting."

Clare retrieved the cigarettes from her bag and lit one. I was tipsy enough to wonder if I could have one too, but I managed to stop myself from asking.

"Anna, have I ever been less than completely honest with you?" she asked.

"Yes."

"Okay, let me rephrase that. Have I ever been less than completely honest with you, apart from when it was in your own best interests for me not to be?"

"Yes."

"God, you're hard work."

I was enjoying this.

"Do you want a third attempt?" I asked. "Perhaps from a different angle. Something like: 'Have I ever actually been less than completely *dishonest* with you'?"

I was pleased with that, but Clare looked unhappy. I decided to help myself to one of her cigarettes anyway, but she slapped my hand away.

"Just tell me what this is really about," I said, getting back to the subject.

"You want to know?"

"Yes. Obviously."

"Louise is moving to London. She wants to be an actress. She needs somewhere to stay."

"Yes, I know all that. Although I still don't understand why she couldn't stay at your flat."

"My flat?"

"Yes, your flat. Or have you forgotten you've got a flat?"

"No, of course I haven't forgotten I've got a flat."

I made a second attempt at a Silk Cut, with the same result, and decided to give up.

"So?" I said.

"So, she can't stay there in case any bad people come looking for me. It would be too risky. And in any case, I'm hardly ever there. And on top of that, I worry about you being lonely, so she would be some company for you."

Inside I was creased up with laughter, but I desperately hoped it wasn't showing.

"That's very kind," I said.

"Exactly. I am."

"And what kind of actress does she want to be?"

"I don't know. Are there different types?"

"Of course there are. Stage, screen, musical theatre."

"Ah yes, I forgot you knew a screen actor once. Remind me how that ended?"

"Oooh." She was referring to a former short-term boyfriend who very nearly murdered me, until Clare came to my rescue. I'd tried to forget, but the image still haunted me. I've never been very successful at relationships, but that was by far the worst. I took another sip of my wine to wash away the taste of the memory. "You know very well how that ended. With a mess on my living room floor."

"Ah yes. Oopsie."

She was playing with me.

"I don't know what kind of actress," she continued. "And the accent is because she grew up in Poland, okay? And that, in a nutshell, is why I haven't often spoken about her over the years, because until she got in touch about moving to London, she was always part of my extended family that I didn't see very often."

It sounded plausible, but was obviously nonsense. It still didn't explain Clare's lack of siblings.

"Just promise me one thing," I said, trying to be serious for a moment.

"Anything you like."

"It's nothing elaborate. I'd be very happy to help. Just promise me I'm not going to find myself immersed in some sort of chaos and end up getting shot."

Clare took slightly longer than I'd expected to reply.

"I'll do my very best to make sure that doesn't happen," she said.

In retrospect, I should never drink wine with Clare. Because the warning signs were there.

"George," said the voice on the phone. "You wanted to speak to me."

"I did," George said as he pushed open the door from the underground car park and emerged on the pavement outside his Battersea apartment. "Thanks for getting back so quickly."

"Is it about your friend?"

"You've heard the rumours then?"

The tone of the voice changed. It sounded more serious.

"I have. You've met young Hamish, I gather?"

"Don't even start me on that bastard."

George unlocked his door, opening it to expose a tiled hallway.

"So how can I help you?" the voice said.

"You know exactly how you can help me," said George.

"I know how *you* can help *me*. But when I asked for your assistance, you didn't seem keen."

"Yeah? Well things have changed."

"So we have a deal?"

George hesitated. Nothing ever came without consequences.

"We've got a deal," he said, at last.

"Wise decision."

He ended the call, but before he could remove his coat, the landline started ringing in the hallway. He picked up the receiver.

"It's me again," said the same voice.

"How the hell did you get this number?"

"That's not important. I just wanted to make sure you weren't going to change your mind, that's all."

The line went dead. The point had been made.

Chapter 6

I WAS fast asleep on the sofa when the doorbell went. It took me a moment to realise where I was and what time of day it was, but then the bell rang again, so I staggered in the direction of the communal hallway, flicking on the front room light as I went.

Louise was standing on the doorstep, by herself. The navy suit had gone, in favour of skin-tight black jeans and a dark grey padded jacket. In my slightly befuddled state, I wondered where she'd managed to get changed. In the back of her car? And then, how come she had a car anyway, when she'd only just arrived in London? There was so much I needed to learn.

"You found it okay?" I asked, once she'd stepped inside, realising I'd just stated the obvious. "Come on in and I'll show you round." She didn't have a suitcase, but she did have a box of chocolates, which was as welcome as it was unexpected. She was taller than me, but there again, everyone is.

I led her through to the front room first, decided the main light was far too bright, so turned the dimmer down and switched on a lava lamp that was perched on top of a bookcase - even though it would take an hour or so to warm up and get exciting. I put the chocolates on the coffee table, wondering how long I should delay getting stuck into them, without looking impolite.

"What a beautiful room," said Louise, with apparent sincerity. I'm not sure what she was used to, back in Poland, but I'd gone for tidy and functional rather than outright flamboyance. The big bay window helped, though. It was what had sold the place to me when I was looking for somewhere to rent. The flat had been painted in neutral colours before I arrived, and furnished with two cream leather sofas, albeit one was larger than the other.

"Thank you. Let me take your coat."

The guided tour didn't take long. I gave her the tiniest glimpse of my bedroom, showed her to hers, reassured her that I had enough spare sheets and pillows to make up the bed, and then took her through to the kitchen - pointing out the bathroom on the way. I like my kitchen, even though I'm hardly the world's greatest chef. It's reasonably modern, with built-in appliances including a dishwasher that I must admit was a higher priority than an oven.

"Tea? Coffee?" I asked.

"Tea please," she replied. "With just a little bit of milk."

That was handy. I didn't have any coffee. I filled the kettle, flicked it on, and put a Yorkshire tea bag into each of two mugs. Nothing but the best for a VIP visitor. Then grabbed a couple of ibuprofen with a glass of water, to fend off what was shaping up to be a late-afternoon hangover.

"So, tell me about the acting," I said, while waiting for the water to boil. "Is it something you've always wanted to do?"

"It is, but opportunities were limited at home. We used to make our own entertainment when I was young. Put on little plays and things. I always loved dressing up and having fun. We didn't have many TV channels."

"I can imagine. It must have been so different." I poured the water into the mugs and started stirring. "Presumably everything is changing now?"

"Completely." She looked wistful. "The restrictions have been removed but now money speaks. If you've got money you can build anything. It's chaos. The queues have gone but there is more violence. Fascists fighting anti-fascists. There's a long way to go."

"Wow. I'm always amazed about how little I know."

I passed her a mug and we took them through to the front room, and each took a place on the larger sofa. I was eyeing the chocolates again, and deciding the threshold had been met, peeled off the cellophane, and offered them to Louise, hoping she wouldn't go for a nutty one.

"Are you still keen to move in, now you've seen it?" I asked.

"I'd love to, if it's still okay with you. When would be convenient with you?"

"When were you thinking? Literally any time from now is good for me. I've got to make the bed, but aside from that it's good to go."

"Really?" Her voice cracked, as though I'd said the kindest thing she'd ever heard.

"Of course. Consider it yours."

"I stayed in a horrible B&B last night," she said, with a little shudder. "I couldn't stand another night so moved out this morning. I found another for tonight but if it would be okay to come here instead, I'd be incredibly grateful."

"You'd be very welcome."

"Thank you." Impulsively she reached across to hug me, but then withdrew almost as quickly, as though unsure if she'd committed a grand faux pas. My smile, I hope, was reassuring.

"The only thing that concerns me is parking," I said. "You mentioned you had a car, but during the week, this street is residents only. There's a public car park a couple of minutes away that I can show you. Not sure what they charge though. You'd be all right tonight, but you'd need to move it in the morning."

"That's okay. It's only a hire car from the airport. I ought to give it back really."

"Perfect." I helped myself to another chocolate, then remembered I was supposed to be meeting a friend for dinner. I still felt full from lunch. What a day. Most Sundays are spent doing housework, reading the newspapers, or sleeping. The clock on my video recorder said it was nearly half past five, which gave me a couple of hours to get ready. I explained this to Louise, but she said she would be okay to stay in on her own. It would give her a chance to get unpacked. And hopefully not burgle me.

"Tell me more about the acting then," I said, keen to know more. "Are you looking at stage or screen? What are the courses?"

"Both. And whatever comes up, really. It's the wrong time of year for drama school, but I've found a couple of part-time ones. There's one starting in a couple of weeks, actually, although I need to know more about it. It's only a one-week introduction."

"Sounds good. Have you done much already? Any Meisner technique?" Her expression told me she'd never heard of it. I expect she wondered how I had, but hoped Clare hadn't told her about my previous failed, yet deadly fling.

"Nothing yet. I've got a lot to learn."

I was desperate to ask about her relationship with Clare, but decided it would be better to approach that once we knew each other a little better. There were more practical issues to address first.

"What are you going to do for money while you're here?" I asked, then wondered if I'd been a bit too personal. Luckily, she seemed unfazed.

"I was hoping to find a part-time job, maybe in a restaurant. I've saved up a bit to get started."

"And do you have any idea how long you're planning to stay in London?"

"It depends on everything really. Once I get settled and find a place, and see how things are going, I'll know more. Or I might go back to Poland, and get a proper job and ... Well, who knows?"

We chatted for another twenty minutes, but then, looking at the time, I apologised and said I had to start getting ready to go out. Louise went to get her bags from the car, giving me time to make up the bed. Then there was a quick lesson in how the TV remote controls worked, before I told her to help herself to anything if she got hungry. That said, I also drew her attention to the takeaway menus pinned to the cork noticeboard in the kitchen, because the cupboards were largely bare.

Shortly before seven, I was ready to depart, but then had a complete rethink on my outfit. I'd already used every ounce of my understanding of fashion psychology ahead of the lunch with Clare, but this was another challenge altogether. I wanted to look self-assured, calm and confident, but also slightly mysterious and seductive, without being tarty. In essence I wanted to give the impression that I could look after myself, and that I was very happy indeed to be on my own, but by extension that anyone not spending time with me was missing out. And if it was their own fault, and they were filled with deep regret, then so much the better. Not that I'm bitter.

I spent longer than normal on my make-up, trying to make the most of my eyes, and thought about tying my hair back, but then decided to let it flow freely, in case I needed something to hide tears behind. I opted for a red dress in the end, with suitably high and uncomfortable shoes. Okay, so it was borderline tarty, but I had a point to prove, and better that than looking like a mouse. A dab of Paris, for old times' sake, and a long, wool overcoat sealed the deal.

Louise was on the phone when I passed through the living room on my way out. I think I took her by surprise. She was whispering with a sense of urgency, and immediately ended the call. I didn't hear what she was saying, but I didn't have time to worry about that.

"You look amazing," she said, turning towards me, slightly flushed. "If you're meeting a man, he's very lucky indeed."

"Thank you." I was grateful for the reassurance. "And I am. Although actually, I want him to realise that he's been incredibly unlucky." That confused her. "I'll explain later." And with that, I headed out into the night.

———

"A glass of something uplifting, my dear?"

Harry Rushton made his way to the drinks cabinet, while Clare removed a copy of the day's Sunday Times Magazine from the armchair and settled down in its place, removing her shoes and tucking her legs underneath.

"Maybe a small Baileys," she said, tracing her fingers over the leather arm of the chair. "Or if not, whatever you're having. Don't open a bottle on my account."

Harry smiled and raised a couple of airline miniatures.

"It pays to travel with the upper classes," he said. "An ice cube, or several?"

"No, thanks, just as it comes." She laughed. "I'm trying to picture you actually buying a plane ticket. Are you getting a bit extravagant in your old age?"

"One has to have one's adventures," he said with a wink, passing her the glass.

Clare smiled.

"I won't ask," she said.

"It's prudent not to."

Harry picked up a remote control, pressed a button, and the gentle strains of a piano edged into the room from the floor-standing Monitor Audio speakers.

"Chopin's Nocturnes," he said. "Frédéric never fails to set the scene wonderfully when the discussion turns to Poland."

"I've always admired your attention to detail."

Clare thought back to the first time they'd met, and how close she'd come to exposing him, when she'd uncovered a scam that subsequently made headlines. He was a rascal, no doubt about it, but she'd been seduced by his charm, and had chosen to leave out his name when she filed her copy. Ever since, he'd been a valuable source of information, and he'd never been less than fair when she'd called upon him.

Harry lowered himself into the opposite chair, and took a sip of his brandy.

"So, my dear, I expect you want to know how it went?"

"I hope she made a good impression?"

He nodded.

"It was quite the whirlwind. She's a very astute girl."

"And Adam was okay?"

"His initial hesitancy was to be expected, but her performance was ... shall we say, *magical*. He will be phoning her this evening to make arrangements to convene tomorrow."

"That's good. Very encouraging."

"And she is fully prepared?"

"Yes, thoroughly." Clare's mind was working overtime, trying to think if there was anything she'd missed.

"And would you care to share? To give me a teeny preview? I have always admired the ingenuity of our Polish cousins."

"Ooh, you never change," she said, her voice laced with affection. "I'd hate to spoil the surprise."

"Ah, but the surprise is an overrated construct, best reserved for the exchange of gifts at Yuletide. I hesitate to overstate my own ability to influence, but as the experienced campaigner knows only too well, there is great currency in being forewarned."

Clare smiled. She had always intended to tell him, but she

was determined to make him work for it. It was all part of the game. But then, she softened. She knew she would never have had the introduction to Adam and his crew if it hadn't been for Harry's willingness to trust her and come to her aid.

"Are you sure this room isn't bugged?" she asked, leaning forward and lowering her voice.

"As sure as I ever can be. And I am devilishly good at safeguarding a confidence."

"Okay."

And so she outlined the plan, giving just enough information to tantalise, but without revealing all of the details. Some things were best kept private, for now. And, of course, she avoided alerting him to the potential danger. Because if everything went well, there'd be plenty of time to analyse the finer points of the strategy, safe from the position of victory. But projects like this were unpredictable, and if the slightest thing went wrong, they had a way of proving deadly.

Chapter 7

DANNY was waiting outside the restaurant when my taxi pulled up, looking as gorgeous and annoying as ever. Bastard. He was my flatmate and closest friend for years until he broke my heart by getting a girlfriend. This was the first time we'd seen each other in over six months.

I didn't know whether to give him a hug or a handshake, but he made my mind up for me with a peck on the cheek, and a smile that reached right to his wonderful blue eyes. I realised I was developing a thing for eyes. Made a change from arms, I suppose. I'd undone my coat in the cab, so he got a flash of red dress. It was all part of the plan to make him see what he was missing.

"You look gorgeous," he said. "Have you done something with your hair?"

I began to have serious doubts about my hair.

"No, but thank, you," I said. "It looks like you forgot to shave this morning." I ran my fingertips over his irritatingly attractive stubble, hoping he'd notice the striking red nails that were as close a match to the dress as I could muster. "Should we?" I indicated towards the door.

He nodded, and then held it open for me to pass. I hoped he'd also notice the sexy shoes. He'd always been a leg man, and heels help. A waitress, dressed in a traditional sari, approached us.

"I've got a reservation for two. Danny Churchill," he said. She checked her list, looking all formal and efficient, and then beckoned for us to follow. I let Danny lead the way, to see if he'd be courteous and pull my chair out for me, but another waiter was already there and beat him to it.

"It's wonderful to see you," he said.

"Likewise. Thank you for inviting me."

"I've missed you."

I stopped myself from saying "I've missed you too" and instead did a "big deal, so there" expression. Or at least I hope it came across like that, and not just that I'd developed a twitch.

"How have you been?" he asked.

"Ooh, it's non-stop parties, Danny. Seriously." God, I hate myself at times. I'm no good at playing the bitch. "No, honestly, I'm okay. Busy, working hard, not much time for anything else. How are you? How's the lovely Lisa? And how's the freelance lifestyle? Have you been working on any decent stories?"

"I'm trying, but it's tough going."

"I can imagine. Still, you're better off away from the Echo, I think, for what it's worth." Danny was an investigative journalist. He'd learned his trade working for Clare in the Daily Echo's special investigations department, until she went off-piste. "I saw a copy the other day and it's gone downhill. It was all celebrity nonsense. I expect they're missing you more than you're missing them. I saw your one in the Telegraph about rogue mobile phone contracts."

"That was bread and butter. It's not going to win any awards." He sounded remorseful. I hoped he was okay. "There are pros and cons of being freelance. People can be less guarded because they don't get intimidated, thinking they're talking to the national press. But equally, having the weight of a newspaper behind you can open doors that it's hard to get access to on your own."

I did feel for him. Yes, he'd broken my heart, but I still cared more than I'd ever be willing to admit, to anyone but myself.

"So how's your job?" he asked. "Do you miss the photography?"

"It's good, and I do, but more than anything I miss being my own boss. That's taken a bit of adjusting. This is still creative in its own way. But actually working for a company and turning up at an office ... I'm not sure I like it."

"You can't go back to how you were?"

"No, not really."

When my photography studio had been comprehensively burgled, Clare had come up with a grand plan. She offered to help me start again, but it wouldn't have been the same.

The waitress came, and waited while we looked at the menus. I opted for the chicken dhansak, obviously. Danny went for an achari chicken from the chef's specialities section, presumably because he was trying to show off. We ordered some wine as well. It probably wasn't the wisest after the lunchtime excess, but hair of the dog, and all of that. It was lovely to see him and yet ... This was what it should always have been like. We were destined to be together. The wine arrived and the waitress poured us each a glass. I swirled it around, trying to make pretty patterns with the light from the candle on the table.

"Are you sure you're okay?" said Danny, puncturing my thoughtful moment of silence.

I wasn't quite sure how to answer that, so I lied.

"Of course, never better."

"What's the matter?"

"Nothing's the matter."

"I know you well enough to know when something's the matter."

How could I tell him that I missed him terribly? That I missed our old flat in Camden? Our old lifestyle, always looking out for each other. The ups and downs, and jokes and fun, his lovely arms, the fact he was the only other person in the whole world I'd trust to make me an acceptable cup of tea. By summarising, I suppose.

"I just miss you," I said.

He sighed, then reached out across the table and put his hand over mine.

"I told you. I miss you too," he said. "We were good."

"The best."

"Better than the best. Even when you were being grumpy."

I wasn't having that.

"I'm never grumpy."

He raised his eyebrows.

"Well, I'm not. Anyway, you didn't tell me how you were getting on with the lovely Lisa."

"No."

I paused, waiting for him to elaborate, which he didn't.

"Set a date yet?"

He sighed again.

"No."

"Do I detect the cheekiest hint of disharmony?"

I looked directly into his lovely eyes. What was going on behind them?

"It's been hard, you know?" he started. "She works long and unpredictable hours. I'm much the same but probably even worse. And there's always so much we can't talk about because of the conflict of interest. She's the police, I'm a journalist, and that's your classic oil and water."

"Are you the oil or are you the water?"

"We take turns." He smiled, but it wasn't one of his most fulsome.

"But you're okay together?"

"We still get on. But I'm beginning to think I'm about as adept at relationships as you are."

"Well, you've learnt from the master there."

"You're still not seeing anyone?" he asked. Did I detect a look of hope, or was I merely fantasising?

"Nope. It'll never happen."

"It will."

"I can pretty much guarantee it won't."

"Yeah, yeah. Anyway. I may be looking for somewhere to live soon."

"Really?" Now I definitely was fantasising. "Is she kicking you out?"

"For your information, she's not kicking me out because I don't actually live with her. I stayed for a couple of weeks when you first evicted me."

"I didn't evict you."

"You ended the lease on the flat, which amounted to the same thing. But the plan was never to live with Lisa."

"Oh." I had the sickening feeling that I might have scored a dreadful own goal in a fit of grumpiness. Not that I'm ever grumpy. "So where have you been living?"

"I rented a studio flat, but it's a struggle," he said. "It's what I mean about freelancing. It's bad enough waiting months to get paid for a story, but then when the rent's due it gets kind of uncomfortable. I think I need to go back to sharing."

"Oh," I said again, acutely aware that I had a spare room, but I'd just given it to a stranger who was almost certainly not related to anyone I knew.

The food arrived. Despite everything, I was suddenly hungry.

"I'm having quite a day of it," I said, changing the subject. "I had lunch with a friend of yours."

"Of mine?"

"Of both of ours. Clare."

"Wow, how is she?"

"You know Clare. Always up to mischief, but nobody really knows what. When did you last speak to her?"

He began to look sheepish, then laughed.

"What?" I said.

"Nothing. I'm just trying to work it out. The last time would have been, oh ... It's been a while." His expression changed, frowning in thought. "About ten hours ago." Then he laughed again.

"And again, *what?*"

"She took me to breakfast."

"Oh, this is superb."

"What's wrong with that?"

"She specifically never mentioned doing that, and even more specifically asked me how you were, as though she hadn't seen you in months."

"Maybe she's just forgetful." He laughed again.

"Ooooh."

"Haha. You're cute when you get in a temper."

"And you should know better than to call me cute."

"You're still in a temper though."

"Did she mention her niece?" I asked, ignoring him.

"Louise. Yes. Apparently she's going to be staying with you. Which is a pity, as I was going to ask if you had a spare room."

"God, this gets better and better." I could have screamed. "So she was telling you that before she'd even asked me?"

"Presumably she knew you'd say yes."

"And are the two of you in cahoots over this? Are you planning some secret assignation?"

He shrugged.

"Not as far as I know. She called out of the blue. Said she was in town and wanted to meet for a catch up."

"Likely story. And you didn't think it was weird that she suddenly had a niece, who we'd never previously heard of, especially given her lack of brothers and sisters?"

"I did kind of wonder about that."

"God." I put down my fork. "I know where this ends. I'll get kidnapped. You'll get shot. And Clare rides in to save the day, all unruffled and glamorous, as though it's just a normal day at the office."

"Let's hope not," he said.

"Quite." I took another sip of wine. It was a big sip, and I didn't argue when Danny immediately refilled my glass.

Harry Rushton stood at the window, watching Clare hail a taxi. When he was confident she wouldn't be returning, he muted the music and picked up the phone.

"She's just departed," he said, when Adam Kirwin answered.

"And?"

"It was a revelatory evening. Naturally, I promised to keep the details confidential."

"Naturally. Although I imagine you're about to tell me."

"Of course." He chuckled, swirling the last of the brandy in his glass. "Her reputation dictates an appropriate degree of caution, but what the eye doesn't see, and suchlike."

"Do you think we can exploit this?"

"Oh yes, dear boy. If you are seated, let me tell you how we can work this to our very considerable advantage."

Chapter 8

"HAVE you got anything planned for Tuesday?" asked Danny, once we'd finished the food, and we were waiting for our empty plates to be cleared.

"What's happening on Tuesday?"

"It's your birthday."

"Oh, that." I shrugged. "I shall try to avoid all mention of it."

"Don't be like that. I'd like to take you somewhere, help you celebrate."

"Celebrate turning twenty-seven?"

"Exactly."

"Should I let you into a secret?"

"Go on."

"Do you remember watching *Neighbours*?" That seemed to confuse him.

"The Australian soap thing? Kylie and Jason and all of that?"

"Exactly the one. I remember watching it years ago, about 1985, and looking at the bloke who played Paul Robinson, the ruthless business chap. What was his name?"

"Paul Robinson, you just said."

"No, stupid, the actor."

"No idea."

"Oh, you do." I thought for a moment, then it came to me. "Stefan ... Stefan Dennis."

"Wow. That's a blast from the past."

"Indeed, but here's the point. I was fifteen at the time and full of hormones and ..."

"You fancied Stefan Dennis?"

"No! Behave. Just listen. I was fifteen, and questioning everything and what it meant to be growing up, and remember seeing him on television and thinking *there is a proper adult. Whatever age he is, that's a grown-up.* No doubt about it. He wasn't old but couldn't be mistaken for a late teenager."

"Okay, and he was twenty-seven?"

"No. You're missing my point."

"So how old was he?"

"Twenty-six. So since the age of fifteen I've had it in my head that when you reach twenty-six you're a proper grown-up. No longer a child, an adolescent, or someone in their early twenties who thinks they know everything, but should know better. So, I was quite happy being twenty-six. I felt I'd arrived. But on Tuesday I'll be twenty-seven and that means I'm at the start of the inevitable decline into middle age, then old age, and - unless medical science intervenes otherwise - a sad and lonely passing, all alone and uncared for, in a nursing home. And that, I think you'll find, is not something to celebrate. Although I appreciate you'll be twenty-eight in a couple of months, so no offence intended."

Danny was laughing at me.

"I remember you made me a cake for my twenty-seventh," he said.

"And you chose that moment to announce your liaison with the detective floozy. So the less said about that the better."

He was still laughing at me.

"It's good to know you never change," he said.

"And again, precisely my point. I *am* about to change. I've peaked. I've had a year of it. And now, on Tuesday, I'll change into an old lady, facing an inexorable decline, which ends with one of those grey perms that old ladies have because their husbands have already died and they've got nothing else to look forward to, apart from a regular trip to the hairdresser, and the occasional conversation with their cat."

"Don't let Clare hear you say that. She's nearly thirty-five. What does that make her?"

"Clare's not human, so the normal rules don't apply."

He stopped laughing and just looked at me, his head slightly tilted.

"I can't imagine you getting old."

"Well, make the most of me today and tomorrow, because from Tuesday onwards I'll be looking for the nearest garden centre - even though I don't have a garden - and more specifically, learning how to knit."

Danny insisted on escorting me home, which was nice, not least because I was tired, wearing shoes that I couldn't walk in, and he offered to cover the taxi fare. I had a tenner ready for the driver, though, and managed to pay before Danny had a chance to locate his wallet. It seemed only fair. We got out of the cab and I steeled myself to give him a farewell, no-hard-feelings hug. It had been a lovely evening. It was good to see him. And I hoped we could do it again some time.

"So this is the new place?" he said. "I've been so curious to see it."

I followed his gaze in the direction of my front door. There was a welcoming glow peeping out between the curtains of the big bay window. It was cold on the street. And I didn't know when I'd see him again.

"Do you want to come in for coffee?" I asked.

A hint of a cheeky smile appeared on his face.

"Do you mean actual coffee or a euphemistic 'coffee' which is actually a cuddle?"

"I actually mean a cup of tea, if I'm being honest."

"Shame."

"Because you'd rather have coffee? I can do you coffee if it makes a difference. As long as you don't mind waiting here while I go to the shop for a jar of Nescafé because I haven't got any."

"Tea's fine, as long as it's not one of your Typhoo punishment ones. I was thinking about the cuddle."

"Wooah."

I stepped back, then turned towards him, hoping I looked vaguely attractive and mysterious in the orange glow of the street light.

"You," I started, "in case you've forgotten, have a girlfriend. And you were quite happy to go off with her last year when I'd have very much liked to have had a cuddle to celebrate your release from hospital. So don't think you can pop round here just because she's kicking you out, and expect me to restart cuddle duties just because you're not getting any at home."

Danny shook his head, possibly in deep regret, but I doubt it.

"She's not kicking me out. And as previously mentioned, it's not my home because I don't live there."

"So you keep saying, but I was speaking metaphorically, or whatever the proper word is when you're trying to make a point after too much wine. Hypothetically, probably. Anyway, the gist of the point remains. You made your choice, without any regard to my feelings, so don't expect me to give you a cuddle as some sort of default fallback, worst-case-scenario option. I can do a platonic hug, but no more than six seconds, and I'll be timing it. And a cup of tea, or even coffee if you absolutely insist on being awkward. And on the upside you might get to meet Louise."

"Wow. Has she moved in already? She didn't hang around."

"Already moved in. Already almost certainly stolen all my valuables and buggered off again. But on the off-chance she hasn't, you'd be more than welcome."

"I didn't know you had any valuables."

"And again I was speaking metaphorically. Or hypothetically, or possibly even in similes. God knows. You're supposed to be the writer. Are you coming in or what?"

He nodded and followed me to the door.

"It'll be weird seeing inside. Recognising your things," he said. "I do miss Rochester Square."

I nearly pointed out that we'd still be living there had he not abandoned me, but managed to stop myself.

"Do you remember when I used to call you Poirot?" I said instead.

"I do. Happy days."

"They were."

And then, as I fumbled to put my key in the lock, and he stood there patiently, waiting for me, the emotions and frustrations of the past twelve months all caught up with me, and I gave up with the key completely and, instead, kissed the two-timing bastard, which was rather nice but I immediately regretted it, because he responded and I felt guilty about Lisa, and I'm not that kind of person.

"Follow me," I said, when I came up for air and finally pushed the door open. "Make yourself at home and I'll put the kettle on."

There was no sign of Louise in the front room, but the door of her bedroom was ajar, and the light was on. Danny was on the larger of the two sofas when I returned with the tea. And that gave me a conundrum. Sit next to him, and risk things getting out of control, or sit opposite and have it look like I was making some kind of point?

I sat next to him, no contest.

"What do you think?" I asked.

"I think it was probably wrong, but I enjoyed it," he said.

"I was talking about the flat, not the kiss, you weirdo."

He laughed, and it was just like the old days, except I hadn't yet checked out his arms. I gave him a hug, but stopped short of a second kiss. He stopped short of touching my legs, and I nearly stopped short of giving his arms a squeeze, but old habits die hard.

"It's lovely," he said. "Are you happy here? You look settled."

Before I had a chance to answer, I heard movement from the hallway.

"Oh, sorry, you've got company," said Louise, poking her head round the door, and then withdrawing just as quickly.

"No, come in, come in," I said, moving slightly along the sofa, away from him. "Louise, meet Danny. Danny, this is Louise. Clare's ... *niece*." He stood up to give her a handshake, which seemed to linger a bit too long. "Come and join us."

"I don't want to interrupt," she said.

"Don't be silly, you're not interrupting anything." I turned to Danny, but he appeared transfixed by the new arrival. Heaven's sake.

"You're *the* Danny?" she said. "I've heard so much about you."

I expect he heard my sigh.

"I hope it wasn't all bad," he said, rather unoriginally.

After a few minutes of small talk, Danny thankfully announced that he should really be making a move, as he had a busy day ahead. I had to be up for work too, and the clock on the video was heading dangerously in the direction of eleven. We all stood together, and I showed him to the door.

"Send me a message when you get home," I said, as he stepped out into the communal hallway.

"I will."

"And thank you for a wonderful evening."

"It was my pleasure, believe me. Louise seems nice."

"Yeah, well you can keep your hands off her, before you start."

"She's far too young for me. I prefer them in their late twenties." He winked.

"Oooh. Go home now before I slap you," I said.

I gave him one last hug, then wished him a safe journey, watched him walk to the main front door and out onto the street. I closed my door. I didn't know whether to be happy about having a lovely time, or sad that it was such a rarity these days. Louise was in her room as I passed, so I called goodnight, asked if there was anything she needed, and then said I'd see her tomorrow. Bed was calling.

I fell asleep almost immediately, but woke up in the night, after a weird and disturbing dream. I couldn't remember the details, but it was enough to make me wonder what my subconscious was trying to tell me.

Chapter 9

Monday, January 20th, 1997

DETECTIVE Sergeant Amy Cranston was waiting patiently, leaning against a pillar, on the top step of the curved entrance to the All Souls church in London's Langham Place. She pulled up her collar against the chill, then thrust her hands deep into her coat pockets. Behind her, BBC Broadcasting House was as busy as ever, with a steady flow of staff and visitors to the Corporation's five national radio stations. But Amy's attention was focused along Regent Street, in the direction of Oxford Circus, scanning the streets for a familiar face as the morning rush hour gathered pace.

"Nice day for it," said a familiar voice, over her left shoulder. She turned and came face to face with Clare Woodbrook, albeit Clare's face was largely hidden under a woollen hat, a scarf and the fake fur collar of her winter coat.

"Is it?" asked Amy.

"Do you mean you're not pleased to see me?"

"It's more a question of whether I'm risking my career by seeing you. You do know I should be arresting you?"

Clare put her finger to her lips.

"Shhh. Let's agree you're not going to do that."

"Let's agree to reserve judgement." Clare always tried to take control, but Amy knew that could be dangerous. "Just because you haven't killed anyone for a couple of years doesn't mean you're not accountable for the things you did previously."

"Who says I haven't killed anyone for a couple of years?" said Clare, dropping her voice.

"If you're joking, it's not very funny."

"I just don't want you to think I'm losing my edge."

"I've got handcuffs, you know. I could take you in now."

"I know."

"So give me one good reason why I shouldn't?"

"I could give you lots of good reasons why you shouldn't. But specifically, if you want a new one, you're going to have to bear with me for a moment."

Amy looked back along Regent Street.

"Are we at least going to go for coffee?" she asked.

"I'd love to," said Clare, "but I quite like it here. If you're planning to ambush me, I can disappear in all sorts of directions."

"Nobody's going to ambush you."

"Do you promise?"

Amy's temper was starting to fray.

"What is this? You're acting like a bloody child. I shouldn't even be talking to you."

"I know, and I appreciate you coming to see me."

"Believe me, I had my doubts. But I'm here of my own volition, on my own, and you'd better decide quickly if you can trust me, because if you don't, I'm going. I'm freezing cold, I've got a million better things to do, including criminals to catch, and lovely as it is to stand here watching the buses, I'm going for coffee."

Amy started walking. Clare fell into step alongside. A minute later, the detective pushed open the door of a small café on a nearby side street and joined the queue of office workers, stocking up on caffeine before heading to work.

"Make yourself useful and find a table, somewhere towards the back," she said. "What are you having?"

"Cappuccino, no sprinkles, please. And thank you," said Clare.

The café was alive with chatter, the air thick with steam and the aroma of coffee and pastries. Towards the rear, two people were placing their empty cups on a tray. They stood up as Clare approached, and she grabbed the table before anyone else could lay claim to it. A few minutes later, Amy joined her.

"What are you doing back in London?" asked Amy, passing over one of the cups.

"I'm just catching up with old friends. How's DCI Rogan Court?"

"Bullshit. And I don't know. I've not worked with him since last year, but I'm sure he'd send his regards. So last chance, what are you doing?"

Clare scooped up some of the milk froth with a teaspoon while looking around the adjacent tables.

"Can you stop being so paranoid?" said Amy.

"I'm not being paranoid. I'm just being careful." Clare lowered her voice again. "Okay, let me run a name by you. George Brandrick."

Amy laughed derisively. "What about him?"

"He's up to no good."

"I know he's up to no good. He's always up to no good. Proving it is our issue."

"How about if I told you of a way in which he would come out of the woodwork just long enough to incriminate himself?" said Clare. "And if, in the process, you'd get an even bigger prize that makes him look insignificant?"

"I'd be interested. Sceptical, but interested."

"Good." Clare paused, looking around one last time. "Let's

drink these and then go somewhere we can't be overheard, and I'll tell you everything you need to know."

———

George Brandrick couldn't face going to the office. Not this early. He dialled Jason's number.

"George," said the bodyguard. "Alright? Any more from Devlin?"

"You don't need to worry about him," George said.

"How come?"

"I've dealt with it."

"Really?"

Immediately, George could feel his blood pressure rise.

"Do I have to remind you who you work for?" he said. "When I say I've dealt with it, I mean I've dealt with it. So you can leave off with the questions. Jesus Christ."

"Sorry, boss."

Maybe this wasn't such a good idea.

"Where are you this morning?" he asked instead.

"I'm out collecting. Do you need me?"

"No, not at the moment." He looked at his watch. "Come and see me this afternoon, though. At the office. There are things we need to discuss. Oh, and Jason?"

"Yes, boss?"

"Keep your wits about you, yeah? Low profile, if you can."

———

"You got your accommodation sorted, then?" asked Adam, leafing through a pile of documents on the desk in front of him, as though looking for something elusive.

Louise was watching him, while helping herself to the freshly-brewed coffee from the machine at the side of the room - partly to steady her nerves, and partly for something to do.

"I did," she said.

"That was quick."

She stopped pouring, wondering if she was still on trial, but it was hard to tell. Adam's attention was in front of him.

"Friends in high places, and all of that," she said. "A friend of a friend offered me a room. She seems nice. Obviously I didn't tell her the reason why I'm in London. I almost feel guilty."

Adam finally stopped what he was doing and faced her.

"It's not a question of feeling guilty. I don't need to tell you that we don't talk to anyone about what we do."

"No, I appreciate that."

"Where is it?"

"The flat? On the edge of Camden."

"Which bit? I know Camden quite well."

Yes, it seemed like a test.

"You know it better than me then," she said.

"And you're sure she has no idea? What did you tell her?"

"That I'm an actress, darling," she said with a pout. "I suppose it's kind of true, in the broadest sense. She definitely has no idea, and obviously I won't be saying. Seriously, you need to know you can trust me."

Adam nodded, subconsciously checking his shirt cuffs.

"I hope I can."

"The trouble is, it transpires she knows a bit about acting," Louise continued, taking her coffee to the sofa. "I'm going to have to read a book on it, in case she starts asking me technical questions. She started last night, something about some kind of technique. I'm supposed to be starting a course."

Adam stood up, and moved over to the large table that dominated one half of the room. He adjusted the projector, plugged it into the socket on the floor, and then focused its beam of light onto the blank wall ahead, before turning the power back off.

"Do you have the slides?" he asked.

"I do." Louise reached into her bag and then handed him a small yellow Kodachrome transparency box. "They're all in order."

Adam checked the first, turned it the right way round, and then began loading them into a carousel.

"And you've got everything else?"

There was a knock at the door.

"Yes, everything we need," said Louise, standing up and heading across to open it. She stood aside to let Harry enter.

"Good morning," he said. "I bear the gift of pastries."

Behind him, Abby and Toby followed, and both nodded in greeting. They were friendly enough, but clearly had reservations. Louise wondered if they were a couple. Both removed their coats and headed to the coffee machine, while Harry collected plates and then laid out a selection of croissants, pains au chocolat, and Chelsea buns on the table.

Toby was full of himself, bristling with the arrogance of youth, regaling his audience with details of a hot date from the night before. Not a couple then. Although judging by Abby's feigned disinterest, Louise suspected there was more to it than that.

Eventually, once everyone was seated, all eyes turned in Louise's direction.

"Ready?" asked Adam.

She nodded, then stood up and took a deep breath. It was time to perform.

Chapter 10

I ACKNOWLEDGE it's a cliché of modern office life, but I was genuinely standing by the water cooler having a conversation.

"Good weekend?" asked Nathan, as I waited for him to finish pouring a cup, so I could take a turn.

"Not bad," I said. I liked Nathan. He worked in sales, but he wasn't your typically pushy salesperson. "Saturday was quiet, but I met up with friends yesterday."

"I thought you were looking a bit delicate."

"You know me too well." I winced at the memory of the double wine session. Not good at my age. "How about you?"

He shrugged.

"Nothing much really. I went to see *Turbulence* on Saturday."

My blank look successfully conveyed that I had no idea what he was talking about.

"Disaster movie with Ray Liotta, set on a plane."

"Oh, okay. Any good?"

"To be honest, it was complete shit." He laughed, stepping aside. "It was my boyfriend's choice, though, so I deny any responsibility."

Wow. Had he just come out to me, or as ever, was I the last to know?

"There you go," I said. "All the more reason to stay single. Cheers." I chinked the water cups together, taking him by surprise, and causing his to spill.

"We'll get you sorted," he said, warmly. "I can think of at least three men here who'd be dead keen to take you out."

"Like who?"

"Phil for starters."

"He's *got* a girlfriend."

"But he's a man. That wouldn't stop him."

I knew it was a joke, but he had a point.

"Anyway, I need to speak to you," he continued, when I didn't ask about the others.

"Really?"

"Follow me."

He led the way out to the rear stairwell. It was an unofficial meeting space for those conversations you didn't want to have within earshot of your colleagues.

"I need your help," he said, once the fire door had closed behind us. Everyone seemed to need my help. I should stop trying to be nice.

"Fire away," I said. He looked awkward, and slightly flushed.

"Obviously, you know we have a whip-round when it's somebody's birthday. And I've been given the task of buying you something for tomorrow. Which should be a surprise, and the idea is that I display my creative spark, while at the same time getting you something you always wanted - but to be honest, you've only been here a few months and I have no idea what you like. So I was thinking, if you can give me a pointer, you'd get something you want and I'll look clever. Win win."

I chuckled.

"Is that it? I thought you were going to ask if I had a spare room."

"*What?*"

"Sorry, it's just what happened yesterday when someone asked me for a favour." I tried to think for a moment. I really wanted to help him, but it was hard. "You know what, though, I'm really not celebrating this year. How do they even know it's my birthday?"

"From your application form, I suppose. But go on, what would you like?"

"A day off?"

"Haha, sorry, I can't arrange that."

I really had no idea. I couldn't think of anything. A book token? Hardly the most creative, even if it would actually be really useful. I like a present as much as anyone, but I wanted nothing to do with the whole thing. A charity donation? That would work, but would also give the game away that he'd spoken to me.

"What sort of budget are you talking?" I asked.

"Everyone's put a fiver in, so about fifty quid."

"Wow. That's very kind." Perhaps a new haircut? Although ironically, nobody would notice because they already thought I'd had one. My brain was fried. "Can I give it some thought and let you know?"

"Of course, but I'm popping out at lunchtime, so if it could be before then, it would be appreciated."

"Okay." I smiled. Subject avoided, at least for now.

"How are you finding it, by the way?" he asked.

"What? Getting old?"

"No, the job. Are you settled in now?"

That was a big question.

"Yeah, I think so. It was a bit of a culture shock at first, but it's interesting. It's nice getting a regular wage."

"You were a photographer, weren't you?"

I nodded.

"So what brought you here?"

"That's a very long story."

He raised an eyebrow. I wasn't sure if he was genuinely interested out of some sort of human compassion, or whether he was just being nosy.

"I had a studio but it was broken into," I said, summarising. "It transpired my insurance didn't cover it, so I lost the lot."

"That's awful."

"It was a traumatic time. In lots of ways." I edged back towards the door.

"Man trouble?"

If only he knew.

"Don't even start me on that," I said, feeling very serious all of a sudden.

"Understood," he said. "You know what? We should have a night out. Blow away the cobwebs and celebrate your birthday."

"Can we avoid the celebrating the birthday bit?"

He smiled.

"Of course."

"Let's do it then. And in the meantime I'll give the present thing some thought and let you know."

He followed me back into the office. I had documents to write and a project to prepare, but now all I could think about was last night, and Danny, and the illicit kiss.

"George Brandrick," said Louise as the first image came up on the wall. "Typical lowlife. Interests include drugs, smuggling tobacco, and various ventures that encourage disadvantaged people to invest in pyramid schemes and the like, dressed up in all sorts of ways, but inevitably resulting in substantial losses."

The picture changed.

"Jason Harrigan. Brandrick's muscle. Not the sharpest. Makes up in force what he lacks in brain cells."

It changed again.

"Brandrick's base in Cygnet Street, Shoreditch. He's got an office on the top floor. There's a communal lobby area with a lift, but that's as much as I know. Access to the lobby is via a fob or keypad when it's locked, but during the day it tends to remain open."

She looked around the table at the four expectant faces.

"Any questions so far?" she asked.

"Yeah, I've got one," said Abby. "Why him, of all the geezers out there, and why are you bringing him to us, babe?"

"Valid questions," said Louise. "To answer the first, then yes, I agree, in one sense he's nothing special. But let's just say, he ripped off someone very close to me, and it's about time he had some of his own medicine. Call it revenge if you like, and yes, it's personal. And as for why I'm bringing him to you, that's easy. Harry and I have a mutual friend. She put us in touch, and I know he's the kind of mark you go for. Someone wealthy, but with a weakness, who deserves everything that's coming to them."

"And his weakness?"

"Money and women."

Toby laughed.

"So he's not a complete bad guy then?" he said, with a mouthful of croissant. But nobody else laughed with him. He looked around the room. "Oh come on, it was a joke."

"Excuse Toby," said Abby. "He can be a knob at times."

Louise took the opportunity to take a sip of her coffee, but it had cooled down too much to be drinkable. She put the cup aside, and looked across to Adam.

"Carry on," he said, dismissing the others with a thinly veiled look of reproach.

"Thank you. So going back to George Brandrick, he's slippery. He's known to the police, but they have trouble making anything stick. He's one removed from the action, always, so whenever things go wrong, there's always someone else to take the fall. So the objective is to smoke him out. Make him put his head above the parapet. But he doesn't work on his own. He's got a team of people around him. A drug supply network, various associates who run his schemes. He's very much the kingpin, but if we can take him down, then there's a chance they'll go with him."

"Wooah," said Toby. "This sounds like you're trying to get him arrested. That's not what we do. Tell her, Adam."

"Toby makes a valid point for once," said Adam, acknowledging his protégé. "We run long cons. That's it. That's our area of expertise. You come up with a plan to take him for money, then I'm interested. But we don't do law enforcement. We don't help the police. In fact, as far as the police are concerned, we don't exist, and I'm extremely keen to keep it that way."

"I appreciate that, and I think you misunderstand me," said Louise. She'd anticipated this objection. So far everything was going exactly as she'd rehearsed. "So there are two aspects. Number one, we present him with a deal that's so good he can't refuse, but we make him think it's his idea. We make him chase us, begging to get involved. And when he does, we take his money and disappear. But then, once it all falls apart, and he realises he's been conned, he's going to want revenge. It's in his nature. So we make sure that he goes down, and goes down properly. But you guys will be long out of the picture by that stage. You can leave that bit to me."

Adam turned to his right, pinching his chin between his thumb and forefinger. Louise watched carefully. It was the second time she'd seen him do that.

"Harry, you're very quiet," he said. "What do you think?"

The older man collected his thoughts for a moment, before giving Louise a reassuring smile.

"I have the benefit of some, shall we say, *inside knowledge* of our friend Mr Brandrick," he said. "I note that Louise has not divulged the details of her personal agenda, and I feel it would be inappropriately forward to press her for the more intimate aspects. But for what it is worth, one can't help but be persuaded by the validity of the objective, nor the suitability of the target."

"Which means?"

"I am intrigued, dear boy. I think we should allow her to give details of what she proposes."

"Okay." Adam allowed himself an internal smile. Harry had prepared him well. But it was important to play the role, making it look like this was the first he'd heard of it. He looked to the other two. Abby shrugged. Toby looked less impressed but finally nodded. He turned back to Louise. "Continue."

"Thank you," she said, pouring herself a glass of mineral water and taking a sip before continuing. "So here's the plan. We create the illusion of a private members' club. We're on the verge of opening up, but one of our investors has delayed things."

"A private members' club?" said Adam.

"A *specialist* private members' club. One with girls. Think of it as an exclusive, upmarket kind of gentleman's club."

"Basically a brothel?"

"Aren't brothels illegal in this country?" Toby interrupted.

"We're not actually setting one up, Toby," Louise continued. "We just give the illusion of setting one up. It never actually exists."

"You look heartbroken, Tobes," said Abby. "You'd like to run a brothel."

"No, I just want to get this straight in my head," he said. "But presumably we'll still need girls, to create the illusion?"

Abby prodded him.

"Behave," she said. "Sorry, Louise, he's full of hormones. He'll grow out of it. Carry on. What would you need from me?"

That was encouraging, thought Louise. The exact dynamics of the group still eluded her, but she had worried that it would be Abby who would take the most convincing.

"What I'd need from you," she started, "is a web site, with an area for members to register for further information. Make it a club, perhaps charging a fee, hinting about what's to come. Very sophisticated, glossy, you know the kind of thing. On top of that we need to create legends for the investors. Perhaps a venture capital company, list of directors, testimonials, all that kind of thing. He's going to check it all out, so it needs to be watertight, several layers deep. And then we need a business plan, full of charts and projections, costs, revenues, strengths and opportunities, all the usual. Is that all doable?"

"Yup. Very doable." She reached out for one of the Chelsea buns, and started to peel the outside layer.

Louise turned back to Adam.

"I've already done research on Brandrick. I know where he drinks, where he does his deals. My proposal is that I go there and make him approach me. Sell him the sizzle, but tell him he's not needed. Make him want it all the more. Have a meeting with him. Tell him again he can't have it. Tease him with the thought of all the Polish girls who'll be coming to work for us, and how it would be a great front for his smuggling and drug operations, but tell him again that it's unfortunate, but he just missed out. He'll be desperate." She turned to Abby. "You know what men are like."

"Treat them mean," she said.

"Keep them keen," added Toby.

"No, just treat them mean," said Abby.

"Exactly," Louise smiled at Abby and then continued, happy that she was forging an alliance. "But then, just as he's reaching peak frustration, we give him a way in. It's going to take an investment, but this is his one chance. But once we get his name on a document and the cash in the bank, we disappear with the money, and you leave it to me to blow it all open, and he gets taken down for running a brothel, trafficking and all sorts else."

"And you think he'll go for this?" asked Adam.

"If I may interject," said Harry, taking over for a moment.

"From what I know of George Brandrick, he will most certainly find the whole construct intoxicating."

"He will," said Louise, focusing her attention back on Adam. "But there is a risk, and like I said at the start, this is kind of personal. So I admit my motivation is to take him down rather than just taking his money, and I know that's a different set of priorities to this team's. So I brought you this." She reached into her bag and then walked around the table to Adam and passed him an envelope. "It's a banker's draft for £50,000. Call it insurance. If we take Brandrick for more than that, you rip it up, and we call it quits. But if anything goes wrong, or we don't make the money, then there's your guarantee that you haven't just worked for nothing."

Adam opened the envelope and inspected the draft carefully.

"It's genuine," said Louise.

"It certainly looks it," he said.

"Harry can vouch for my integrity. You keep hold of that. Obviously I have to trust you not to cash it yet, but hopefully you won't need it. But keep it somewhere safe, and that's your guarantee that I'll do everything I can to make sure this is a success. I couldn't do this without you. I understand it's a leap of faith for you to work with me, but hopefully this is the first of many things we can do together."

Harry reached out and turned off the projector. The fan slowed down and stopped, its whirring replaced with silence.

"So are you on board?" asked Louise.

Adam gave one last look at the others, then stood up and offered Louise his hand.

"We're on board," he said. "We'll spend the rest of the day planning the details, but I think it will be a pleasure to work alongside you." He kept his eyes on his shirt cuffs as a handshake sealed the deal.

Even allowing for the frequent paranoia that came with the territory of his business interests, George seemed on edge. Jason was used to his moods, but today he seemed particularly troubled.

"How did you sort out Devlin, then?" he asked.

George sat back in his chair, and put his feet up on his desk, crossing his legs at the ankles.

"Yeah, and what did I tell you? Shut up about it and move on."

"Understood, boss. But you wanted to see me?"

"I need you to do a job for me."

"Go on." He rocked back on the two hind legs of his chair.

George hesitated, perhaps aware of the levity of the request.

"I've been asked for a bit of assistance on a little project. Call it a favour for a favour. There's a woman you might have heard of. Clare Woodbrook."

Jason shrugged and shook his head, taking the moment to stretch his arms out, then putting his hands behind his head. As ever, his biceps strained the fabric of his close-fitting shirt.

"Vaguely. Possibly. No idea who she is though."

George found a picture on his computer and turned the screen round, so Jason could see it. He summarised her career highlights, from her time as an investigative journalist to the art fraud that marked her switch to the dark side, and the rumours of her involvement in shady deals throughout mainland Europe since.

"She looks fit. And she's never been caught?" asked the bodyguard.

"Officially? No. Unofficially, she flirts with the police. She's got friends on the inside, and she helps them out in exchange for them turning a blind eye."

"So she's an informer?"

"Kind of. Anyway, the point is, I need you to find her for me."

"Because?"

"You don't need to worry about that."

Jason brought his chair down with a crash, frowning.

"Okay. So where am I looking?" he said with a scowl. "And what do I do when I find her?"

"I don't know where you'll find her. But she's got plenty of enemies, and plenty of people who might be nervous if she's back, both here and outside London. So eyes peeled, all right? Ask around. But be careful, she's not someone you want to mess with. When you find her, bring her to me, and we can have a little meeting."

"You don't want me to hurt her?"

George considered that for a moment.

"Not yet. Not from the outset. Give her a chance to speak to me first, but after that, we can do a risk assessment and act accordingly. Understood?"

"Clear as." Jason liked the sound of that.

"Now get yourself out there," George concluded. "But be subtle. If she sees you coming ..." He paused, looking for the right words, but struggled to find them. "Well, let's just say, it would be better all round for both of us if she didn't."

Chapter 11

THE flat was empty when I arrived home from work. I had no idea where Louise was, but just as I started to worry, I heard her key in the door, and a moment later she appeared in the front room.

"Hiya," I said from the sofa. "Good day?"

"Constructive," she said. I was continually impressed by her command of English. "I've been round some of the acting schools, then I met up with friends for coffee, and I popped into Foyles to get some textbooks." She showed me a carrier bag, then put it on the chair while she hung up her coat.

"Oh, and I took my car to the car park. I don't think I'll be using it, so I'm going to take it back, although I've put the keys down somewhere, so if you come across them, let me know. I'm worn out now," she added with a smile, as she turned back towards me, and then collapsed onto the sofa opposite.

Given my recent fascination with eyes, I couldn't help but notice her beautiful, crystal clear, pale brown pair. They were captivating, albeit accentuated by a subtle touch of eyeliner. She was so young, and so clear-skinned, and looked so pure that my previously-latent maternal urge wanted to wrap her in something soft and protect her from all of the harm in the world. Especially if she was prone to hanging round with the likes of Clare.

"Would you like a cup of tea?" she asked me.

"I would, but honestly I'm a nightmare when it comes to tea. I'll make it," I said. Tea is not something to be trusted to a novice.

She smiled at me.

"Clare warned me about that," she said. "So I put a bottle of Champagne in the fridge this morning as a backup. And I thought I could buy you a takeaway, to say thank you for having me. Your choice."

"Wow. I could get used to this." Despite the previous day's excesses, it took less than a moment to decide on the Champagne. "That's very kind. But you don't have to get me a takeaway. Honestly, it's no bother."

"I'd like to. Indian? Pizzas?"

I was tired. It had been a long day. The prospect of not having to cook was suddenly as appetising as the thought of an American Hot. I nodded.

"Normally I'd say Indian, but I had one yesterday. Pizza would be divine."

As we tucked in, we chatted, and it felt like Louise was already an old friend. She was smart, witty and entertaining, and I resolved to keep her away from Danny at all costs.

"So tell me more," I said. "Do you smoke? Have any dangerous hobbies? How do you know Clare again?"

"I do smoke occasionally. I know it's bad, but I will stop soon. But of course I won't smoke in the flat."

"Don't worry about it. Clare doesn't seem to."

"No, but it would be rude. As for hobbies, nothing dangerous. I used to play piano. I try to do a bit of magic but I'm not very good. I like photography."

"Really?"

"Yes, when I can."

Wow. We'd never run short of things to talk about at this rate.

Louise stood up and took the empty boxes through to the kitchen, then returned with the Champagne and topped up our glasses.

"I used to be a photographer," I said.

"Yes, Clare said. Apparently you were the best."

"I don't know about that. I did okay. Long story. I'd love to see some of your pictures."

"I don't have any with me, sadly. They're all back home. But next time I go back I'll bring some with me. I'd love to get your professional opinion."

"What do you take pictures of?"

"Cities mainly. People. Candid things."

"Sounds good. And you must show me some of your magic tricks."

She laughed and looked embarrassed.

"They need work. I'm still at the beginner stage."

"Well, we seem to have made the Champagne disappear," I said, looking at the empty bottle.

She smiled, and we raised our glasses, toasting something, although I'm not really sure what.

"I really do appreciate you putting me up," she said. "It's very kind. I should be out of your way in a few days. I will look to find somewhere of my own."

"Take your time. Really, it's a pleasure having someone here. It saves me buying a cat."

She laughed. I realised she still hadn't elaborated on how she knew Clare, and was just about to have another go at it, when my phone pinged with an SMS message from Danny.

Great to see you last night. We should do that more often. x

. . .

Louise disappeared to the kitchen and I studied my phone, reading the message again and again. It was enough to send my mind in all sorts of unwelcome directions, recalling the highlights of everything he'd said to me.

Was he serious about looking for somewhere to stay? Would that be every dream come true or - more likely - a total disaster? Could it ever be like the old days? There was so much to think about. Part of me wanted to text back immediately and offer to send him a key. He could even share my bed if he wanted to. We'd done that before, platonically, countless times.

Yet what was I thinking? It couldn't be like that, could it? Not after what he'd done to me, deserting me for Lisa. And yes, I know, it was my fault because I'd never told him how I'd felt, and both he and Clare had made me well aware of the fact. Clare had repeatedly told me that he would have done anything for me had I not relentlessly given the impression that I wasn't interested. So really I knew I couldn't blame him, but obviously I did, because I'm me and I'm always right, as far as my own opinion goes. Irrespective of whether it's technically correct.

"Is it okay if I come back in?" Louise's voice cut into my thoughts. I didn't reply immediately, not really taking in what she was asking.

"Oh, gosh. I'm sorry," she continued. "That must have sounded very rude. I'll go to my room."

I shook my head.

"No, it's me, sorry, I was miles away. Yes, of course, come in. Treat it as your home. Sorry, I just had a phone message from Danny."

"Is everything okay?"

"Yes, it's ... Well, it's another long story." Time to change the subject, albeit onto something related. "Do you have a boyfriend?"

"No." She shrugged. "I don't like macho young boys who

think they have something to prove. And I'm wary of the older ones because they're single for a reason."

A woman after my own heart.

"I've loaded the dishwasher," she continued. "I hope that's okay."

Part of me felt like she was trying too hard, but a bigger part was prepared to accept that she was actually a nice, considerate person. And I could certainly get used to having her round. If she offered to do my ironing, I'd ask her to move in permanently.

"Who are you sending a message to?" asked Lisa.

Danny put down his phone, far too quickly. He could feel his face colouring.

"Just a friend," he said, hoping that would be the end of it.

"Which friend?"

"Anna." He held his breath, expecting the next question. But when it didn't come, he felt even worse. The silence was more oppressive than a full-blown argument. Instead, Lisa was concentrating on the TV. Danny had never found *The Brittas Empire* funny. Lisa wasn't laughing either, but she seemed intent on looking at the screen rather than him.

"Are you okay?" he asked at last, reaching across the sofa, to rest his hand on her leg. Lisa shifted her position slightly, but she didn't respond and hold his hand.

"Lisa?"

She pressed the mute button on the remote control.

"I'm fine. Just tired."

"Are you sure?"

"Danny, I... " She sighed. "Look, it's been a rotten day. Jessica woke up early and made a total fuss when I dropped her at playgroup this morning, and then work's been tough, all right?

I'm a bit stressed, and I don't want to have an argument about it."

"Nobody's arguing," he said. "I'm just worried about you, that's all."

"Yeah? Well, there's no need to worry. There's nothing you can do about it. I want to switch off and not think about it, okay?"

That was the end of that. She restored the volume, but she still wasn't laughing. The message was sinking in.

"I should be getting home," said Danny. "I'll leave you in peace. I think an early night would do us both good."

Lisa muted the volume again. Her face looked thunderous, but softened as Danny reached for his shoes and started tying the laces.

"Look, I'm sorry," she said. "You know I can't talk about it."

"I know."

"I wish I could, but ..."

"Don't worry," Danny interrupted. They'd been here so many times before. "But if there's anything I can do, you will let me know?"

She nodded. Danny gently squeezed her leg, and this time she returned the gesture, squeezing his hand.

"I'm free tomorrow," she said, in a softer voice. "Mum's taking Jessica for the evening. Let's have a proper date night. I think it'd do us good."

Danny's first thought was Anna's birthday, but he tried to shake it. It wasn't right.

"Great idea," he said. "What could you fancy? Restaurant? Cinema? Theatre?"

"I don't know what's on at the cinema. Is *Jerry Maguire* still on? I'd have loved to have seen that. It's probably too late to get tickets for the theatre."

"How about this then, we go up to the West End, find a restaurant, go to the cinema after."

"Unless you just want to come round here and rekindle a bit of passion." She said the words, but Danny didn't see the enthusiasm reflected in her eyes.

"No, you're right," he said. "We should have a night out. There are precious few opportunities as it is."

But then she didn't look too enthusiastic about that either.

"Can we afford it?" she said.

Please, not this again.

"Oh come on."

"We're neither of us made of money, Danny. And you haven't been paid in I don't know how long."

"I know." He struggled to keep the exasperation out of his voice. "I'll stick it on a card if necessary."

"I can't ask you to do that."

"Fine, we'll stay in then."

It took a moment for the tension to subside.

"I'll tell you what," said Danny. "Let's go out, have a lovely time, but just try to keep the cost down."

"Okay. Good plan."

"It'll do us good."

"It will. Should I come to yours and pick you up at seven?"

"Perfect. See you tomorrow."

Danny smiled as best as he could and then kissed Lisa goodbye, before showing himself out for an evening alone.

It was nearly half past nine by the time I texted Danny back, and even then it was just a simple *"Yes we should."*

I very nearly added *"and if you're serious about needing somewhere to stay, we should discuss it, because I'll have my spare room back soon"* but thought better of it. Because if I once started that ball rolling, there was a chance that he'd say yes, and things would escalate beyond all control. And that was too much to take in, especially as I wasn't feeling my best.

I'd put it down to the heavy Sunday, but then remembered a theory of biorhythms, in which you were likely to be poorly just before your birthday because it was the anniversary of the most difficult part of your mother's pregnancy. And I already had issues with that. If she'd pushed just a little bit harder in the final stages, I'd have been born ten minutes earlier, and then I would have gone through life being on time for everything.

There was a ping, but it wasn't a reply from Danny. It wasn't even from my normal phone. It was from the special phone that Clare had given me, so that we always had a way of keeping in touch. Making sure the thing was charged up for the very occasional call or message was a bit of a faff, but it was a small price to pay for the number of times she'd saved my life. And while I hoped those days were over, I always felt bizarrely privileged to hear from her. I opened the message.

How's Louise? I hope she's settled in okay and she's not causing you any problems.

I sent a message back.

Yes, she's lovely. She seems happy and it's a pleasure to have her here. She's in her room reading at the moment, but she treated me to a pizza which was very nice. I think I'll miss her when she goes. :-)

I got a reply almost immediately.

· · ·

That's great news. You know where I am if you need me. And thank you again for helping. x

I decided to have an early night. It was a good excuse to curl up with *Bridget Jones's Diary*, which I was finding strangely reassuring. And anyway, there was a lot to think about. Not least that if Louise had other friends in London, who she'd met for coffee, why wasn't she staying with them, rather than with a complete stranger?

Chapter 12

Tuesday, January 21st, 1997

DANNY was up early. It was a special day. And even if Anna was in denial about her birthday, it was a great opportunity to demonstrate that he could be thoughtful, hopefully help rebuild bridges, and have a laugh in the process.

He didn't know what time she went to work, but he thought eight would be a good time to arrive. That way he could leave a present outside the door to her flat, so she'd discover it as she left for the day, while minimising the chance of anyone stealing it from the communal hallway. There was a card, a bottle of wine, and a ball of wool and two knitting needles.

The first challenge was getting through the outer door, but he was in luck. As he was approaching, one of the tenants of another flat was leaving, and with a short sprint, he managed to catch the door before it swung completely shut.

The hallway was cold, with two ground floor flats - Anna and her next door neighbour - and a staircase that led to the other flats above. He stood on the stairs as he unpacked the presents, getting ready to leave them. Then Anna's door started to open.

Danny leapt upstairs, his heart racing, desperate not to be caught, hoping that Anna wouldn't look up and see him.

But it wasn't Anna who stepped out into the hallway and then closed the door gently behind her. It was Louise. And she was dressed to kill, with impeccable make-up, in a short royal blue coat, short skirt, black sheer tights, and high heels. His first thought was wow! But there was something about her demeanour that looked both furtive and purposeful, and immediately his investigative instincts kicked in. Who exactly was she? What was she doing here? Where had she come from? And why was she leaving the house so early in the morning, so elaborately dressed?

There was no reason to assume she was up to anything untoward. And yet, something didn't look quite right. Maybe it was the connection with Clare, or perhaps just the way she seemed to be trying to sneak out unnoticed. Danny only had a moment to think, but his brain was working overtime. And his suspicions were definitely aroused. In that moment, he decided that for his own peace of mind, he would have to look into it.

He waited until Louise left through the main front door, then quickly arranged the presents and followed her out onto the street. But despite looking both ways, he couldn't see her.

And then she stepped out from a bus shelter, where she'd paused to light a cigarette, protected from the morning breeze. She continued walking, quickening her pace. Danny fell into step, a considerable distance behind, but close enough that he could watch without being noticed.

Louise crossed the road, weaving in and out of slow-moving traffic, then turned abruptly into a narrow alleyway between two shops.

Danny hurriedly crossed the road, but by the time he got to the end of the alley, Louise was about halfway along. It was too narrow to follow without attracting attention, but he was sure it was a dead end, leading nowhere. He paused, watching. Then a young man, with the gait of a disaffected teenager, emerged from a doorway further down, wearing dark jeans and a down jacket with the hood obscuring his face. From a distance, Louise appeared to hesitate, but she didn't stop.

Danny felt in his pocket for his compact Nikon Zoom 500 camera, then held it at waist level, sacrificing the comfort of looking through the viewfinder in favour of discretion. He stood on the corner, glancing to his right, ready at any moment to disappear from view if Louise looked like turning. He pressed the shutter release, several times, capturing the moment on film, even if he wasn't sure quite what was happening.

He peeked round the corner and watched while Louise stopped to talk to the man. The conversation seemed to be intense. Then she reached into her pocket and gave him an envelope. Was it money? The man handed her a small package in return. It looked like drugs. Danny shot a few more pictures, hoping they would be in focus. Hoping that the lens was pointing in vaguely the right direction. And then, as Louise started to turn, he slunk back into a nearby shop doorway, to see what happened next.

A moment later, she returned to the main road, and continued walking in the direction of the Tube station. Danny followed again, closer this time, as he was protected by the ever-increasing number of other people walking in the same direction. Her actions were curious enough that he felt wholly justified in his surveillance.

Louise walked down to the southbound Northern Line platform. When the train arrived, Danny seized his chance and jumped onto the adjacent carriage. She got off at Goodge Street and he followed her again, until she entered the lobby of a hotel. He expected her to stop at reception, but she didn't. She carried on, straight past, and from his vantage point on the street outside, he watched as she entered the lift and disappeared from view.

There was no sign of Louise when I woke up and got ready for work, but her door was closed so I decided she must be sleeping. I thought about waking her, but then remembered I wasn't her mum, and she was a grown adult, albeit only just. Unlike me, who had woken up a year older than I wanted to be, hoping nobody would notice.

As I left the flat, I nearly tripped over several packages on my doorstep. But then, when I saw the birthday wrapping paper, I knew they weren't there by accident.

I took them inside. It was a beautiful card. Danny had chosen well, even if I could remember specifically telling him not to make a fuss. But when I opened the first gift, I found it easy to forgive him. I like wine, may have mentioned it. Especially expensive wine, and to be fair, he hadn't skimped. The wool and knitting needles, though ... They were the actions of a cheeky git.

I couldn't help but smile. And then the smile deepened. This could be good. If Danny was trying to work his way back into my affections, I could have a bit of fun: make him suffer, and play hard to get. Which I appreciate I've done before to my own detriment - but far from being deterred by past failures, I proudly embraced them as all part of life's learning.

Tuesdays are normally my London Underground day. I've never been a fan of the Tube but I've been trying to come to terms with it, one small step at a time. It's a work-driven objective. If I'm out with colleagues, I get funny looks if I catch a bus or taxi while the others go on a train together. At best, it's antisocial. At worst it looks like I'm on the same spectrum as those who would rather climb thirty flights of stairs than risk fifteen seconds in a lift (although I'm not belittling them - it must be tough having a phobia that doesn't even have an official name). I'm not scared of the Underground as such. I just don't like it. So every Tuesday I've been travelling to work by Tube to try to get more acclimatised.

But not on my birthday.

Danny called when I was in the back of the cab, heading to the office, but obviously I didn't answer. He called again, and left a message this time. I should call him immediately. Haha, well he could wait for a bit. All part of the game.

My desk was decorated with balloons, streamers and a big, albeit slightly tired-looking banner saying Happy Birthday, and midway through the morning there was a cake. I like cakes, and I was really touched that they'd made such an effort. I still felt like the new girl, but I was beginning to feel accepted.

Nathan gave me my present from the whip-round - a month-long pass and two personal training sessions at the gym, just down the road from our office. Nobody had been more surprised than me when I'd thought that would be a good suggestion, but there was method in my fast-developing madness. It wasn't the sort of thing I'd buy for myself, and yet somewhere, deep down, I knew I should do something to work off the effects of excess wine, especially now I was entering middle age.

Not that I'd ever tell Danny of course. He'd find it hilarious. He tried to ring me several more times throughout the morning, but I kept my phone on silent so I wouldn't be tempted to answer. I'm such a tease.

Danny slammed the phone down once again. He would have tried Anna at work but didn't know the name of her company. It was so frustrating. But she had to know what he'd discovered about Louise.

In desperation, he called Clare on his version of the private phone.

"I need you to be honest with me," he said when she answered.

"I always am, Danny. You're not turning into Anna are you?"

He ignored the question. He wasn't in the mood for jokes. In any case, her voice was faint above the busy London traffic.

"Okay, so be honest with me. Who is Louise?"

"In what way?"

"You know in what way."

"I'm not sure I do."

Danny could feel his patience ebbing away, and it was showing in his voice. He paused for a moment while a siren made it pointless to continue. He edged back into a doorway to try to shield himself, but the benefit was marginal. Eventually the police car passed, and he was able to continue.

"Where does she come from? How do you know her? How *well* do you know her? What is she doing here? Why is she staying with Anna?"

"That's a lot of questions."

"With good reason."

"Why so many questions?"

"Can you please just answer them?"

"Okay, I will." Clare paused. Danny waited.

"Well?" he said eventually.

"I'm just weighing things up. I will answer them, of course, and any others you can think of, all to the best of my knowledge. And I think you'll get a brilliant story out of it. But the phone isn't the best place to do it."

"What sort of story?"

"The sort of story we used to do. It's exposing the bad guys."

Danny was intrigued, but it didn't help ease the frustration.

"So can we meet?"

"That was the delay. I was checking my diary. When is good for you?"

"This afternoon? This evening?"

"I could do this evening. As long as you're happy to travel."

"I'll travel. Where on earth are you?"

"You know, that's the first time I've known anyone add 'on earth' to a question and actually mean it."

"Clare, please."

It was exasperating.

"Warsaw."

"*Walsall?*"

"No, Warsaw. In Poland. Not the Walsall, north west of Birmingham."

"How am I supposed to get to Warsaw? And what on earth are you doing there?"

"That's a less relevant use of the phrase."

"Christ. Just tell me."

"I'm sorting out some things. I like Warsaw. It's one of my favourites. And as for how you get here, if you can get to Heathrow it's about two and a half hours via British Airways. Hold on one moment."

Danny sighed and looked at the traffic while he waited for Clare to return. He left the doorway and started heading in the direction of the nearest Tube station. It was ridiculous to think he could travel to Warsaw. A taxi was parked at the side of the road, belching out thick black diesel fumes, so he crossed to the other side.

"I'm back," said Clare. "There's a flight this afternoon. If you can get to the airport in the next four hours or so, they still have seats."

"This is madness. I can't get to Warsaw. Apart from anything else, I'm freelance now, I don't have an expense account, or the money for last-minute flights across Europe. Never mind a hotel."

"I knew you were going to say that. So here's the deal. Can you physically get there?"

"Get where?"

"Heathrow."

"I could physically get to Heathrow."

"In the next four hours?"

"Yes. I'm not at home but it wouldn't take long."

"Okay, perfect. Do that. I'll buy the ticket. You can pick it up at the BA ticket desk. It'll be a flexible return flight, in your name. I'll get you picked up at the airport here, and don't worry about accommodation. I'll sort that out for you."

"This is still madness."

"It's important, Danny. Do you want me to tell you about Louise?"

"Of course I do, but I can't ask you to pay for flights and hotels and all that, never mind travel halfway across Europe on a whim."

"Consider it already done, and it's only two and half hours. It would take longer than that to get to Sunderland on the train. Now get off the phone and go and pack a suitcase. Bring enough for a few days. I think you'll like Warsaw."

The line went dead. Danny stood motionless for a moment, wondering what he'd just agreed to. He looked at his watch. There would just about be enough time to drop off the film on a one-hour processing service and then get home before leaving for the airport. But there was one other thing he had to do.

Once the film had been handed in, he dialled Lisa's number. It went to voicemail.

"Hi," he said, feeling dreadful. "It's about tonight. Really, really sorry but I'm going to have to cancel. A work thing has come up. I'll make it up to you. Call me when you can. And sorry again."

He wasn't confident that she would ever return the call.

Chapter 13

LOUISE and Adam's crew had a long, intensive day of brainstorming, planning and preparation. The more they worked on the details, the more she was confident that the project would be a success. She had to hope so. Clare's £50,000 banker's draft was at stake.

She'd made an effort with her outfit for the dress rehearsal, and Toby had clearly been impressed. She still wasn't sure if he trusted her, but she knew she'd made an impression. Part of the plan was for the two of them to have a drink together. It was strictly professional, and expertly scripted, but Toby hadn't been able to resist making suggestive remarks about what they could do together afterwards. And yet she knew that despite all of his youthful exuberance, he was a valued member of the crew. Harry had explained Toby's pivotal role in a previous project, which brought down the mastermind of a pension transfer scheme that had defrauded hundreds of elderly people out of their life savings.

By late afternoon, however, she was starting to get anxious. She wanted to get home and change before Anna arrived back from work, so as to avoid any awkward questions. Harry picked up on her concern, and suggested that they should have a break and be fresh for the evening, when the first stage of the plan was due to be put in motion. Luckily, Adam agreed.

But as she left the hotel and headed out into the late afternoon traffic, a woman with short hair and a black trench coat, tied at the waist, approached her.

"Louise?" she said.

"I am."

DS Amy Cranston introduced herself and offered a hand to shake.

"Clare told me all about you," she said. "How are you finding London?"

"It's big and noisy but I'm learning my way around."

"You're looking very smart. Have you been visiting anyone?" She nodded back in the direction of the hotel.

Louise was on her guard. She didn't know how much Amy knew.

"Just a friend."

"Okay."

Amy took a step back, and Louise could feel that she was being assessed.

"How well do you know Clare?" asked Amy. Where had that come from?

"Reasonably well, I think."

Amy nodded, as if trying to decide whether or not to believe her.

"Well, let me warn you," she continued, "she does unconventional things. They get results, occasionally, but she doesn't always stick within either the letter or the spirit of the law. We don't chase after her because -" Amy frowned, as though choosing her words carefully.

"Because she's helped you out in other ways," Louise finished. "She's like a super-informer."

Amy's eyes narrowed. The stare was unsettling.

"That's one way of putting it. But don't think it gives you carte blanche to do anything you like. The situation could change at any time, and it doesn't extend to her friends and colleagues."

"Understood."

"So if you do anything illegal, even if it's under Clare's instruction, I'm warning you that you will be stopped. And we'll be keeping a close eye on you."

"That's good to know. But don't worry, I am not going to do anything bad. I'm aware I am a visitor in this country. I will be, how do you say it? Playing it safe."

"I'm glad to hear it."

Louise looked at her watch.

"Is there anything else? It's just that I'm running late for something and I should really be making a move."

"No. That's all," said Amy.

"Well, thank you for the, er, warning." Louise smiled, but it didn't reach her eyes. "I will be sure to be careful. It's been a pleasure to meet you."

"Let's hope it is next time, too," said Amy, before turning to leave as suddenly as she'd arrived.

Worth knowing, thought Louise. She knew she'd have to be extra-careful. But she couldn't explain to Adam that she was now under police surveillance. There was no turning back.

To be fair to him, Danny tries. I'd fully intended to call him back at lunchtime, but Nathan suggested a birthday excursion for sandwiches at Pret A Manger, and I could hardly refuse.

"How's your birthday so far?" he asked, as we walked down the street.

"It's actually been all right," I said.

"Did you get lots of cards and presents?"

"No, only a couple, but I told everyone I know not to bother." I didn't want to go into how I didn't really have very many close friends, aside from Danny and a mad woman called Clare.

"I bet you'd have never imagined being here, on your last birthday. That's what's wonderful about this industry. It's all changing so quickly."

I had to think back.

"This time last year I was preparing to fly to Venice to do a photo shoot for a hat company."

"Wow, that's amazing. And yet now you're here, slumming it with us."

"Honestly, it wasn't as glamorous as it possibly sounds. But yes, you're right, I suppose. I'm pretty sure that four years ago I'd never heard of the Internet. I'd certainly never sent an email."

"We live in exciting times."

"You think?"

"Of course. Don't you?"

I didn't really know what I thought. But I couldn't shake the feeling that the 1990s were a bit of an anticlimax. Not as much fun as the '80s, and primarily something we all had to get through to have the exciting dawn of the new millennium, whatever that would entail.

"I'm twenty-seven," I said. "When I was growing up we had exciting things like Duran Duran and loads of other really good bands. Depeche Mode. Ultravox. Then there was the Cold War and the constant threat of it all kicking off, and it was dangerous, but weirdly it made you aware of your circumstances, your own vulnerability, and you could imagine how exciting it would be to be a spy. But now it's all celebrities and Richard Branson crashing his balloon. Britpop and the Spice Girls, and Princess Diana faffing around with Dodi Fayed. I don't know. I just think young people today are missing out on the excitement we had."

"Well, I'm twenty-one and I don't think I'm missing out."

"You're twenty-one?"

"Do you think I look older?" He seemed a touch offended.

"No, not all. I just ... I just don't know. I never really considered it, I suppose. Well, now I do feel old."

He laughed.

"You're not old. You haven't even reached your prime yet."

"Nathan, I beg to differ. Anyway, there's an election soon. That might change everything."

"If Tony Blair gets in? I hope so."

"Exactly. And then I suppose we've got the millennium to look forward to, although I imagine it'll be that Prince record, wall-to-wall for an entire year, and frankly I've heard that enough already."

He laughed again.

"Sometimes I wish I was straight," he said. "I think we'd have got on famously."

"I still think we're going to get on. And it's better, anyway, because we don't have to worry about any of that emotional crap, because if there's one thing I'm shit at, it's relationships. Anyway, when are we having our night out?"

"Definitely soon." He put his arm through mine, and it was strangely comforting.

Lunch took longer than it should have done, and I didn't have a chance to ring Danny when I got back to the office, as I was called into a content strategy meeting. By the time it finished, I was starting to feel guilty, so the first thing I did was call him. But there was no answer, and when I tried again a few minutes later, his phone appeared to be switched off altogether. That's annoying, I thought. And then a familiar worry began to resurface. Had I messed it up again by playing hard to get? Surely he couldn't be that sensitive, could he? But he wasn't me, and therefore he wasn't rational, and God knows what he was thinking.

What if he'd been calling about something important? What if he was in trouble?

I headed home for a birthday evening with Louise, but with a growing sense of worry, resolving never to play hard to get again.

Chapter 14

DANNY emerged from baggage reclaim at Okecie International Airport in Warsaw, still not quite believing he'd agreed to the trip. And now he was here, it seemed like an even more ridiculous idea. He knew very little about modern Poland, apart from what he'd seen in the news a few years previously, when it broke free of Russian rule. He didn't understand a word of the language, didn't have any of the local currency, and felt uncomfortable at the thought that he was handing over all control to Clare Woodbrook. At best she was a good friend, and he enjoyed her company. But she was never far from trouble.

A middle-aged man in a dark brown suit was holding a board marked "Danny Churchill", so he tried to introduce himself, but the man didn't speak English, and instead just indicated for him to follow. Immediately, Danny tried to assess the risks. What if this was not the person that Clare had arranged? It might be anyone, taking him to anywhere.

The journey could have been through any of countless cities in Europe. Open roads gave way to residential development, then steadily heavier traffic through streets lined with shops and scenes of construction. Danny tried to get his bearings, but his view was hampered by the darkness, and the combination of lashing rain and spray from other vehicles. The driver turned up the heating to de-mist the windscreen, making the car uncomfortably hot and airless. On the radio, familiar mainstream pop gave way to unintelligible voices in a language that he could not understand at all.

The sense of unease didn't abate until the car pulled into a bay outside a block of apartments in the city centre, just past the Centralna railway station. The man fetched Danny's case from the boot, and then indicated to a door in a covered passageway, running down the side of the building. Shivering in the cold, Danny pressed the buzzer, and waited for a response, feeling helpless and at the mercy of others.

"Do you need a hand with the bag?"

He turned to find Clare, standing under an umbrella, smiling at him. The door buzzed, and she led the way inside.

"Well done for making it. What do you think of your room?" she asked, once they'd picked up the key, and made their way to the fourth floor.

"It's all right now I'm inside, but the corridors looked like a prison," said Danny. "What's with all the metal grilles?"

"It used to be residential," said Clare, as if that was explanation enough.

Danny rested his case on the floor by the bed, and then checked the bathroom. The whole apartment was small, but there was room for a sofa and a small kitchen area. It was clean and functional, and there was even a small balcony, which could be a welcome addition in the summer.

"It looks much better than it did from the outside," he said. "Although I have no idea how long I'm supposed to be staying here."

"Me neither at the moment. A couple of nights, though, possibly. Do you have anything to be rushing back to?"

Danny thought of Lisa. He still hadn't spoken to her since leaving the voicemail. He shook his head.

"Good," Clare continued. "Do you need a bit of time to get freshened up? I was thinking of taking you to dinner, because I imagine you must be starving."

"No, just a couple of minutes. I need to make a quick call." But when he looked at his phone, it showed no signal.

"What network are you on?" asked Clare.

"Orange."

"Ah. They don't have roaming agreements yet. You can borrow mine if you like."

"Won't that give away your number? You do know I'm calling Lisa."

"That's a valid point, Danny. And I don't mean my normal phone. I mean a separate one."

"How many phones have you got, for heaven's sake?"

Clare's expression indicated that she'd never actually counted, nor thought it was anything unusual to have more than one.

"I have different phones for different things. One for business. One that only you and Anna have access to. This is a different one, that's just a short-term thing that I change often."

Clare reached into her bag for her Motorola StarTAC 85 clamshell phone, and passed it over.

"It's +44 for the UK, then the number, minus the zero. I'll wait outside," she said.

"Perfect. I'll be five minutes."

Danny tried Lisa's number, but it went to voicemail again. He thought about leaving another message, explaining he was in Warsaw, but decided against it. They had a rule not to discuss work with each other. He tried Anna again, but that just rang and rang. Finally, he gave up, and joined Clare outside.

The restaurant was only a short walk away, but Danny was glad of the warmth when they got inside. The decor was modern, with black floor tiles, black tables, and subdued lighting aside from the occasional strategically placed spotlight. It looked seductively upmarket, and the kind of place where deals could be done, or where lovers could have a secret, illicit liaison.

Clare ordered wine, and then waited for Danny to look at the menu, and make his selection from the delicious-sounding steaks on offer. Once the order was placed, she got to the point.

"So, you want to know all about Lucy?" she said.

"Who's Lucy?"

"Sorry. Louise." Danny thought he detected the hint of a blush, but it was difficult to know in the subdued lighting. "I call her Lucy for short sometimes."

"Right. Because Lucy's got fewer syllables?"

Clare shrugged, then smiled.

"We'll stick with Louise, shall we?"

"You're the boss."

"Ah, if only, Danny. Alas those days have gone. I've told you. I work for you now."

"And to quote you, 'if only'." Danny took a sip of his wine. He didn't normally drink red, but it was delicious. "So, tell me about Louise."

Clare made an elaborate show of removing a packet of cigarettes and a lighter from the clutch bag on the table between them, then lit one, and waved the smoke away.

"Okay," she said at last. "But do you promise not to be angry with me?"

I was forced to go for a birthday drink with my colleagues after work, which kind of seemed to be labouring the point, but I could hardly say no. But I managed to keep it to just the one, explaining that I had a friend staying with me, and needed to get home. That raised a few eyebrows. Nathan nudged me, then leaned in close to whisper.

"They'll be heartbroken."

It took me a moment to realise what he meant. I thought about explaining that it really was a friend, and not a hot date, but then thought better of it. Whoever these mystery - and probably mythical - admirers were, it wouldn't do any harm to encourage them to leave me alone.

When I arrived home, Louise was on the sofa. She immediately stood up and gave me a happy birthday hug, but then stepped back, looking shy and awkward, as though worried she'd overstepped a boundary again. She offered to leave me in peace and go to her room, but I told her not to be silly.

"I don't know if Auntie Clare warned you about my cooking," I started, trying to suppress a giggle at the ongoing charade, "but I'm going to attempt some form of pasta thing for tea. You're more than welcome to join me."

"That's very kind," she said, looking genuinely touched. "But unfortunately I've agreed to meet a friend for dinner tonight."

"Probably wise." Hmmm. Another friend. The plot thickened. I was desperate to ask her about her friends, but I didn't want to look too intrusive this early. I'd get it out of her, though. Eventually.

"Oh. I got you a birthday present," she said, with a great big smile. "One moment and I'll get it for you." She headed towards the door, in the direction of her room.

"You didn't need to get me a present."

"I know, but I wanted to, to stay thank you."

A moment later she was back, with a small, beautifully-wrapped rectangular box.

"This is for you," she said. Her eyes were wide open, as though seeking approval. The urge to nurture her was overpowering.

I took the box to the big sofa, and she sat opposite me, perched on the edge of the smaller one. The wrapping paper revealed a burgundy leather box, and when I opened the box I was speechless.

"I hope you like it," she said.

I very nearly cried. It was beautiful. A Ceylon sapphire pendant necklace that perfectly matched the ring I'd stolen from Clare. However much had that cost?

"It's absolutely gorgeous," I said, when I finally found my voice. "But seriously, you must have spent a fortune. You shouldn't have, but it's divine."

"I had a little bit of help with the money," she said, sheepishly. "And with choosing it. Here, let me help you."

My phone started ringing but I ignored it. I leaned forward and she helped me fasten the clasp so I could see what it felt like. It felt expensive. I could sense the spirit of Clare in the room alongside us. I was aware that she knew about the ring. She'd caught me wearing it. But it was her own fault for deliberately leaving it down the side of a chair, when she was on the run. She hadn't asked for it back, but instead had bought herself an even bigger one to replace it. It was one of my most treasured possessions, and now it had a friend.

"Thank you so much," I said, giving her a hug. "That's way beyond the call of duty and incredibly kind. I shall treasure it."

Louise said she had to get ready, and when she returned, twenty minutes later, she looked stunning in a black dress, heels, and a gorgeous royal blue coat.

"Wow," I said. "You look fabulous."

"Do you like it? I bought it today."

"You look amazing. It suits you." God, I was starting to feel old. I offered to give her a lift to wherever she was going, but she insisted on taking a taxi, telling me she couldn't expect me to go out, especially on my birthday. I wasn't going to argue, but I was starting to feel increasingly protective.

It was surprisingly lonely in the flat once she'd left. It had only been a couple of days, but I was amazed how quickly I'd got used to having company. I tried Danny again, but his phone was still off. The playing hard-to-get thing had, indeed, failed to serve its desired purpose. Now I was the one calling Danny repeatedly. I imagined him looking at his phone and chuckling. Or maybe locked in some sort of romantic clinch with Lisa, seduced by one dangle of her handcuffs, which wasn't what I wanted to be thinking about, today of all days. So there it was. My birthday, spent on my own, worrying about him, and worrying about my young houseguest, having no idea what I wanted to do with my life. From the arm of the sofa, the knitting needles were taunting me.

I tried Danny one last time before settling down for a night in front of the TV, trying to laugh at *Harry Enfield and Chums*, and then thinking of Clare when it was followed by an Inside Story documentary about female spies and honey traps. I sent her a message, thanking her for her part in the present, but she didn't reply either. There are times when only a cup of tea will do.

Chapter 15

"I CAN try not to be angry with you," said Danny. "But the mere fact you say that makes me think there's a good chance I will be."

Clare looked at her watch. Danny felt the urge to do the same. After the two-and-a-half-hour flight, and with the one-hour time difference, it was already nearly 10pm.

"I hope you won't be," she said. "It is kind of a long story, though, and it's already rather late."

"I didn't come all the way to Warsaw to be fobbed off, or to be in bed before midnight."

"No, although there are lots of opportunities for a single man to be in bed before midnight in a town like Warsaw. How is Lisa, by the way?"

"Lisa's fine."

"Are you still living with her?"

"I was never living with her."

"But you're still together as a couple? It's just that if you're not, the women here are beautiful and intelligent and I could introduce you to some friends of mine ..."

The food arrived. The steaks looked delicious, and were

immaculately presented, alongside side orders of various vegetables.

"So getting back to Louise," said Danny, once they'd made a start. His patience was wearing thin. And yet he found it hard to really lose his temper with Clare. He knew her well enough by now to understand her games. And she would forever be on a pedestal, as the woman he'd always looked up to, even if her recent career had been substantially less admirable.

"Who is she?" he asked.

"She's a very good friend of mine."

"But not your niece though?"

"No."

"And is her name actually Louise?"

"No."

"But you call her Louise because ...?"

"Because it's easier than her real name."

"Which is?"

"Agnieszka. Which I can spell for you, if you like, but I'll warn you now, it's got a z in it."

"She's Polish then?"

Clare nodded.

"I suppose that figures. And you're here because of that?"

Clare nodded again.

"What is she doing in London?" Danny continued.

"Working."

"Working doing what?"

"Officially trying to be an actress, but she has a few sidelines."

"I can imagine. Such as?"

"I don't know. Probably bar work, waitressing. You'll see once she gets settled."

Danny was unconvinced but decided to come back to that later.

"Have you known her long?" he continued.

"Quite a long time, yes."

"And how well do you know her?"

Clare shrugged, looking thoughtful.

"Not as well as I'd like."

"But you trust her?"

"Implicitly."

Danny sat back, trying to gather his thoughts. He wasn't sure he was getting anywhere.

"So why are you in Poland?" he asked.

"I'm going to come on to that."

"Do you want to come on to it now?"

"In a moment."

It was exasperating.

"You know the most important thing to me?" he said. "Whatever you're up to, you've arranged for Louise, or whatever her name is ..."

"Honestly, it's easier to stick with Louise."

"... you've arranged for her to stay with Anna. And I want to know why, because I don't know what you're playing at, but if Anna is involved and gets hurt in any way, physically or emotionally, I'm going to be furious."

"Anna is safe. I promise you. I've told you, I'm a good person. I try to do the right things. To help people."

"Oh shit." Danny suddenly looked startled.

"What?"

"Can I quickly borrow your phone again to make a quick call to Anna, just to check she's okay. Wish her a happy birthday?"

"Of course. You can use the special Anna phone. One moment. I hadn't realised it was her birthday. That's unforgivable."

"I wouldn't worry. But it would be nice to know that she's okay."

"Of course."

Clare reached into her coat pocket and withdrew another Motorola, and passed it across.

"You still have feelings then?" she said.

Danny took a deep breath and sighed.

"Of course. She's my best friend."

"Still?"

"I'd like to think so."

"Despite what you did?"

"What did I do? Tell me. You're clever. Tell me, please, what exactly I did wrong. You know what she's like. *'I don't do relationships.'* *'Why mess up a friendship?'* We lived together for what? Seven years. We even slept in the same bed on countless occasions, largely thanks to you ..."

"You're welcome," Clare interrupted with a mischievous glint in her eyes.

"And she didn't ever give me any indication that she ever wanted more. But I did. Love. Passion. Sex ...."

"And again, I could arrange those while you're here, although probably not the love and passion bit."

Danny ignored her.

"But she didn't ever want that. At least not with me."

"She did."

"But did she? Not until I met Lisa."

"Oh, Danny." Clare shook her head. "Look, call her before it gets too late and then we can continue this conversation."

———

There was nothing else for it. I decided to have a bath. The water was running, and the bubbles were growing tremendously when I heard my Clare phone ringing. I quickly turned off the taps and ran back to the front room, but it stopped just before I got there.

I dialled her back immediately, and the call connected, but the line was dreadful. She sounded like a robot, and every other syllable was missing. I thanked her for the gift and said it was lovely, but I didn't know if she could hear me either. And then the line went dead. I tried calling back, but it couldn't even make a connection. So much for the wonders of technology.

So it was back to the bath for a leisurely soak, then an early night with Bridget Jones. I hoped Clare was okay. I hoped Danny was okay. I hoped Louise was okay. Oh, and there was another thought. Maybe Danny wasn't answering his phone because he was out on a hot date with Louise. I wouldn't put it past him. I wanted to wait up till she arrived home, primarily to see if she'd smudged her lipstick, and had a particularly guilty expression, but after one chapter, I was asleep before I'd even had the chance to turn out my bedside light.

I didn't sleep well, though. My mind was too active. Sometimes I think I get a sixth sense when I know that something is going wrong.

Chapter 16

AT a table in an expensive, seductively-lit bar in the West End of London, Louise was in the midst of a furious argument with Toby.

George Brandrick was enjoying the show. It had gone well beyond a standard lovers' tiff, and looked on the cusp of turning violent, and he couldn't help but admire the young woman. Both in terms of her spark and devilishly sexy demeanour. At one point she got up and stormed off, but then came back and threatened to pour a drink over her companion. George couldn't make out all of the words, but it was spectacular entertainment.

He tried to get closer, to hear what she was saying, but he was caught out when she turned towards him, looking furious.

"And what the fuck are you looking at?" she snarled.

George turned away, embarrassed to be caught, but still tried to keep an ear on the row. Then the young man said something to her that made her angrier still. He stood up.

"Get your own fucking drink." At least, that's what George thought he'd said. Either way, he turned and departed. The woman sat there for a moment, as though waiting for him to return. But when he didn't she made her way to the bar.

"Sorry about that," said Clare. "The line can be bad. But at least you know she's okay."

"Yeah, I suppose." Danny continued with his steak, but he was frustrated. It had been Anna's birthday all day, and he still hadn't managed to speak to her properly. She'd said thank you for the present, though, in between the words cutting out, so at least that was something. "It's weird. I used to be so relaxed, thinking we were immortal, but now I keep worrying about her."

"That's understandable."

"I know, but I've got enough on my plate worrying about you."

Clare was visibly surprised.

"Me?"

"Yes, of course you. I do care about you, you know."

"Well, that's very nice to know, even if a bit unexpected. And likewise."

Danny pushed his knife and fork to one side and took another sip of the wine. The candle on the table was flickering between them. It gave Clare's skin a golden glow. She looked well, and yet who really knew what was going on in her world?

"Are you safe here?" he asked.

Clare looked thoughtful for a moment.

"I think so. It's a very safe city," she said. "As long as you don't get caught up in the riots."

"Riots?"

"The fascists and the anti-fascists. It gets a bit lively sometimes."

"Right. Anyway, I mean - " Danny leaned forward and lowered his voice, "- from the police."

Clare's thoughtful expression turned quizzical.

"As far as I know. I've not done anything wrong for a very long time."

"It's what, ten months since you killed someone?"

"Oh, please." She sat back. "Anyway, that was an accident. He was a bad person. I only wanted to teach him a lesson. It wasn't my fault he had a bad heart."

"Even so, though. You can't keep doing that."

"I don't!" She sounded offended, but the frown was soon replaced by a grin. "You should come to my room. Check it for bodies. Give everything a thorough inspection."

Danny noticed the wink and laughed.

"If I didn't know you better, I'd think you were flirting with me."

"Who says I'm not?"

He laughed.

"Do you know how often I dreamed about something like that? But can you imagine? What would Anna say?"

"We'd have to keep it secret."

"You'd be okay with that. I'm rubbish at secrets. She'd kill me. Both of us."

"It'd be fine. I'll teach you self-defence."

Danny knew Clare was joking, but he was enjoying the chat. And yet he knew it was time to get serious. Clare had finished eating as well now, so it was as good a time as any.

"You know the weird thing?" he said. "I do think a lot of you. I assume you know that."

"I'm flattered."

"Oh, come on. You were everything I aspired to be. Until, well, let's say when we stopped working together. And I don't want to offend you ..."

"But?"

"There is a 'but'. And here it is. But I don't know if I believe a word you've told me tonight."

"About what?"

"About Louise."

He waited for her to respond, watching for any change in her expression, but she was the past master at utilising silence.

"I rang you," Danny continued, knowing that he'd have to be first to flinch, "and you said you couldn't discuss Louise on the phone, so I had to get a flight and now, here I am, a thousand miles from home, and yet you've still not said anything even remotely contentious. Okay, so that's not her real name, and she works as a waitress occasionally. So what? Big deal. If that was all it was, you could have told me that on the phone."

Danny reached into the inside pocket of his jacket and withdrew the photos he'd taken that morning, then took a final look before handing them across.

"So, no offence, and excuse the language, but I think you're talking bullshit," he said. "This was Louise this morning."

Clare picked up the pictures and looked through them before placing them face down on the table beside her plate.

"Where did you get these?" she asked.

"I took them. I saw her leave the flat, and I was curious. So I followed. And if I'm not mistaken, she's buying drugs. Then she goes into a hotel, all dressed up. I don't think it's too much of a leap to think she's not turning up to work in the restaurant."

"So you're saying what?"

"I don't think you need me to spell it out, do you?"

"Try me."

"Clare, don't pretend to be naive. This is me, not some idiot you just met."

"So, you're saying what? That she's working as some kind of high-class call girl? Obtaining drugs for clients?"

"That's exactly what I'm saying. It's certainly what it looks like."

"Danny, I trained you well." She paused, then picked up the pictures and handed them back. "Although sadly, not well enough."

Clare returned her phone to her bag, but not before turning

the opening slightly towards him. He couldn't fail to notice the grip of the gun.

So far, so good, thought Louise. And it had been fun playing with Toby. The secret to a good improvisation is to understand the motivation of your character and then think quickly, and adapt to circumstances, playing off your partner, and trying to outdo them while they try to outdo you. And it was so much more exciting to do it for real than it had been practising in the hotel suite. They'd strayed from the rehearsed script but that gave it so much more life and authenticity. Had it not been for Toby nudging her leg under the table, she would almost have believed his fury herself.

The bar was crowded, but she felt that a drink was the least she deserved. Waiting patiently, but edging forward, she became aware of a presence getting ever closer. And when she finally reached the front of the throng, she knew that it was almost time for act two.

"Martini and lemonade, please." She had to raise her voice to be heard over the general hubbub of the club.

"Ice and lemon?"

"A little bit of both, please. Actually, can you make it a double?"

The barman nodded and set to work. A minute or so later he placed a glass, two-thirds full of clear liquid, on a small paper coaster.

"I'll get this," said a voice from over her shoulder. She turned and came face to face with George.

"No, you're all right," she said, then turned back to the barman and went to hand him a twenty-pound note.

"I insist," said George. "It's the very least I can do to make amends for overhearing your conversation."

Louise ignored him.

"Can you take it out of this please?" she reiterated.

"Pablo, add it to my tab, thank you," George continued, raising his voice for the benefit of the barman.

Louise sighed and shook her head.

"Listen," she said, turning back to George, her eyes narrowing, "I am quite capable of buying my own drink. I am not in the mood to be dicked about by men. Okay? So if you've paid for it, you can also drink it. I'm out of here."

She pushed past him, and headed back through the crowds in the direction of the exit, not turning when she heard George call out after her, and stopping only to collect her distinctive royal blue coat from the cloakroom.

Danny didn't like the change in Clare's expression. The mask of joviality had vanished.

"What did I tell you about taking things at face value?" she asked.

"I don't."

"So you say. But you assume Louise was buying drugs?"

"I know what I saw."

"Okay, but let's analyse that. What you saw was two people on a London street, admittedly quite a narrow one, talking to each other. They swap something. It could have been anything."

"Oh, come on. Credit me with some intelligence, please."

"I'm trying to. Which is why I'm disappointed when you jump to conclusions."

Danny didn't know whether to laugh or scream.

"All right then, you tell me your theory about what she was up to."

"I don't need to have a theory. I know exactly what she was doing."

"Which was?"

"I'll tell you. Buying information."

"*What?*"

"A zip disk."

"Information about what, though?"

Clare looked at her watch, then toyed with the sapphire on her right ring finger.

"I'm going to tell you everything," she said. "I promise you. But there's a lot to tell, and I need to show you some places and meet some people, so it really isn't one for tonight. I'll tell you everything, but it's one for tomorrow."

Danny started to protest, but Clare put up her hand to stop him.

"I'm not being evasive, honestly. I'll give you the summary now, so you know it's not a wasted journey, and I didn't bring you here just for fun. There's a story, I'm going to need your help, and it's definitely one for clear minds."

"So the summary?" asked Danny.

"The summary is that Louise is in London on a mission, putting right some wrongs, and getting close to someone who needs to be exposed. And yes, it's personal, because the person concerned was responsible for the death of her father."

"Wow. And she's staying with Anna because?"

"Because she can't stay with me, because I'm not there, and I didn't want to put her up in a hotel. I want to know she's looked after, and I trust Anna to do that."

Danny sat back, trying to take it all in. There were countless questions, but he sensed that was as much as he was going to get for this evening.

"Let's get back and get to sleep," Clare continued. "Tomorrow is going to be a busy day."

Danny nodded.

"Okay," he said. "But when we meet tomorrow, I need you to be honest with me like you've never been before."

Chapter 17

Wednesday, January 22nd, 1997

OR the first time in living memory, I woke up on the morning after my birthday without any form of hangover. In fact, I felt better than I had for a few days, as the biorhythmic malaise appeared to have lifted, and I had a whole year ahead of me before I had to worry about getting older again.

Obviously I avoided looking too closely in the mirror in case I'd turned spectacularly grey and wrinkled overnight, but I actually felt quite lively, even though Wednesdays are a bit of a no-man's-land in terms of days of the week. I frankly can't see the point of them. I quite like Mondays, which admittedly, puts me in something of a minority, but the start of a new week is invigorating, with a clean slate, and lots of time to explore the potential of new opportunities. By Tuesday you're into the flow of the thing. On Thursday you're either in a panic about what you haven't got done, or starting to look forward to the weekend. And Friday is an excuse for a party (albeit in my case that normally involves a takeaway and the thought of a nice lie in.) Wednesdays, though, are a bit shit.

So I was feeling unexpectedly cheerful when the phone rang. Yes, I was aware that I'd stuffed things up with Danny again, but I enjoyed being single, and choosing which side of the bed to sleep on, and not being woken up by someone else fidgeting and snoring. So, if he'd taken the hump, it was his loss, and I wasn't going to give it another minute's thought.

Why, then, was my first thought that I hoped it was him calling me? And then I realised it couldn't be as it was the special Clare phone.

"Good morning and happy belated birthday," she said. "I'm so sorry I missed it."

"That's okay."

"I hadn't realised what day it was. I do apologise. Did you have a nice time? Did you get lots of presents?"

"I had a lovely time, thank you. Just a quiet night at home. And a couple of presents. Louise gave me a very nice necklace."

"Did she?"

"She did. Apparently someone helped her to choose it, so I should really be thanking them as well, but she didn't actually tell me who it was."

"Hmmm. Interesting. Presumably someone who thinks a lot of you, though."

"Presumably. It was very kind, anyway."

I wedged the phone on my shoulder while reaching for my coat, aware that I'd have to be leaving for work soon, or I'd need to take the Underground, and it wasn't even the day for it.

"How's she settling in?" asked Clare.

I looked around, aware that nothing had really changed.

"I'd hardly know she was here. She went out last night. I was asleep before she got back."

"Have you seen her this morning?" There was a hint of concern in her voice.

"Not yet. She definitely made it back, though. Her shoes are by the sofa. I think she's having another lie in. She's not one for getting up early." Had she deliberately left the shoes out so that I'd know she was home, and therefore not need to worry, or disturb her? Probably. "Have you heard anything from Danny, by the way? He tried to call me yesterday morning, and I tried ringing back a couple of times, but there was no answer." There was no need to be specific about the number of times I'd tried.

"I have, and yes, sorry, he's been having phone trouble. He did call you last night though."

"Did he?"

"Yes. He borrowed this phone, but the line was awful."

"Ah. Was that him? I thought it was you. It sounded like a robot." All of a sudden my spirits were well and truly lifted.

"It was. I'll tell him you were asking about him if I see him."

"Thank you."

I think she could sense that I was eager to get out of the door - not least because I rattled my keys quite close to the microphone - so we ended the call, and I set out for work. It seemed odd that the two of them were suddenly spending so much time together, but I owed it to my sanity not to ask why.

"You're genuinely scary when you're angry," said Toby. Louise returned the smile.

"I told you, I want to be an actress." By the time Anna was leaving for work, Louise was already in the hotel suite for a team debrief.

"How do you think we did, boss?" asked Toby, turning to Adam.

"You were both fantastic," he said. "It looked for all the world like you were properly going for it. Well done, the pair of you."

"Did you see what he did after I left?" asked Louise. "Do you think he noticed the coat?"

"He definitely did," said Adam. "He started to follow and then stopped, but kept his eyes on you all the way to the door."

"Perfect."

"Remind me why the coat is important, babe?" said Abby, joining in. Unlike Adam, she hadn't been there to witness the performance, but her time would come.

"Because I want him to know that it's me," said Louise. "At the moment I'm just some Polish girl in a bar, and if he saw me again he might think he recognised me, but not be sure. Or he might have forgotten about me altogether. But if he sees the coat again it's a - what do you call it?" She turned to Adam.

"Memory trigger."

"Exactly. A memory trigger. He sees the coat, he knows it's me. It reminds him of last night, and he's going to be much more likely to approach again because he can't stand rejection."

There was a knock at the door. Toby was closest so he opened it. Harry came in, bearing brown paper bags.

"Good morning, my dear thespians," he said, with a nod to Toby and Louise. "I bear the gift of breakfast."

A selection of muffins and pastries were laid out on the table, while Abby fired up the coffee machine. When the small talk subsided, Adam called the group to order.

"So, last night went well," he said. "It's an encouraging start. We're going to strike while the iron is hot, if you can forgive the cliché, Harry."

Louise smiled to herself. Harry was from a different, more colourful era.

"So, next steps. We're going to press right on," Adam continued. "Let's discuss the plan for today. It's time to start reeling him in."

Chapter 18

DANNY was nearly finished in the shower when he heard a firm knock at the apartment door. He hastily grabbed a towel and padded across the room. Looking through the spy hole, he saw Clare, as well dressed as ever. There was nothing for it. He'd have to open the door.

"Ooh, Danny," she said, looking him up and down. "I didn't know you cared."

"Come in," he said, trying to adjust his stance. "Help yourself in the kitchen if you can find anything, and I'll quickly get dressed."

"No need on my account."

"Can you please stop pretending to flirt with me?"

"Who's pretending?" She winked. "I'm teasing, but I do like the stubble. It suits you."

"I forgot to pack a razor."

"You look all rugged and manly."

Danny sighed, and Clare decided to change the subject.

"I'll make tea," she said.

"There's no milk."

She reached into her bag, pulled out a white bottle, covered in Polish writing, and waved it in Danny's direction.

"I've thought of that. I can't promise it'll be up to Anna's standard but I'll try."

Danny grabbed his clothes and disappeared into the bathroom. By the time he emerged, Clare was on the balcony, smoking a cigarette. Danny joined her. Daylight afforded Danny his first proper view of Warsaw, and one of the city's many construction sites. Skyscrapers had started to emerge - dwarfing the concrete communist tower blocks, although the skyline was still dominated by the huge Palace of Culture and Science.

"It'll be nice when it's finished," said Clare. "The general idea is to hide the Palace, because it was built by Stalin. But that's ironic because the Russians built tower blocks to hide the churches. If you're into construction, this is the place to be."

"It must be exciting, though," said Danny. "I know I wasn't here before the Curtain came down, but even standing here, you get an impression of how much it's changing."

"Mainly for the best," said Clare. Danny let that pass for the moment.

The sun was bright, and the sky largely cloudless, but the temperature was still close to freezing. Clare flicked the stub of the cigarette into the car park below, and then they went back inside and sat at the kitchen table.

"I was going to make toast but we forgot to get bread," Clare started. "I'll take you out for breakfast somewhere, but first ..."

"You promised to tell me everything."

"Indeed. So, here's the story. And I promise that to the best of my knowledge, this is the truth, the whole truth and nothing but the truth, as they say in court."

Danny raised an eyebrow.

"It might be a useful discipline to master one day," she added.

"Quite." He couldn't help but smile. He couldn't imagine Clare ever being prosecuted for her crimes, although it was an omnipresent threat, lurking in the background. He occasionally wondered how much that pressure affected her actions. Whether it led to a certain mental instability. But now wasn't the time to digress.

"Bear in mind I've done a lot of the work on this. We're getting towards the end of it now, but I'll give you all the background so you've got the full picture, okay?"

"Please."

"Right, well, starting at the beginning: Agnieszka - Louise - is someone I've known for a long time. Her father - let's call him Greg - was an investigative journalist over here, and an old friend of mine."

"Greg, because his real name also has a z in it?"

"Two. It's spelt G-R-Z-E-G-O-R-Z although you pronounce it Zheh-gorsh. I stick with Greg, though. It's easier."

"Indeed. And you said *'was'*."

"Yes. He died recently."

Danny shivered, as though the temperature had just dropped. She'd mentioned it the night before, but he hadn't really taken it in.

"Sorry to hear that. Illness?"

Clare shook her head, looking about as serious as he could remember.

"Suicide, officially."

"Wow. That's awful."

"It's not quite that simple, though, because I don't think he did commit suicide. I think he was murdered."

"Oh God." Danny let that sink in for a moment, appreciating that the stakes had just risen, exponentially. "Because?"

"Because he was in a prison cell at the time."

"Which would make it hard."

"Although not impossible, which is what they were counting on."

"What had he done? To end up in prison."

"Again officially? He'd killed someone in his apartment, but I don't think he did that either."

Danny took a deep breath and whistled, then rubbed his temples with his hands, his brain kicking into gear.

"So, let me see if I'm getting this. You're saying he was framed? Then murdered as a cover-up?"

"Kind of. I'm saying he was framed so that he'd get arrested, and that once he was in a cell, somebody had all the time in the world to do whatever they wanted to do to him. I think he knew things that were valuable for some people but dangerous for others. Somebody either wanted to find out what those things were, or they wanted to make sure he never repeated them. Either way, he didn't wake up one morning."

"But who? Why? What were the things?"

"That's what I've been trying to find out. He was a good person. He did a similar job to us, exposing corruption." Danny didn't think it was the right time to point out that Clare's career had ended. "But that meant he occasionally mixed in bad circles, and fell out with the wrong people. So I've been trying to find out what he knew. What he was working on. And then, as for who killed him, there are two aspects to that. Who pulled the trigger and who issued the order."

"And that's why you're here?"

She clicked her fingers, and pointed at him.

"You're good. And yes, kind of."

"Jesus. It all sounds horrendous. Poor Louise." He thought of the innocent young girl, back in Anna's front room. She was so beautiful and open, and yet all the time she was living with deep and recent inner pain and turmoil. He felt his admiration growing. "It's weird. I only met her briefly, but I could tell there was something going on behind the smile. But I had no idea it was anything like this."

"Quite. Louise and her father were very close. Her parents

split when she was young, so she lived with her dad, and they doted on each other."

"And so why is Louise in London?"

"I'm coming onto that. Bear with me. I haven't finished the background yet."

"Okay." Danny paused, momentarily lost in thought. "Where's her mother?"

"She's long gone," said Clare. "Just upped and disappeared one day." She took another cigarette from the packet, almost instinctively, but then stopped. Danny crossed to the sink and ran some water into a cup as a temporary ash tray, and passed it over.

"I don't want to smoke in your room," said Clare. "It wouldn't be fair."

"It also wouldn't be the first time." He smiled, grateful for a temporary moment of levity. But it didn't last. "Feel free, honestly. And in the meantime, how much progress have you made? Have you worked out who killed him yet?"

"I'm getting there with all of it. But it's been difficult. He was on remand, mixing with other prisoners, and any one of them could have done it. For obvious reasons that's hard to investigate. I've been trying to get into the prison to speak to the guards, but I don't speak Polish and they forget how to speak English if you start asking awkward questions, even assuming they know any in the first place. It's very much a brick wall. But it's not about who killed him, it's about who issued the order."

"Any success with that?"

Clare looked away momentarily, then lit her cigarette. When she spoke, her voice was quieter than before.

"That, I'm afraid, is a bit closer to home," she said.

"Not one of your associates?"

"*What?*"

Danny realised what he'd said.

"Sorry."

"Christ. Is that how little you think of me? Are you trying to insinuate that I'm somehow behind this?"

"No, of course not, it's just when you said closer to home..."

"For God's sake." Clare's voice carried unexpected fury. "That's the most ridiculous thing I've ever heard. Why the hell would I be investigating if it was me? And do you really think that's the sort of thing I'd do? Can you and everyone else finally begin to believe me when I say I'm a bloody angel?"

"Emphasis on the bloody, occasionally."

"Ooh." Clare couldn't hide her exasperation, and stood up. "I hate to swear, but can you please *piss off*?"

"Sorry. Again."

She walked across to the kitchen window, her back to Danny. There was an empty silence in the room. Danny tried to punctuate it with another apology, but she raised a hand to silence him. She turned on the tap and extinguished the cigarette in the flow of water. When she eventually turned back round, Danny thought she looked smaller than normal. She was dabbing the corners of her eyes with a torn-off sheet of kitchen roll.

"I don't know why I bother. I really don't," she said, with an uncharacteristic quaver in her voice. "I'm constantly judged because of one mistake four years ago."

"I'm not judging you. It was a joke."

"Yeah, well, it's not funny."

"I admit that." Danny stepped forward and extended his arms for a hug. She looked hesitant but eventually returned the embrace. Now wasn't the time to mention that his comments weren't based on the murders of her business partners four years ago, but the other bodies that she'd added to her tally since. None of them had been innocent, but she was ruthless when she wanted to be.

"I'm sorry," he said again, gently tightening his grip. It felt strangely intimate, as though she was vulnerable and he was the protector. He'd never felt like Clare needed protection before.

Eventually she stepped back, but the awkwardness remained as they re-took their seats.

"You, of all people Danny," she said with a sigh, but then stopped him when he tried to apologise again. She'd clearly had enough, and the clock was ticking. "Let's move on."

Danny nodded, and took a sip of his tea. It wasn't as bad as he'd feared.

"As I was saying, it might sound counter-intuitive but we don't need to worry about who actually killed him," Clare continued, in a voice that was slowly returning to a more familiar timbre. "They're already inside, and would have been following orders. I doubt it was personal. It might take a while, but I'll find out who it was one day and I'll deal with him."

Danny thought that rather proved his earlier point, but knew better than to mention it.

"As for who issued the order, I've got theories."

"Such as?"

"It's a question of understanding Greg and knowing what he was involved in, and who he might have upset. Whoever it was had a motive. But maybe it wasn't a question of silencing him. We can't assume anything. That seems most likely but did he owe somebody money? Had he stitched anyone up? Understand the motive and you'll know where to look."

"And have you made any progress on that?"

"A bit. And given everything going on in Warsaw at the moment, I've come to the conclusion that the most likely scenario was that he was investigating some large-scale corruption. But don't forget we've got the other murder too. The one he was accused of. Did he kill that man in his flat? If so, maybe he was executed in revenge. And even if he was innocent, he could have been executed in revenge by someone who *thought* he'd done it. But I don't believe he did it, so I've been trying to find out who the victim was, and why he was killed, and why it was done to implicate him. As for who pulled the trigger in the apartment, the cleanliness of the shot had the mark of a professional, so I started thinking it was a local hitman, your average gun for hire."

"Average in your world. Any form of hitman is far from average for a normal person."

Clare let that pass.

"I'm pretty sure I worked that out," she continued, undaunted. "He won't be doing it again, because he was thorough at the execution, but less so at covering his tracks. There's a national park about ten miles north-west of here. The body of a known hitman was discovered by a couple of hikers, partially buried. Albeit the wrong side of also being discovered by the local wildlife."

"I wonder how that happened?" Danny stopped, immediately worried that he'd overstepped the mark again. Luckily, Clare seemed unfazed.

"Nothing to do with me, anyway. I don't know whether he wanted more money or threatened to talk, but either way, my theory is that whoever hired him also made sure of his silence."

"This all sounds brutal."

"It is. So you don't need me to tell you that we have to be careful. But when we discover the truth, I really believe you'll have a fantastic story, because it's going to involve corruption, murder, and all sorts, both here and back home. I want to take you to the apartment, show you around and see what you make of it. But some of the answers are back in London too."

"Meaning?"

"There are definite links to people back there, so I've been investigating those too."

"Do you have names?"

She nodded.

"Yes. One in particular. Like I said, I've been working on this for a while. Ever since Greg first got arrested. So it's quite advanced already." She paused, as though deciding whether to cross some invisible line. "Louise is in London because she's going to get close to him, earn his trust. And then, when she's done that, she's going to gather evidence, and bring him down. That's the theory, anyway."

"And get her revenge in the time-honoured fashion?"

"You think she's going to kill him?"

"I thought it best to ask."

Clare shook her head.

"Louise isn't a killer. And just killing him would miss the point. It's about bringing down the entire organisation."

"And the person?"

Clare paused, her brow creased in concentration. She reached for the cigarettes again, but stopped herself before taking one out. Eventually she continued.

"There's a local lowlife called George Brandrick. He's a known gangster, but nothing sticks. He's into drugs, smuggling tobacco and all sorts. He's got connections, and to be quite brutal about it, he's the sort of scum I went into this business to bring to justice. The police struggle to pin anything on him, but I know what he's up to. So do the police. But as ever, there's a difference between knowing what someone does and having the evidence to prove it in court."

"And that's who Louise is targeting? How is she going to get close to him?"

"It's a bit complicated. Another friend of mine, from back in the day, is what you'd call a gentleman thief. He's now part of a long con crew, so I spoke to him. Louise is working with them. And by the time she's finished, Brandrick will be exposed. In the process, she gets revenge for the sake of her father."

"Are they actually going to do a con?"

"That's the plan. In fact it'll all be over long before things get to that stage, but nobody knows about that. Apart from me and Louise, obviously. And now you."

"Wow. And how do I fit in?"

"It's time to document it. When this all hits the fan it'll be making headlines. And I'd rather give that to you than anyone else. You'll have unprecedented access, and when the editors come calling, you'll be able to name your price."

Clare looked at her watch. The morning was already slipping away.

"Now, though, I want to take you to Greg's apartment. Show you around, and see if you can spot anything I missed. Look through any paperwork we think might be of interest, and basically give the place a thorough going-over."

"You've been before?"

"Last Thursday. Then later on, we're going to meet one of his former colleagues. I'm pretty sure I'm on the right lines with all of this, but I trust and value your judgement. Always have. You know that."

"So we're going to get going now?"

"We are."

"Can I say one thing, then, before we go?"

They both stood up. Clare reached across to Danny's jacket and passed it to him.

"Of course. As long as it's not another joke." She smiled, and in that moment it looked like he'd been forgiven.

"I just want to say thank you. That's all. For bringing me here and being honest with me."

"Always, Danny. You know me."

But that was the trouble. He knew her only too well.

Chapter 19

"CAN I take your coat, madame?" asked the maître d'.

Louise scanned the restaurant. It was more modern than she'd expected, and more brightly lit - helped by a skylight that ran the length of the dining area. To the left there was a view to the kitchen, where immaculately-dressed chefs were hard at work, despite the early hour. Most of the tables were still unoccupied, but she spotted Abby, alone, reading a newspaper towards the back.

"No, thank you, it's fine. I'll keep hold of it," she said.

"Okay. If you'd like to follow me. Your friend is here already."

Abby put down the newspaper and rose to shake Louise's hand as she approached. They introduced themselves as though they were strangers, despite having said goodbye only a couple of hours before.

A young waiter approached and asked if they were ready to order.

"Just a few more minutes, babe," said Abby. Louise had her back to the restaurant, so was relying on Abby to keep watch. Abby, in turn, studied the menu while remaining vigilant for any new arrivals.

"Are we having a starter?" asked Louise.

"I suppose we should," said Abby. "We ain't in any rush. What do you fancy? What do you normally eat in Poland?"

"We're too busy drinking vodka all day to worry about food," she said, with a wry smile. "I'm thinking the pumpkin soup to start and then the turmeric battered haddock, but what are trompette mushrooms?"

"Show me."

Louise pointed to the pumpkin soup on the starter section.

"I haven't got a Scooby, love," said Abby. "Mushrooms in the shape of a trumpet? I'm always suspicious of restaurants that try to sound all posh and sophisticated, while knowing that no normal punter has a clue what they're on about."

"You and me both."

"On a similar theme," Abby continued, "look at this, babe. The mackerel comes with cucumber raita ice cream. As a starter. I mean, what the fuck? And I was looking at the roast fillet of hake, but what's a razor clam piperade when it's at home, aside from something lethal?" She paused. "Oooh, hello, posh voice on. Don't look behind you."

"He's here?"

She nodded. It was time to perform.

George Brandrick took a table by himself, in the next row, exactly as they'd been told. So far so good. Abby and Louise started chatting in slightly raised voices, pitched just loud enough that their words would carry. They discussed mutual fictional acquaintances, their absence of boyfriends, and then, as the starters were cleared away, Abby announced it was time to get down to business.

"Before we do that, I'm just going to pop to the, er, ladies' room," said Louise.

"Powdering your nose?"

"That's one word for it."

"Naughty. Leave some for me."

Louise laughed, stood up and then walked straight past Brandrick without giving him a glance, but close enough to make him notice, even if he hadn't already spotted the coat on the back of her chair. A few minutes later she took a different route back, so she wouldn't have to look him in the eye, while pausing on the way for a quick flirtatious exchange with one of the waiting staff.

"So, business," she said, when she was back in her seat.

"Indeed. Tell me how I can help you."

"Okay." She picked up her glass of sparkling mineral water, swilled the liquid round for a moment before taking a sip, and then chinked it back against Abby's wine glass as she replaced it on the table.

"Sorry," she said. But the fractional raise of Abby's eyebrows was enough to confirm that the noise had captured Brandrick's attention. "So, the club. It's looking good. We're nearly ready to go."

"Do you have the girls?" asked Abby.

"The girls? Lots and lots of girls." She laughed. "Trust me, the girls are easy."

"As it were." Abby laughed.

"Well, yes, there is that. But I mean in terms of availability, girls aren't a problem."

"So what is the problem?"

"Robbie."

"Robbie?"

"Yeah, Robbie. He's being a dick."

"In what way's he being a dick?"

Louise paused for a moment while the main courses arrived.

"We've all had to show proof of funds," she continued, while starting to tackle the fish. "And that was fine. He did that. But now it comes to putting in the actual account, he's, er, well, he's being a dick."

"Do you think he doesn't have the money?" asked Abby.

"I don't know. I genuinely don't. I mean, I know the man. I

feel guilty because I introduced him, and I know he should, in theory, have pots of money. But he hasn't paid up when he should have done. He's made promises he hasn't kept. And now none of us can get hold of him."

"Shit. Sounds ominous."

"Well, it is, because none of the others want to make up the deficit on my say-so. I can't do it, and it's a bit late to be getting anyone else in. But unless we get on with it we're going to lose the premises."

"But you thought I might be interested?" Abby took a mouthful of hake, and then washed it down with a sip of wine.

"I thought it was worth a chat. I mean, I don't know if it's your kind of project. And I know the whole girls thing might make you nervous, but the returns are there if we can get this off the ground."

"What sort of returns are we talking?"

"Big. Let me call Adam and get him to fax you through the business plan. Take a look at it and see what you think. But I don't think you'd be disappointed. And obviously ..." She stopped, and tapped the side of her nose.

"Obviously what?"

"Well, you know. Do you need me to spell it out? Captive audience. Let's just say there are significant potential revenue streams that we couldn't put in the business plan, for, er, legal reasons."

"Understood." Abby looked deep in thought. "It sounds very interesting. I must admit, it's really not good timing for me at the moment because I've just committed to a big project elsewhere, but this sounds, shall we say, spicy."

"In more ways than one."

"Indeed. And you'd need a decision?"

"Soon as. We should've signed for the building on Monday. Obviously, the longer we leave it, the higher the risk. How's the hake, by the way?"

"Gorgeous. And the haddock?"

"A bit fishy." They laughed. Conversation returned to non-business subjects and then, once the plates were cleared away, Louise asked for the bill.

"I'm getting this," she said.

"Are you sure?"

"Of course. It was me that invited you, even if it was your choice of restaurant. It's the very least I can do."

"Well, thank you. We must do this again some time. And that'd be my treat."

"I look forward to it. And who knows? We might even end up as partners."

Abby scrunched up her face.

"I have to be honest and say not to get your hopes up. I'll have a look at the plan, but even if it's as spectacular as it sounds, my issue will be liquidity."

"I understand. But thank you anyway. And if you have any rich friends that you think might be interested, please let me know. Discreetly, obviously. It goes without saying that for now, the plan is for you and you only. It needs to be shredded if you're not interested."

"Of course."

The waiter came and Louise paid the bill.

"Right," she said. "Back to work."

"Are you up to anything exciting this afternoon?"

"Not as exciting for me as it is for Adam. We've got a meeting with some of the Polish girls to check out their, erm, credentials."

"He's going to find it hard to control himself."

"Luckily for Adam, he probably won't have to."

"Tut tut, naughty naughty."

"Hey, boys will be boys."

They stood up. Louise made a show of putting on her blue coat, and they made their way to the door. At the entrance they kissed cheeks and Abby set off, while Louise lit a cigarette and started tapping numbers into her phone. The Shoreditch street was busy with office workers, buses and taxis, and felt cold after the warmth of the restaurant.

A moment later, a familiar voice came from behind her.

"So, we meet again."

She turned, and gave George a quizzical frown.

"Do we?"

"Last night? At the bar?"

A flicker of recognition crossed her face.

"Oh. Were you the, erm ...?"

"I bought you a drink. Then you fucked off, not to put too fine a point on it." George lit a cigarette of his own.

"Ah yes. I remember," Louise replied. "But I did tell you not to."

"Yeah? Well I don't always do as I'm told."

"Quite." She snapped the phone shut and put it in her coat pocket, then turned to walk away.

"You could make up for it by letting me buy you one now," he called after her.

"No thank you," she said over her shoulder. George started to walk after her.

"I insist."

Louise stopped and turned to face him, her expression cold.

"Sorry, Mr whatever-your-name-is. That's very kind, but no. I have to get back to work. I've got a busy afternoon. And I'm not looking for romance at the moment."

"Who said anything about romance?"

"Wow, that's even worse. You're looking for a quick legover, is that it?"

George raised his arms in protest.

"No, no, no. You misunderstand me. I thought we could have a little business discussion."

"A business discussion? Christ." She shook her head in

disbelief. "Have you been earwigging my private conversations again?"

"Not deliberately, but I couldn't avoid overhearing some of it."

Louise looked suitably offended.

"Unbelievable."

But George was unrepentant, and not giving up.

"Look, if you don't want to go for a drink, my office is about three doors away. You could come with me and we could have a discussion there."

"That's even worse." Louise sounded exasperated. "Do I look like the kind of girl who'd agree to go to some office with a complete stranger she's only just met? Give me some credit. I don't even know your name."

"I didn't mean it like that. And it's George. George Brandrick." He extended his arm for a handshake. Louise hesitated for a moment, then dropped the cigarette to the floor, stubbed it out under the toe of her black suede ankle boot, and reached out to shake his hand.

"Louise," she said.

"Pleased to meet you, Louise. So what's it going to be? Drink or office?"

"You don't give up, do you?"

"It's not something I'm known for."

She sighed.

"Okay. If it'll stop you stalking me, I'll agree to a drink. But it'll have to be a quick one."

"Of course." He smiled. Louise couldn't believe quite how easily this was all going. With one final look along the street, she followed George back into the restaurant.

Chapter 20

THE restaurant was still busy, but George led Louise to a quiet area by the entrance that was usually reserved for customers waiting for a table. With the lunch service well underway, the waiting area was deserted, and there was little chance of being overheard.

Louise asked for a cappuccino. George protested at first, suggesting something stronger, but finally relented and followed suit.

"So, tell me a little bit about yourself," he said, while they waited for the drinks to be prepared.

"Is this a job interview?" Louise looked suitably unimpressed. "You're the one who keeps listening in to my conversations, so I think you already know more than I'd like you to. Tell me about you. Who you are, why you're stalking me."

George laughed.

"Listen, my darling, I'm far from stalking you. I come in here every Wednesday as long as I'm working from my office. But I do a bit of this, a bit of that. I'm what you'd call an entrepreneur. Where's your sexy accent from, by the way?"

Louise was unmoved.

"If you're going to start coming on to me, I'm going leave you to it, irrespective of whether it's the second time you've wasted money buying a drink."

"Hey, I'm just being friendly. Let's omit the word sexy, if it means that much to you. But you've got a lovely voice. That's not my fault."

"Fine." Louise relented. "I'm from Kielce, which you've probably never heard of." George shrugged and shook his head. "There you go then. It's in Poland. Introductions over. But seriously, as much as it's a pleasure to meet you, whatever your name is – sorry, I've forgotten already ..."

"George."

"- George, you said you wanted a business discussion. About?"

He lit a cigarette and offered one to Louise, but she refused. The coffees arrived, and he handed the waiter a ten-pound note to cover them.

"I couldn't help overhearing your conversation," he started. "It sounds like you're in a spot of bother."

"No, not really." Louise scooped some of the froth with a teaspoon, mainly so she could avoid any form of eye contact.

"That's not what it sounded like. Some form of club? An investor not coming up with the required funds on time? Something about missing out on the deadline for the premises?"

"Jesus. Do you know how invasive that sounds?"

But George didn't appear bothered.

"If you want a private conversation, I suggest you don't do it in public, okay?" he said. "It's not my fault I heard what I heard. Ears don't have an off-switch."

"Okay, lesson learned. So what of it?"

George exhaled smoke, then wafted it away.

"If you're looking for an investor, I might be interested. I'm in the entertainment industry in the broadest kind of way. And I'm always interested in an investment if there are benefits in return."

Louise smiled, although it didn't reach her eyes.

"Oh, George, you're like a freshly-cleaned window."

"What the fuck does that mean?"

"It means I can see right through you. Are you interested in the investment or the fact we were discussing girls?"

"I can't pretend that there's not a certain appeal in both."

"I thought as much." She took a sip of the coffee and looked at her watch. "Well, thank you for your interest, but - and please don't take this the wrong way - I don't know anything about you. I don't know who you are, what you do, what kind of a reputation you have. And I work as part of a team, so please don't take this the wrong way either, but even if you told me you had unlimited resources, I'm not going to put my reputation on the line by vouching for you to the others."

"And likewise, I'm not going to make an offer of investment when I know fuck all about the opportunity, not to put too fine a point on it." He stubbed out the cigarette. "But I think we should have a proper meeting. Bring me the business plan. I'll have a look and if it washes its face, I'll make you an offer. Then you'll know whether it's worth your while to do your due diligence on me."

"I'm afraid the business plan is confidential, so that's not happening," said Louise. "For all I know, you might be the Inland Revenue or the Vice Squad."

George laughed again.

"That sounds ever-more intriguing. I'll tell you what. What time do you finish work this afternoon?"

"Five-ish. Sometimes later. Why?"

George took a business card from his wallet and handed it over.

"Come and see me at my office. I'll be there till seven. Bring a colleague if you're worried you can't trust me. I know you've got to rush off now, but we can have a longer chat. You can outline the plan, even if it's only verbally. How does that sound?"

"It sounds like a waste of time, if I'm being honest."

"Fine. Do your own fucking thing then. Very best of luck with it."

George sat back. He didn't look happy. It was time to turn on the charm. Louise leant forward, letting the loose neckline of her dress fall open a little.

"Okay, I'll tell you what I'll do," she said. "I'll come to your office. But I'm not making any promises. I'm not going to be able to go into too much detail, but I'll tell you the outline. Would that make you happy and stop you from following me?"

George chuckled.

"Just after five?"

"Probably nearer six, but I've got your number so I'll call you when I'm on the way."

"I'll look forward to it. I have a good feeling that we might work well together. You seem to have spirit, and I like that."

Louise drained the last of the coffee.

"Until this evening then. And thank you for the drink this time." She stood up and offered her hand. George shook it.

"I look forward to it," he said, before watching as Louise fastened her coat and headed for the door, without once looking back.

———

By the time Louise made it back to the hotel suite, Abby had already briefed Adam, Harry and Toby on the details of the lunch date.

"Come in, come in, dear girl," said Harry, opening the door to let her through. "I believe a small semblance of a toast is in order."

Louise smiled.

"It's still early days," she said, "but we're getting there." She took off her coat and collapsed onto the sofa, at the opposite end to Abby. "I'll tell you what, though – the food was divine, but if this keeps up, I'm going to need to go on a very strict diet."

"Abby said you did great work," said Adam, his expression warmer than she'd ever seen before.

"It was a team effort." She leaned across to high-five Abby. "We basically had a competition to see who could say the word 'girls' the most."

"I think it was a draw," said Abby with a smile. "Good effort, though, babe. It was fun winding up the old pervert."

"It was."

Abby offered coffee, but Louise asked for mineral water instead. Toby stood up from the armchair opposite and said he would get it.

"So, how was the meeting afterwards?" asked Adam.

"I watched from behind a bus stop, and saw him come out," added Abby.

"It was good. He wanted to know more, obviously, and asked me to visit him at his office once I've finished work. How's the business plan coming, by the way? All sorted?"

Abby nodded.

"It's all done, babe. We've just got one final proofread then it's good to go."

"Perfect. So yes, he wants me to do that, and I said I would, obviously, but now - " she looked at her watch "- it's nearly two. I shall give it an hour or two then a call to cancel, tell him I'm not feeling well."

"He'll be so frustrated," said Abby, with a conspiratorial smile.

"I hope so. That's very much the plan."

Chapter 21

CLARE led Danny past the Palace of Culture and Science, and then through a succession of busy streets, until finally they reached one of the city's many parks. The open space gave respite from the traffic noise and sounds of construction.

"Warsaw is a lot more beautiful than I expected," said Danny, his breath fogging in the air.

"It's a nice place," said Clare. "Even the communist towers have a certain Brutalist charm. I'll take you to the Old Town later, if we've got time. You can still see bits of walls that are riddled with bullet holes, even though it's all been rebuilt. You feel the weight of history. It's kind of humbling, really. Hold on a moment."

They paused next to a fountain, while Clare checked her phone. Danny walked round the far side of one of the rococo sculptures to give her a moment of privacy, and take in his surroundings. An immaculately-dressed mother was sitting on a bench on the far side of the fountain, watching her young son playing. She called out to him to come closer when an elderly couple walked nearby with their dog, and he ran happily into her arms.

Clare emerged, putting the phone back into the pocket of her big, black coat.

"Sorry about that. It was a message about a meeting this evening," she said.

Danny fell into step alongside her as they continued through the park. There were cyclists, lots of people walking, and even one young boy on a skateboard.

"I wonder what they make of it all," he said, as much to himself as Clare. "I can imagine that eight years ago it was all so different."

Clare nodded, putting her arm through his. They looked for all the world like a courting couple.

"It was, but in general they're not complaining. There's a lot to do, but it's coming round after decades of oppression. At least they don't need to spend all day queuing for a loaf of mouldy bread any longer."

"Did that really happen, or is that just an urban myth?"

"Oh, Danny. Believe me, it really happened. But that's not even the start of it."

They left the park, and a few minutes later, Clare indicated to a block of flats on the opposite side of a busy dual carriageway. They joined the throng of people waiting at the traffic lights. Red lights halted the six lanes of traffic. A yellow tram was stationary on one of the two lines in between the carriageways. Once they were on the far side, Clare led the way to the end of the building, and eventually to a double glass door at the rear. She pushed it open and told Danny to follow, but with a finger to her lips to warn him to be quiet.

Inside there was a small kiosk, selling chocolate, cigarettes, magazines and newspapers, and then a bank of four lifts behind a pair of floor-to-ceiling metal security grilles.

"It looks like another prison," Danny whispered.

"Believe me, you don't want to see inside an actual Polish prison," Clare whispered back. "Now shhhh."

She approached the kiosk. A middle-aged woman sat behind the counter. Danny got the impression that they might be the first customers of the day, but she didn't look bothered. Clare said something that he didn't understand. The woman shook her head and looked away, uninterested, but Clare didn't give up. She reached into her pocket and withdrew some paper money and handed it across. The woman looked at it, nodded and, without a word, wrote a number on a piece of paper before handing it to Clare, along with a key.

"Thank you," said Clare, in English. But the woman had turned away again, and didn't acknowledge her. Clare led the way to the security grille. She tapped the number from the paper into the keypad. The door swung open and Danny followed her through to the bank of lifts. Once inside, Clare pressed the button for the eighth floor and Danny decided it was okay to speak.

"What was all that about?" he asked.

"Nothing much. It was a bit of a pantomime really. She looks after the key but won't hand it over unless you make it worth her while."

"Old habits?"

"Something like that. Some parts of Warsaw have developed quicker than others."

The lift opened into a corridor, lined with wooden doors. The whole place looked surprisingly clean and well-kept.

"Are you ready?" asked Clare.

Danny had no idea what he was walking into, but by now there was no going back.

Downstairs, the woman in the kiosk waited for the lift doors to close, and the metal security grille to swing back into place.

She watched the light on the lift show the eighth floor, just to confirm that they had stopped in the right place. Then she picked up the phone the man had left her, and made a call to the only number that was programmed into its memory.

Chapter 22

"WELL, I wasn't expecting that," said Clare.

"No."

Danny walked through the front room and checked the bedroom, but it was the same story. Everything had been cleared. There was no furniture, nor anything in any of the built-in cupboards. The bathroom was similarly bare. The only indication that the apartment had ever been lived in was the indentations on the carpet where furniture had once stood. And the remnants of an ominous dark stain in front of the window.

He joined Clare in the kitchen, where she was checking the cupboards, but they were all bare. There wasn't even a layer of dust on the work surface. Clare put her finger to her lips and Danny nodded in understanding. Just because the place was superficially empty didn't mean that someone hadn't left a listening device.

After one last look around, Clare led the way back to the lifts. They dropped the key at the kiosk and headed out onto the street. Once they were safely out of earshot, Danny spoke.

"So much for going through his things."

"Sorry about that."

"Presumably it wasn't like that when you were there last week?"

"No." Clare continued walking. "Let's go and get coffee, and we can assess this."

A few minutes later, they stopped at a small café, on a pedestrianised street, under the shadow of the looming Palace of Culture and Science. Despite the cold, Clare suggested taking a table outside. Danny waited while she went inside to order. She appeared unsettled.

"Aside from anything else, it's Louise I feel sorry for," said Danny, once she joined him with the drinks.

"Why Louise?"

"Because if that's her dad's apartment and someone's cleaned it out, that's all her family history. Photo albums, any souvenirs, I don't know - books, records, clothes, anything she had there, and more importantly, anything to remember her dad by. You don't think she's cleared it all to storage, do you? Especially if she's got to sell it, or end the lease, or whatever she's got to do with it."

"No," said Clare with a head shake.

"You're sure?"

"Absolutely sure, Danny. First of all, she's in London. Second, I told her I was taking you there and why. And third, I'm not a hundred percent sure it isn't still classed as a crime scene. In any case, I've told her that I'll look after everything this end. She needs to concentrate in London, getting close to Brandrick."

"Okay, then, but who?"

"Presumably whoever ordered his execution."

Danny paused for a moment, watching the activity on the street. It wasn't busy, but there was a steady trickle of shoppers. Clare pointed to a man in a suit who was approaching, on the far side of the street.

"Watch this one," she said. The man looked nervous, slowing down and checking over his shoulder before finally hesitating outside a doorway between a convenience shop and a travel agency. He pressed the bell. A moment later the door opened and he disappeared inside.

"One-nil to me," said Clare.

"What are you on about?" asked Danny.

"Punter spotting. That's a brothel."

"Really?"

"You say that as though you immediately want to go inside and check for yourself." She laughed. "I can't take you anywhere."

"No," Danny protested, but he knew she was only teasing him. "I just wondered how you knew."

"Because it's a growth industry. Have a look around. Admittedly it's not quite Amsterdam or Hamburg, but it's quite seedy in places."

They watched as the door opened again, and a different man, dressed just as formally, exited onto the street and started walking away at pace, without looking back.

"He's had his moment," said Clare.

Once the customer had disappeared from sight, conversation returned to the apartment.

"I must admit, it worries me," said Clare. "Whoever we're dealing with is clearly organised. They've got influence, and they're one step ahead."

"Are we safe, sitting out here? I mean, aside from hypothermia. What if they're watching the place? They'd know we were investigating. They could have followed us."

Clare considered that for a moment.

"It's a valid point. But that's not necessarily a bad thing. I've always found that's when they become vulnerable. You're right, though, we should be vigilant."

"Okay, and what now?"

She looked at her watch.

"We should think about food. Then tonight I've arranged to meet a guy called Anatol Rudyk who used to work with Greg. He's still at the newspaper, and he might be able to give us a bit of background, tell us the kind of things he was working on, and hopefully point us in the right direction."

"Sounds good."

"Although when you meet him, don't mention Louise. It's best for everyone if we keep this quiet. We're finding out information - not giving it away."

"Makes sense, I suppose. And in the meantime?"

"In the meantime we could go back to yours, if you like. I can recommend a snooze. It could be a big night. In fact, we could both do that ... We could sleep together."

"You're on fire. Is it hormones, do you think?"

Clare chuckled.

"Actually, I need to check in with Louise, as well, to see if she's making progress." She stopped and the smile faded from her face. Danny followed her eyes up the street to where a man in jeans and a parka was standing, with a camera, pointing the lens directly at them.

Clare stood and Danny followed. The man lowered the camera and started walking away from them, then looked over his shoulder. When he spotted Danny and Clare heading in his direction, he quickened his pace, and then started to run. Danny didn't need any further instruction, and set off at pace in pursuit, with Clare close behind although she couldn't keep up with Danny's speed.

The man turned down a side street. Danny was gaining, but when he arrived at the corner, he was just in time to see the man getting into a black Audi, which roared away into the distance. It was too far away to see the licence plate. A moment later, Clare caught up with him.

It took her a moment to get her breath back.

"I think that answers your question," she said, still panting. "I think from now on, we're going to have to start being very careful."

On an absolute whim, I popped into a hat shop on the way home from the office, and bought a fedora. I don't know why, and I don't know if I'll ever be brave enough to wear it in front of anyone I know. Perhaps it was my subconscious, reminiscing about the photoshoot for the hat company. Either way, I thought it suited me, and in a show of defiant fearlessness, I wore it all the way home, monitoring the reactions of others. Nobody collapsed in a heap of laughter, which I took as an encouraging sign.

It was safely back in its box by the time I arrived home, though, just in case Louise thought I'd turned into a nutcase. I don't know why I was worried about her opinion, really, but for some reason it seemed to matter. I'd come to the conclusion that I was in no rush for her to move on.

She was on the sofa when I got in, reading a book on Meisner technique, which I knew was something to do with acting, even if I couldn't remember exactly what. She looked up and smiled at me when I walked in, which was nice, and then announced that she'd made us a lasagne for tea, which was totally unexpected and even nicer. I followed her to the kitchen to check on its progress, half expecting to find a scene of chaos, but instead it was quietly bubbling away in the oven, and everything else was safely being cleaned in the dishwasher.

"I didn't even know we had the ingredients for a lasagne," I said, realising that I wasn't exactly sure what went into one.

"We didn't but I went to the shop," she said, as though the whole thing had been as effortless as having a snooze on the sofa. "Anyway, how was your birthday? Sorry I missed you this morning."

"Oh, don't worry, and it was fine. Very quiet, but that's what I wanted really. I went to bed and read for a bit. It was blissful." I hoped that didn't sound like I was glad she was out of the way.

Oh God. It probably did. "How are you, anyway? I see you've started reading up on the acting."

"I'm okay. And yes, although I'm still looking for courses. And a flat. Sorry."

"Hey, don't apologise. I'm feeling incredibly pampered at the moment." I was more concerned that she'd get frustrated, hanging round my flat all day, and move out because of the sheer boredom of sharing my lifestyle.

It wasn't long before the lasagne was ready, and it was even more delicious than I expected.

"Where did you learn to cook like that?" I asked, in true admiration, but she just passed off the compliment, saying it was nothing.

"Are you up to anything this evening?" she asked instead.

I thought for a moment, in case there was something I was supposed to be doing that I'd forgotten about, but nothing sprang to mind.

"Not much," I said. "If you play chess, I'll give you a game of that, if you fancy it."

"I do, but I'm a bit out of practice," she said with a mischievous glint. By out of practice, I suspect she meant she was one rung below grandmaster level. "I'm actually supposed to be going out again, to meet a friend for a drink. I'd love you to come as well, if you'd like to."

"That's very kind, but I've got work in the morning."

"It'd be fun, though. You could wear your new hat."

That alarmed me.

"How did you know I'd bought a new hat?" I had visions of Clare stalking me, and phoning her with the news.

"You came home carrying a hat box," she said.

"Oh, yes." I should really try to be less paranoid. I blame my friends.

"So, would you like to?" she persisted. "It's only a couple of drinks in a private members' club, so probably not the most exciting, but I'd love to take you, kind of a belated birthday celebration."

"You'd nearly persuaded me until you added that last bit."

"Okay, forget the birthday. It'd still be fun, though."

I was about to protest again, saying I had nothing to wear, even though that would be blatantly untrue, but then, the thought of meeting one or more of Louise's mysterious friends stoked my curiosity.

"I'd be honoured if you could come," she continued. "Apart from anything else, it'd prove that life begins at twenty-seven." The wink was clearly learnt from Clare.

"Okay," I said, pushing aside thoughts of the potential for disaster. "I'd love to."

I had nearly an hour to get ready, so headed for the shower. Seriously, what could possibly go wrong?

Chapter 23

TWO hours later I was seated on a low-slung sofa in a club somewhere close to Covent Garden, albeit without the hat. It was a bit more upmarket than I was used to, with a firm but friendly receptionist who insisted I should sign in as a guest. The club was styled to look a bit like a library, with paperbacks and hardbacks dotted around on shelves, and I assume the idea was that members could borrow them to read while they supped overpriced wines and spirits. Louise looked gorgeous in a dark grey dress, but I confess my attention was on the man opposite, whom she'd introduced as Adam. He was a bit dishy, albeit not normally the kind I go for. I tend to look for a mental connection as well as a purely physical one, but he had a certain aura that could turn me.

I was trying to work out if he was romantically linked to the fourth member of our group - a rather glamorous and super-cool black girl with blonde streaks in her impressively-styled hair. Louise had introduced her as Abby but hadn't mentioned any connection between her and Adam, other than they were all mutual friends.

We were making good progress with a rather delightful bottle of Kiwi Sauvignon Blanc, but my attempts to find out more about Louise and her curious friends were being thwarted by the number of questions they kept asking me. We'd discussed my photographic career, and then all the usual questions about my current job, like what exactly does a content producer do? At one point, perhaps inspired by the literary surroundings, I announced that it was my ambition, one day, to write a novel based on adventures I'd had with a rather colourful friend. Louise, however, didn't take the bait, and instead let Adam lead the conversation.

Eventually I managed to get a question in.

"So, are you all actors, then?"

Abby let Adam answer.

"Yeah, kind of," he said. "Obviously we've got other jobs as well, but I think there's an ambition there."

"I want to see some more of Louise's magic," said Abby, changing the subject again. All eyes were on Louise, who'd turned bashful all of a sudden.

"Oh yes," I said, turning towards my house guest. "You mentioned you did a bit of that."

"She's good, ain't you darlin'?" said Abby.

"I'm just a beginner, really," said Louise, with a hint of a smile that suggested it was an understatement. But Adam was removing a cufflink from his shirt and handed it to her.

"See if you can make this disappear," he said. "And I'm going to watch carefully."

Louise held it up to the light, taking a good look at the sparkling purple glass that might actually have been an amethyst.

"I can make it disappear, but I can't promise I can get it back again," she said.

"I'll take my chances."

"Okay, your risk. I'll try."

She enclosed it in her fist, and then coughed slightly, as though to clear her throat.

"Sorry, I'm going to need a sip of wine, to make this work," she said, then reached out for her glass with her other hand, all the while keeping her fist clenched and in full view of the rest of us.

"Here goes," she said. "Three, two, one." She blew on the back of her hand, but then looked nervously at the rest of us. "I'm not sure that's gone as planned."

"What's happened?" I said, fascinated.

"Well, it's definitely disappeared," she said, turning her hand round so the palm was upwards, and then unclenching her fingers. I couldn't help but laugh. She looked so concerned, but nevertheless it was brilliant. "The idea was for it to reappear in your pocket," she continued, looking at Adam, "but I don't think it has."

He immediately patted down his jacket, but came up blank.

"So where is it?" I asked.

"I don't know," she said. "I told you, I'm still learning that bit."

"Is it on the floor?" asked Abby.

"I don't know," said Louise. "It might be."

We pulled the table out and all moved our legs to see if we could see it on the carpet, but there was no sign. Louise looked thoughtful, then clicked her fingers.

"I know where it's gone," she said. "Anna."

"What?" I said.

"Are you sitting on it?"

"I don't think so." I stood up. There was nothing there. I checked behind the cushion, but still nothing.

"No, it's gone, then," she said. "Sorry about that. Maybe if someone could pour me another glass of wine?" She nodded to the ice bucket in the middle of the table.

"I think it's empty," said Abby.

"Give it a go, just in case."

Adam reached for the bottle, then stopped.

"Oh, very good," he said, retrieving the cufflink from the bottom of the ice bucket, then holding it up for us to look at. Louise looked nonplussed. I had no idea how she'd done that but it was deeply impressive. The obvious devilment behind her innocent eyes was both amusing and slightly alarming.

Suddenly, though, her expression changed. I followed her eyes to a middle-aged man with a close-cropped beard who was standing at the bar, staring in our direction.

"Are you okay?" I said. She looked far from okay.

"Yes, I just think I've seen someone I recognise." She stood up. "I'll pop over and say hello. Back in a moment."

And with that she departed. I looked to the others, but none of them seemed particularly concerned. Maybe I was just imagining things. Or maybe I'm just used to things taking a turn for the unexpected worse.

Louise walked past George until she was out of sight of the table, and then waited for him to catch up with her.

"We must stop meeting like this," he said.

"We must. I'm back to thinking you're stalking me."

"So this is what you cancelled me for?" He nodded back in the direction they'd come from. "I thought you were supposed to be unwell."

"It's business, George. Something important that I had to sort out."

"Looks like it." The sarcastic tone was unmistakeable. "You have glamorous friends. Who's the other girl? She looks inviting."

"They're colleagues. I know what it looks like. But believe me, this is business. Or at least I hope it will be."

"I've told you, I can help."

"And I've told you, I don't think you can."

Louise turned, as though to head back to the table, but George reached out and gripped her arm. She tried to shake free, but the grip only intensified.

"The bar owner is a friend," he said. "You couldn't make the meeting, so let's have a chat now. We can borrow his office."

"I need to be getting back."

"And I'm not taking no for an answer."

"Fine," she said, then shook her arm again, and this time he let go. "Five minutes."

George led the way past reception, through a curtained-off area to a staircase. At the top he opened a door to an office. Another man was already in there, reading a newspaper.

"Jason, give us a moment will you?" said George. Jason got up and left, pulling the door closed behind him. George took a seat on the sofa, and patted the space next to him. Louise hesitated for a moment and then joined him, albeit keeping a distance between them.

George looked at his watch, then continued.

"So, let's cut the crap. What do you need?"

"I shouldn't even discuss this with you."

"Humour me."

Louise rubbed her forehead, and then swept her hair back.

"In terms of facilities? Premises and girls to work there."

"So basically you're setting up a brothel?"

"No! Well, possibly a hint of that."

George laughed.

"You're playing a dangerous game, my love," he said.

Louise gave an exasperated sigh.

"You haven't seen the business plan. I'll show you the plan, but I don't have it on me. And yes, there are elements that are, shall we say, adult in nature, but the primary issue is that we've found an existing place that we could take over tomorrow, if our friend stumps up his share of the money."

"Where's the place?"

"Not far from here."

"Would I know it?"

"I expect so."

"How much do you need?"

Louise sat back, and crossed her legs.

"This is where I stop discussing it, because the ownership structure is, shall we say, complicated."

"In what way?"

"In the way that it's all deniable if things go wrong. It won't go wrong, but certain aspects require discretion."

"And the girls?"

"Which girls?"

"The ones you're recruiting."

She hesitated, then fixed him with a determined expression.

"We have those. But we need to pay flights and accommodation. That's what we were discussing tonight. The other girl is assisting with logistics."

"Maybe you could take me over and introduce me."

"No! Seriously, it's fine. Everything is under control."

"But if your backer doesn't come through?"

"Then we have an issue. But personally I still think he will."

"Sure?"

"Reasonably."

"So not sure then?"

She shrugged. George took a packet of cigarettes from his pocket and offered her one. She accepted, and he lit them both.

Louise softened.

"George, I like you. I really do," she said. "You seem like a straight man."

He nodded.

"I'll come to see you tomorrow. At your office. I promise I won't cancel. I'll get hold of the latest business plan and show you. It's probably too late, but if you still want to know more after that, I can arrange a meeting to introduce you to my partners. Okay? But I'll warn you now, it's not my decision. They're fair but they're serious and they're not going to be keen on changing direction this late in the day."

"Fair enough. But if it saves the day?"

"Then maybe. But you'll have to convince them as much as they'll have to convince you."

"I think you'll find I can be very convincing."

He reached out and put his hand on her exposed thigh. She lifted it off and put it down on the sofa, but ran her fingers over the back of his hand as she did so.

"I'm sure you can," she said, with a smile. "But for now I'd better get back before they come looking for me. Okay?"

He nodded.

"I very much look forward to it."

"Me too." She stubbed out the cigarette and then rose from the sofa. "Until tomorrow."

Louise let herself out and made her way back downstairs to rejoin the others.

***

I was relieved to see Louise walking back towards us. She'd missed the arrival of the second bottle of wine, but Abby had poured her a glass anyway. It was just as well, as there wasn't much left.

"What happened there? Who was that?" I asked when she retook her place beside me.

"Oh God," she laughed. "I just made an idiot of myself." She looked embarrassed, and a little bit flustered.

"How come?"

"It was nothing. Just somebody I thought I recognised from back home, but it wasn't him. I got chatting anyway. I seriously need to get my eyes tested."

"Are you sure?"

"Yes, seriously. First thing tomorrow, I'll make an appointment at whatever the place is called."

"An optician."

"That's the one."

Her English was usually so good, I occasionally forgot it wasn't her native language.

Before long, Adam announced that he had to be up for work in the morning. I knew I should be saying the same, but it had been a fun night. Adam, being chivalrous, suggested that Louise and I should take the first taxi, and they'd get the next one. I still hadn't worked out if they were a couple.

Once we were home, I thanked Louise for a great time.

"Thank you for coming," she said.

"And I was very impressed by the magic. You have to tell me how you did that."

She smiled.

"It was nothing. Seriously, I'm not that good. Normally I'd have time to prepare something, but they sprang that on me."

"I know, but even so, it was brilliant."

"Ah, you're very kind. But making it disappear is easy. It's all about sleight of hand. The rest was just a distraction, which is why I did the cough. Then I had to take attention away from the ice bucket, so when Abby got us to look at the floor, it was perfect."

"But I didn't see you go near the ice bucket."

"It must have been magic then."

I felt yet another rush of admiration.

"Well, I thought it was amazing."

"Thank you."

After a goodnight hug, I headed to bed for another chapter of Bridget. But I couldn't concentrate on the words. I kept thinking about the man in the bar. I wasn't convinced he was a random stranger. It looked a lot more serious than that.

Chapter 24

A THOUSAND miles away in Warsaw, the night was getting lively.

Danny and Clare had only just arrived at the neon-lit bar when a large man in his late forties, with thinning hair and a greying beard, came over and introduced himself as Anatol Rudyk. His brown suit looked well-worn, and not particularly well-tailored. They all shook hands and Anatol led the way to a relatively secluded corner, far enough from the nearest loudspeakers to make conversation just about possible over the pounding electronic music.

"So you knew Grzegorz," he said, once they were perched on stools around a small circular table. It was a statement more than a question.

"He was an old friend," said Clare. "I used to work for a newspaper in London. We crossed paths years ago. He helped me on a piece about Lech Wałęsa and Solidarność, just before the Wall came down. Helped me make sense of it all."

"They were interesting times."

"They were. But you look around now and the change since 1989 is incredible."

"All of Europe is changing," said Anatol. "It's still hard and we have a long way to go, but no more black market for currency vouchers, eh?" He laughed. "Let me organise drinks. Vodka?"

"That's very kind, but just lager for me," said Danny. "I don't really drink spirits."

"Nonsense! You must drink vodka in Warsaw."

Danny looked to Clare for support, but none was forthcoming. Their host made his way to the bar. Danny offered to go with him, but Anatol waved him away.

"Danny, put your tongue away," said Clare, as they waited for him to return. "Have you never seen a lady before?"

"What is this place?" He tried to take his eyes off the pole dancers gyrating on the main stage area, but it was proving hard.

"It's not a strip club, before you get excited. They're merely part of the decor."

Before long, Anatol returned, with a waitress in a short black dress and fishnets following close behind. She was carrying a silver tray with three glasses and a bottle of iced vodka, and placed it down on the table before leaving. Anatol opened the bottle and started pouring a measure into each of the glasses.

"You know when the Rolling Stones played here in 1967 we paid them with a car full of vodka?" he said. "Although they weren't allowed to take it with them. That was quite a night." He gave a glass to Danny and Clare. "*Na zdrowie!*"

"*Na zdrowie,*" said Clare, lifting her glass and chinking it against the others.

"Cheers," said Danny, deciding against attempting the Polish, lest he should make a mess of it. He took a sip and flinched.

"So, what is your interest now?" Anatol asked them, looking from one to the other.

"We want to pay our respects and know what happened to Grzegorz," said Clare. "When I heard the news I couldn't believe it. It came as such a shock."

"It was a great shock to all of us. He was always, how do you say? Indestructible. Like a lion."

"Did you know him well?" asked Danny.

"Yes, I worked with him for many years. Not so closely. I do mainly news, but we were friends. Good friends." He took another gulp of vodka and waited for Danny and Clare to do the same. Danny flinched again, his throat burning, but the big Pole was necking his as though it was water.

"What about the man he was supposed to have killed?" asked Clare. "Do we know anything about him? Who he was, where he came from, how and why it turned violent?"

Anatol opened his hands in a dismissive gesture.

"No, it is a mystery what happened. We tried to find out about him. He was ... An informer? Is that the word?" Clare nodded. "We think he was helping Grzegorz with a story, but as for why he ended up dead? We don't know."

"Do you know what he was working on?"

"He didn't tell me. He didn't talk much about his stories until he published them."

"So you've got no idea."

Anatol swept his arm around the room.

"Look around you. Look around the city. You can see how much it is changing. That presents opportunities but also attracts people who are maybe less honest. Who can turn things to their advantage." He shrugged. "Poland has always had corruption. It still has corruption. But now it's more property and planning than queue jumping and pairs of Levis. *Na zdrowie.*"

Clare raised her glass again. Danny followed suit. He was still struggling with the vodka, but the third sip seemed to go down slightly more easily. Perhaps he was becoming acclimatised. More likely, his taste buds had already been scalded into submission.

It was becoming clear that Anatol wasn't going to provide the breakthrough they'd been looking for. He continued to answer every question, and was at least trying to be helpful. But Danny decided to try a different approach, before the vodka really took hold.

"Do you know anyone else who is investigating?" he asked. "Or anybody who would be nervous if they knew we were here, asking questions?"

"No. Maybe." Anatol paused, as though trying to consider all the ramifications. "Perhaps if someone was happy that he was no longer working on a particular story, they wouldn't be happy if you were asking questions. But I don't know."

"But do you really think he committed suicide? Why would he do that?"

"That is what we are told, but I don't know why. Maybe he had money problems or health issues. Or maybe he just didn't like the thought of spending the next thirty years in prison."

Beside him, Clare stubbed out a cigarette, and then, unhelpfully, refilled their glasses. Danny gave her a filthy "what are you doing?" look, but she had a mischievous expression that told him they were in this for the long haul. But Anatol was running out of information, and as his mind started to go fuzzy, Danny found his eyes wandering around the room. There were so many beautiful women. He found himself looking at one in particular, who made eye contact and smiled at him before he had a chance to turn away.

A few minutes later, he looked again. She was chatting to her friend, laughing and drinking, and then she caught his eye again. This time she waved. Danny quickly looked away, but Clare had noticed, and wasn't going to let him off so easily.

"Excuse my colleague," she said to Anatol. "He seems to be unable to resist the lure of the local ladies."

Their host laughed.

"Polish girls are the most beautiful in the world," he said. "Although our Ukrainian neighbours would tell you differently." He turned around to see who Danny had been looking at. "Ah, yes. You have very good taste, my friend."

"Sorry," he protested, finding the situation funny. "She waved at me. I'm innocent."

"Not that innocent, eh Danny?" said Clare, apparently enjoying his discomfort.

"What's that supposed to mean?"

"You're not averse to going to the odd massage parlour, if my memory serves me correctly."

"That was for research! And nothing happened."

"Research." Clare did the bunny ears thing, and laughed.

"You know it was research." He sighed, exasperated.

Anatol was confused.

"Excuse Clare," said Danny. "She has a strange sense of humour. I was investigating a people-trafficking ring back in London and ended up going to a massage parlour, but only to get information, and they threw me out, which is the bit she forgets to mention."

"Steady, Danny," Clare interrupted. "Your friend is coming over."

He looked up in horror, but she wasn't wrong. The young woman and her friend were approaching. Anatol stood and pulled another couple of stools close so they could join them at their table. Danny was mortified. But there again, she was one of the most beautiful women he had ever seen, with her high Slavic cheekbones, long flowing hair and intensely seductive kiss-me lips. And the vodka was beginning to wash away his inhibitions.

"Girls, come and join us," said Anatol in English. "This is my English friend, Danny, and his colleague Clare. And you are?"

"Małgorzata, and this is Karolina," said the one who had caught Danny's eye. She extended a hand in Danny's direction, her eyes sparkling. "It is a pleasure to meet you."

While Danny returned the handshake, and then felt his heart flutter as she let go, but trailed her fingertips over his palm, Anatol signalled to a waitress, held up a glass and two fingers. A moment later, two more glasses arrived.

Małgorzata sat next to Danny. Underneath the table, their knees touched. Her friend seemed more interested in Anatol, and before long, Anatol's arm had snaked around her. There was lots of laughter, and conversation that Danny didn't understand. More vodka flowed. The woman got ever closer. She touched his arm, and then his leg. Danny turned to Clare, looking for support, but she seemed to be finding the whole thing hilarious.

"Danny," said Clare, beckoning to him. By now, he was feeling very much the worse for wear. He leaned over, although trying to stay upright was proving to be an increasing struggle, and he was grateful that he didn't have to lean too far. Clare tilted her head to whisper into his ear.

"She's probably a prostitute, no disrespect," she said. "I'm not saying you couldn't charm the ladies, but I suspect it's not just your body she's interested in."

"What am I going to do?" he hissed back.

"Go with the flow. Go on, I'll treat you."

"You're trying to get me into trouble."

Clare leaned back, and put up her hands in a mock protestation of innocence. Danny gave her a look of daggers. But despite how much she was clearly enjoying the show, Danny was grateful when she called a halt.

"We need to be getting back to the hotel," she announced. Małgorzata protested and told him he must come back again, and he said he would, despite knowing that he would probably never see her again. What if she wasn't a prostitute? But he already had a girlfriend. And oh God, what would Anna say if she could see him now?

Danny tried to stand up, but the change in posture suddenly made his legs feel hollow and he gripped the table for support while saying his farewells to Anatol and Małgorzata, and accepting a kiss on the cheek from the other woman, whose name he was struggling to remember. With a final look back, they headed to the door. He knew he might struggle to remember much about the night, but he thought he would never forget the way she blew him a kiss.

By the time he was back on the street, the cold air and fatigue added to Danny's sense of disorientation. Clare was far from sober, but seemed much more in control, and he was glad she was there to supervise the taxi.

The journey back to the apartment passed in a blur, but Danny was aware that he had his arm round Clare at one point, while part of him couldn't quite equate their current closeness with the woman who seemed so distant at times, and with whom he had once shared an office, in a constant state of reverence.

Clare paid the taxi driver, then helped Danny out of the car, into the building, and up to his room. By the time they got there, all he wanted to do was lie on the bed and close his eyes, and try not to think about the state of his head the next morning. Clare approached with a glass of water and told him to drink it. He propped himself up and did so.

"What time is it?" he asked.

"Just gone one."

"Please tell me we don't have an early start tomorrow."

"I can tell you, if it helps. It wouldn't necessarily be true, though."

"God."

Danny closed his eyes for a moment, but when he opened them, the room was still spinning.

"I'm never drinking vodka again," he said. But when he turned round, Clare was nowhere to be seen. Then he heard noises from the bathroom and she reappeared, looking almost as sleepy as he felt. He had no idea how far she had to go to get back to her place.

"Would you like to stay?" he said. "I'll have the sofa. Or most likely the bathroom."

"That's never going to happen, Danny. I know you're the expert in platonic bed-sharing, but it would be better if I went back to my place, in case I'm tempted to take advantage of your slightly inebriated state."

"You're getting worse. Are you getting broody or something?"

Clare's expression changed. And then she told him about the child she'd lost the previous year, and suddenly the mood changed, and all he wanted to do was apologise, and give her a hug, and make everything all right for her.

"There's nothing you can do, Danny," she said. "These things happen. It wasn't meant to be. Keep drinking water, try to stay out of trouble and I'll come back in the morning to give you a lift to the airport."

"Are you flying back with me?"

"No. I'm making my own way back."

"Do you have your own plane?"

"No, of course I don't have my own plane. Who do you think I am? I'm not made of money. I have friends with planes who let me hitch a lift occasionally."

It was so much to take in, but now wasn't the time.

"Sorry about Anatol," said Clare. "I thought he'd be able to give us more insight. But still, it was a fun night. What happens in Warsaw stays in Warsaw, and all of that."

"It was," said Danny. But in his mind he could still see Małgorzata, and wondered where she was now. There was no logic to the world, sometimes.

"You're still keen on the story?" asked Clare.

That took him a moment to process.

"Yes," he said at last. "On several conditions."

"Go on."

"Number one, that it's genuine, above board, and there's no secret agenda."

"I promise."

"Number two, that nobody gets hurt. Anna specifically, but me, you, Louise and anyone else who might be involved."

"Also promised."

"Obviously. And number three, that there's nothing illegal."

"Mmmm."

"What do you mean, mmmm?"

"I mean you won't have to do anything illegal. Louise and I might have to stretch the boundaries a bit from time to time, just to make sure Brandrick is thoroughly implicated. But it won't be for personal gain, and it will be justifiable when the day of judgement comes."

"Fine."

Danny was too tired to argue. He didn't even think he'd have the energy to get undressed, although he knew he should.

"Do I at least get a goodnight kiss?" asked Clare, before she left. But Danny was already fast asleep.

Chapter 25

Thursday, January 23rd, 1997

L OUISE sat at the table while the others tucked into Harry's daily selection of pastries, and finished reading the business plan. It all seemed to check out.

"And you've built the websites and created the legends?" she asked, turning to Abby.

"Yup. All done, babe."

There was a laptop on the table. Louise pulled it to her, clicked the icon to connect to the internet, and then typed some of the web addresses into Netscape. It all seemed to stack up. She couldn't have been more impressed.

"It looks fantastic," she said. "But if I'm going into the lion's den with this, it needs to be not just watertight but bombproof."

"It's both of those," said Abby. "I ain't an amateur."

Louise was prepared to believe it. Every link she clicked led to a new page of content and information, even linking out to what looked like news sites, with articles on her co-investors. Had she not known it was all complete fiction, she'd have sworn it was true.

"I can't thank you enough," she said.

"My pleasure, babe," said Abby. "Although feel free to suggest to Adam that I'm worth a pay rise."

"One thing at a time," said Adam. But even he seemed to be in a particularly good mood.

"Right," said Louise. "I ought to call George and let him know I'm on my way."

The others wished her well as she retrieved her coat, and then headed to the door.

Danny woke up, feeling nauseous. His eyes flickered half-open, squinting at the thin bar of light that sliced through the gap in the curtains. Then they opened wide. There was a dark figure on the sofa, watching him. He caught his breath. Clare. Or was it? The figure was motionless. He heaved his head off the pillow, trying to ignore the throbbing. Then he heard the familiar voice.

"Wakey wakey, it's 7am," she called. "Who's your friend?"

"What friend?"

Danny took a moment to process the question, then turned on the bed and nearly leapt out of it in shock. There was a woman lying face down next to him, still dressed, but partly covered by a blanket.

"Jesus. I've got no idea," he said, putting distance between them.

"You're a dark horse. I very much remember leaving you here on your own."

"You did. I ..." But nothing made sense. "I'll wake her up."

He nudged her, but she didn't move. Clare opened the curtains, and that was when he noticed the bruises on the woman's neck.

Danny leapt off the bed, his head spinning, then rushed to the bathroom to be violently sick. What on earth was going on?

When he was sure his stomach was empty, he tentatively left the bathroom. Clare was standing over the body, giving it an inspection.

"This will enhance your reputation as a ladykiller," said Clare, but Danny couldn't see the funny side.

"Believe me, I have no idea who she is, how she got here, or who killed her," he said, his voice laced with panic. "And I certainly didn't have sex with her."

"I believe you. And I'm not proposing a forensic examination," said Clare. "We've got to give the girl some dignity. It does present an issue, Danny, I'm not going to lie."

Clare turned the body over so she could see her face. Danny winced and turned away.

"Oh, it's your friend from last night," said Clare.

"The prostitute?"

"Former prostitute by the looks of things. What was her name? Something beginning with M."

Danny tried to think back, but the night was a blur.

"I remember. Małgorzata," Clare continued. " Although it's best not to ask how to spell that. It's got a Z and one of those funny Ls with a line through it."

Danny started to feel nauseous again, but it wasn't just the excess vodka.

"Jesus, Clare. What's going on?" he asked, backing towards the bathroom. But Clare didn't seem to be sharing his sense of panic.

"I'm not one hundred percent sure, but let's hope she's not discovered until we're safely out of the country."

"But I didn't kill her."

"I believe you. Really. I think the police might take a bit more persuading."

"But I didn't! For fuck's sake."

Danny sat on the floor, grateful for the wall behind his back, while Clare searched the body for identification. But there was nothing apart from a roll of cash in a clutch bag, some make-up, a packet of cigarettes and a lighter.

"I think the best thing we can do is to get out of here as quickly as possible," she said. "Although please have a shower because, well, frankly, we'd all benefit from that. Then I'll get you to the airport and I'll sort this out."

But Danny wasn't listening.

"You promised me nobody would get hurt," he said, anger rising. "And now there's a dead woman, whose only crime seems to have been to try to talk to me in a strip bar."

"We don't know that chatting you up was her only crime," said Clare.

"Can you stop taking the piss and be serious for a minute?" Danny's voice was bordering on hysterical. "There's a young woman dead. She had everything to live for. And now she's here, because of me. Of us."

"I am being serious. But we're not the bad people here, Danny. Yes, it's a tragedy and my heart bleeds, but she's not the first victim in this, and we need to keep cool heads and find out what's going on, or she might well not be the last. Now please, get in the shower, get dressed, and we can start dealing with this."

Danny nodded, his head in turmoil. He was in no fit state to compute what he was seeing. He lost himself under the shower, the scalding water doing its best to pump life into his body. He wanted to stay there forever, thinking of little else than the jet, washing away the physical and mental pain. But time was of the essence. After a few minutes he wrapped himself in a towel and returned to the bedroom to fetch clean clothes.

"I'll pop out on the balcony for a cigarette while you get dressed," said Clare, opening the door. But as she stepped out, the glass window in the door exploded. Instinctively she ducked, letting out a scream, and threw herself back into the bedroom.

"What the fuck was that?" asked Danny.

Clare crawled back towards the door, keeping low. Wedged into the wall was a piece of metal, a sharp one. It had missed her head by inches.

"A crossbow bolt," she said, sounding more scared than Danny had ever known her to.

No further words were necessary. Danny grabbed his clothes, while Clare edged along the floor and re-closed the curtains. Her face was even paler in the semi-darkness.

"What now?" asked Danny, terror adding vibrato to his voice.

Clare didn't answer. She was sitting on the floor, with her head in her hands.

"Clare?" he urged again.

She looked up, as though coming out of a trance.

"Priority one is to get us out of here," she said. "And try to avoid being killed in the process."

Chapter 26

JASON scowled as he met Louise at the fifth floor lift door and showed her through to his boss's office. He stood at the entrance, keeping watch. George directed her to a chair in front of his desk.

"You have something for me?" he said, clicking with his mouse, and then turning the computer screen away so he could give her his full attention.

"I have the plan," said Louise. "But it's not really something for an audience, no disrespect." She looked back to Jason, who was standing silently, watching.

"I don't have secrets here," said George. "Don't mind him."

"But maybe I do have secrets."

She hesitated, and eventually George nodded. Jason stepped back into the corridor, and closed the door behind him.

"Okay, but before I show it to you I still need to know more about you," said Louise. "Who are you? What do you do? For all I know, you could be working undercover for the police."

"I'm sure you've done your research on me."

"I have. But that makes me even more suspicious. If the police turn a blind eye to you because you're supplying information ..."

George stood up, and moved round to the front of his desk.

"I assure you, there's nothing for you to worry about," he said, reaching out for the folder she'd placed on her lap. "Give me the plan, and leave it with me and I'll come up with a proposal."

"I'm afraid I can't do that," said Louise, her grip intensifying.

"You can't expect me to make a decision based on a five-minute read-through."

"I don't expect you to make a decision anyway. You're the one chasing me. But I can't leave this with you. You have no idea what I had to go through to persuade them to let me take this out of the building. It's the most confidential of all confidential documents."

"Fine."

He took the folder and returned to his desk.

"Take your time. I'm happy to wait," said Louise, crossing her legs to reveal an expanse of thigh. She followed his eyes down to her legs. "If there's anything you need to ask me, feel free."

George started to read, then tapped a couple of times at his keyboard, leafing forwards and backwards through the document. Eventually he turned back to her.

"Some of these additional revenue streams. They're vague," he said.

Louise nodded.

"Why? What does 'miscellaneous and ancillary' mean?"

"Do I need to spell it out for you?"

"It would be appreciated, yes."

"I think you should use your imagination. There's the club itself, but it opens up opportunities for more, er, stimulating revenue generation. And the movement of funds, if you catch my drift."

He nodded.

"Interesting."

Another few moments passed.

"There's no mention of the premises. It's all very cagey on the specifics. It talks of option A and option B."

Louise shrugged.

"The building is not confirmed. I told you. Option A is ready to go, but it needs us to move very quickly. With option B we have more time. It's not as easy and the start would be delayed. The plan covers both. We know where they are, but we can't risk the deal in case the document is leaked."

"But you can't tell me where the premises are?"

"We can't put it in the business plan, but I can show you." She watched his eyes for any reaction, and was pleased to see a spark of enthusiasm. He was so easy to play. "We'd have to be discreet. We can't go in there like we're about to own the place. Can I trust you?"

"Of course you can trust me."

Louise thought he was the last person in the world she could trust.

"Will Igor be coming?"

"Igor?"

She nodded in the direction of the door.

"Jason," said George.

"Jason? What sort of name is Jason for hired muscle?"

"I'd advise you not to repeat that in his earshot."

"Noted. But I'd prefer it if it was just you and me. I'll introduce you to Harry. He's the money man."

"Jason will be with me. That's non-negotiable. When are we talking?"

"We have to act fast, so this evening?"

"And where?"

"It's not far from here, don't worry. I'll call you later and tell you where."

"You can't tell me now?"

"That wouldn't be appropriate."

George sighed. Louise crossed her legs again, and ran the tip of her tongue over her glossy dark purple lipstick.

"It will only be a quick meeting, George," she continued. "I'm probably only going to have half an hour free, but I'll show you the place and you'll meet Harry. I'll call you." She stood up and reached out for the folder. George gave it one last look and then passed it over.

"Could I interest you in a little drink now," he said. "To discuss things aside from business?"

She frowned.

"I'd love to, but I have a meeting to attend. About staff recruitment." The insinuation was clear. "But we'll chat tonight, and get to know each other even if it's just for half an hour. Some things are better not rushed. I'm looking forward to it."

The journey to Okecie airport was fraught. Danny was relieved to see that Clare had a car waiting at the back of the apartment building, and that they both managed to reach it without being shot, but that was a rare bit of good news amid the carnage. Neither of them spoke, both too preoccupied with watching out for danger, expecting at any moment to discover they were being followed.

Their driver pulled into the short stay car park and killed the engine.

"What are we going to do now?" asked Danny, feeling desperate.

"I'll tell you what you're going to do," said Clare. "You're going to run, and catch the 10.30 flight. Then I'm going to meet you back in London, late this afternoon." She asked the driver for a pen and a piece of paper, then wrote something down and handed it to Danny. "That's my hotel and room number. It's near

Bond Street. You should be back about - " she looked at her watch and then her eyes narrowed as she did the calculation "– just gone two, allowing for the time difference, so three-ish by the time you're leaving the airport. I'm going to have to dash now because I've got to fix things, but I'll meet you there at, say, five-thirty?"

"How are you going to get back by then? It's another country, a thousand miles away."

"I've told you, I've got a friend who can give me a lift. But it's going to be tight. Believe me, nothing would make me happier than coming back with you on BA, and making sure you're safe, but scheduled airlines and major airports are not an option for me."

Danny sat back and closed his eyes.

"I'm not sure having you around qualifies as keeping me safe," he said.

"Well, I think my track record proves otherwise."

"Your track record?" He opened his eyes and fixed them on Clare. "Chaos follows you."

"Because we do a dangerous job," she said. "But I told you, we're not the bad people. We just pursue the ones who are."

Shaking his head, Danny looked out of the window at the grey morning sky. A plane was coming in to land, and he followed its progress until it disappeared behind the terminal building.

"And what if you're not there by five-thirty?" he asked. "What if something happens to you?"

"Nothing is going to happen to me, and I will be there. If I'm running late, I'll call you, but it'll be fine, I'm sure. But only if you get going now, because I've got a busy couple of hours ahead."

"Okay." Danny knew it was pointless to delay things any longer. After collecting his bag, he set off on the short walk to the terminal. He didn't look back, but instead broke into a run, partly to ensure he caught the plane, and partly because he was aware that the longer he was outside, the more he was a target – but with no idea who had him in their sights.

Chapter 27

THE first thing Danny did when he cleared Heathrow passport control was to call Lisa. But he could tell from her tone of voice that she hadn't forgiven him for cancelling their date night.

"I said I was sorry," he said.

"And that was it? You didn't think to call me since?"

"I've been away, out of the country. I didn't have a phone."

"Yeah, I'm sure."

He sighed, exasperated.

"How are things there?"

"Oh, they're brilliant. I had a lovely time on Tuesday. My mum came round and took Jessica for the evening so I was able to stay in by myself with an indulgent Pot Noodle and all the excitement of a Conservative party political broadcast. You missed a great night. How about you? Where have you been, anyway?"

"I'm not sure I can say. Sorry."

"Can you come round tonight?"

Relationships weren't supposed to be like this, were they? What happened to the happy times?

"I don't know that I can, sorry. I don't know what's happening tonight."

"There's a surprise."

"It's not like that! I have to work. I'm on a story. What can I say? You know the deal."

"It looks like it."

Neither spoke for a moment, to let the pressure subside. Eventually, Lisa broke the silence.

"Is this the way it's always going to be?"

"What do you mean by that?"

"I mean it's not working, Danny. Not for me, anyway. I thought I could do this, and I know it's as much my fault as anyone's, but I don't want to go on like this."

"What are you saying?"

"I'm saying I need a break."

"From?"

"From us. This. I'm sorry. Just give me space, okay? Give me time, to sort my head out. I'll call you."

"And there's nothing I can say in the meantime?"

"No, I don't think so. Goodbye, Danny."

And she ended the call. Danny made his way to the Underground platform, feeling confused and desolate, then, when the train came, he took a seat in the relatively deserted end carriage, with his bag between his knees and his head in his hands.

When he walked into the hotel room, Clare was on the phone. She ended the call.

"How do you do that?" he asked, in genuine amazement.

"Do what?"

"Cross borders like a ghost walking through doors. Do you not need a passport?"

"I've got a passport," she said with a pout. Danny tried not to laugh.

"Oh, don't look all hurt. It's a valid question."

"I've got a passport," she insisted.

"Can I see it?"

"No."

"Why not?"

"Because the picture is not one of my most flattering."

"You can hide the picture. I'm curious about the rest of it."

"No."

"Okay. Well, I'm done here, then. Good luck with Greg."

He turned to walk away, knowing she'd call him back.

"For heaven's sake. Okay."

Danny sat on the bed while Clare delved into her handbag. Eventually she held out her passport for him.

"That says Suomi on the front," said Danny, once he'd taken it. "Isn't that Finland?"

"Your point?"

"Kaarina Mäkinen?"

"And again, I'm not sure exactly what you're getting at."

He handed back the passport. Clare offered to make a cup of tea, which he accepted.

"So how did you leave things in Poland?" he asked, as they waited for the kettle to boil.

"I sorted it, Danny. And I've just brought Louise up to speed on it all."

"What do you mean you sorted it? You can't just dispose of a body. She was a young girl. She'll have parents and friends and all sorts of people who are looking for her. People who love her, who are worried sick."

"I know."

"So what do you mean you sorted it?"

"I mean you don't need to worry about it any more. It probably wouldn't be wise to return to Warsaw in the foreseeable future, but as far as you're concerned, just forget it ever happened."

"That's the most ridiculous thing I ever heard. I woke up ..." He instinctively looked around and lowered his voice, although they were the only two in the room and the door was closed. "I woke up next to a dead girl. And I'm pretty sure I didn't kill her, so that means somebody else must have been in my room. So excuse my naivety on these things, but telling me not to worry really doesn't work for me. Who was she? Why was she there? And who the fuck strangled her?"

"You're looking at me as though I know all the answers."

"I kind of assume you do."

"And what have I told you about assuming things? Anyway. Onto happier news: I'm taking you for another night out."

"No, no, no, no, no, no, no."

"I acknowledge your enthusiasm, but honestly, it'll be fun."

"It won't be fun. You'll get me drunk and I'll wake up next to another dead person."

"Oh, Danny," Clare shook her head and smiled, while pouring boiling water into two mugs. "You're so cynical."

"And with bloody good reason."

"Well, the good news is, there's nothing to be cynical about. We're going to a club."

"You are, I'm not."

"You sound just like Anna. Do I have to let you beat me at chess so I get my own way, or should we just agree that I'm going to get my own way eventually anyway, and save ourselves twenty minutes of discussing it?"

Danny lay back on the bed, put a pillow over his face and pretended to scream.

"Why? What sort of club?" he said when he resurfaced.

"Just a club. A private members' club."

"And are you a member?"

"Ah, kind of. Enough to get in. With a couple of guests."

"And why?"

"It's a two-birds-one-stone scenario. I'm interested in the person who runs it and I want to see our Mr Brandrick in person."

"Oh, this gets worse."

Clare emptied a couple of capsules of milk into each cup and passed one over.

"What do you mean 'interested in the person who runs it'?" he asked.

"I think he might be up to no good."

"I expected that. But in what way?"

"He's Irish and I think he's running the club as a front to support the IRA. Money laundering, counterfeiting, a bit of smuggling."

"Prostitution?"

"No, which I appreciate will be a let-down for you. But the IRA doesn't get involved in prostitution, or drugs. It's against their moral code."

"But blowing people up is morally okay?"

"They'd argue that was legitimate. I'm not making excuses for them."

"Well, I'm still not going."

"You are and we're going to take Anna. It'll be good for you two to spend some time together."

"I'm going back under the pillow." Danny lay back down, and grabbed two pillows this time.

"It'll be a great night," Clare continued.

"It really won't."

"Oh come on. Don't be such a spoilsport."

"I can't hear you."

"We're just going for a drink. It'll be like the old days."

Danny looked out from between the pillows.

"The last time you took us both for a drink, it was to a gay swingers' club."

"Precisely. And we had a great night. I can't promise this will be as colourful. Anyway, we can call it a birthday celebration."

"I wouldn't advise bringing the birthday into it."

"Okay, a non-birthday celebration. Class reunion. Drink your tea and we'll go and tell her the news."

I was lying on the sofa, desperately trying not to fall asleep, and aware that Louise was up to something food-related in the kitchen. I was also aware that I should at least make a token effort to help her, or it would look like I was taking the piss. And then the doorbell rang.

"I'll get it," she called. Oh, heavenly. I went back to closing my eyes. A moment later, Clare and Danny walked in, looking like a pair of naughty schoolchildren.

"At last," I said, sitting up, and hoping I hadn't just made a mess of the remnants of my make-up. "Don't worry about returning my messages. Good evening, Clare."

"It's not Danny's fault," said Clare. "I took him to Warsaw."

"To where?"

Louise seemed less interested in Auntie Clare making a trip to her motherland than I might have expected. She offered to make drinks, but they both said they'd just had one. I thought it would definitely be taking the piss if I was the only one to say yes, so I declined as well, even though I'd have quite liked a cup of tea.

We spent the next few minutes catching up, chatting about my birthday, and changing the subject whenever I asked anything about Warsaw. Eventually Clare got to what I thought might very well be the point of the visit.

"Anyway," she said. "We want to take you for a night out."

I looked to Danny, who responded with a *don't blame me, it's not my idea* kind of expression.

"When?"

"Tonight."

"Why?"

"To have a non-birthday drink. On me."

I thought about it, but only long enough to come up with a polite way of declining, which in retrospect possibly didn't sound as polite as I'd hoped.

"That's very generous, but you could achieve the same effect by just buying a bottle of wine from the shop down the road, and save us all the whole faff of going out. I'd be happy to share it with you."

"But you enjoy going out," said Clare.

"Since when do I enjoy going out?"

"You've always enjoyed going out."

"That was back in the day. Anyway, I was out last night. I've got to stay in and learn how to knit." I nodded in the direction of Danny's present, which was perched on the arm of the smaller sofa.

"Please. It'll make him really happy."

"Don't bring me into this," said Danny.

"Ignore him," she said. "He gets confused, poor love."

I looked from one to the other. To his credit, Danny appeared embarrassed, but Clare was ominously excitable, and that normally only means one thing.

"It's a work night," I said, putting up a final protest. "Some of us have jobs to go to in the morning."

"I promise to have you back home and in bed no later than midnight."

"But why do you want me to come?"

"Because I like you. And you might meet a lovely man."

I glanced at Danny again, to see his reaction, but he shrugged and looked even more embarrassed, which was open to interpretation. I thought about asking if I could take Nathan from work, as we'd still not managed to arrange a night of our own, but decided that might come across as spiteful.

"You're bad," I said instead. And then got up to start the process of getting ready - after hastily consuming Louise's latest delicious creation.

Chapter 28

I WAS out of the shower, nearly dressed, and applying eyeliner when there was a tap at my bedroom door.

"Come in," I called. Danny poked his head inside, and I beckoned him to sit on the bed. "I'm nearly ready."

"That's okay. I just wanted to apologise about the phone messages. I tried to call you lots of times, but then by the time you called me back, I was on the way to Warsaw and didn't have a signal."

"Don't worry about it. What did you want to talk to me about anyway?"

"Just to wish you a happy birthday. And to say thank you again for a wonderful evening."

"But your message said I had to call you back immediately. It sounded urgent."

"Did it?"

I think he could tell from my face that I was neither convinced nor in the mood for bullshit, but actually I was pleased to see him and I didn't want to start an argument.

"Let's hope we have another of those wonderful evenings

tonight," I said instead. "And I promise I'll try not to kiss you again."

He smiled at that, but noticeably failed to say something like, *Don't let me stop you, in fact how about we get started now?*

Instead, I stood up and asked him to help fasten my new Ceylon sapphire necklace.

"Where did you get this from?"

"It was a present from someone," I said, trying to sound all coy and mysterious, but the look on his little face was almost heartbreaking. "Louise."

"Louise? Louise gave you this?"

I nodded.

"With a bit of help from Auntie Clare I suspect. Actually, come with me, I need to go and ask them where we're going and how we're getting there so I can choose the right shoes."

He nodded, and followed me out of the room, but just before we reached the front room I put my arm out and stopped him dead. Clare was standing, giving Louise a hug. But more than that, she was holding her hand, and running the fingers of her other hand through Louise's hair, brushing it away from her face. Then, to cap it all, she leaned in closer still and kissed her on the forehead. I backed up immediately, as quietly as I could, taking Danny with me, back to my room. We closed the door.

"Did you see that?" I hissed.

"I did," he whispered back.

"You don't think ...?"

"It looks like it."

"But ... But you don't think she's a bit young for her?"

"Experienced older woman. It's quite seductive."

"What? Oh, here we go."

"It's a known thing."

"Let's not even get started on that. But do you really think ...? It would explain a lot."

"I don't know. But it certainly looked like it. Listen, Clare told me a lot about Louise in Warsaw. It's too much to go into now, but I'll fill you in when we're on our own."

"I look forward to it." I was struggling to take this all in, anyway. "Perhaps she's not as young as she looks. That can be a thing, can't it? Clare said she was nineteen, but what if she only said that to throw us off the scent? Maybe this is what tonight's about. They're both coming out and want us to be there to witness the happy occasion."

"You are terrible."

"What do you mean?"

But he was laughing at me.

I quickly made a decision on the shoes, deciding it was another opportunity to show off my sexy new boots. The novelty had yet to wear off. With a final touch of lipstick and a dab of Poison, I was ready.

"How do I look?" I said, brushing down my dress.

"Gorgeous," he said, which was nice.

"Perfect. Let's see if we can go and find these lovely men she was talking about."

He immediately had that expression again.

"Only joking," I added. "I've already found you."

I led the way back down the hall, trying to make as much noise as I could without it looking like the work of a madwoman.

It was a different club to the one I'd been to with Louise the night before, but it had a similar kind of set-up - just without the books. This time, though, Clare was in charge, and she led us to a quiet corner in one of many alcoves. It was on a slightly raised platform, but my view of the rest of the venue was largely obscured by plants, railings and a curtain. The subdued lighting didn't help either, but I thought Clare could probably see everything from her vantage point. Danny sat next to me. Louise, meanwhile, who looked utterly gorgeous in a red dress, sat next to Clare, and seemed slightly on edge.

The drink started to flow and then an elderly man approached us, wearing a cravat, and looking for all the world like a well-to-do country squire. Louise introduced him as Harry, and said he was a tutor at the acting school she wanted to enrol at. He suggested going to meet some of the other staff and students so she made her apologies and left us. If there was to be a big announcement, it would have to wait.

True to her word, Clare was on her best behaviour and it was a very pleasant evening. At one point, another man came over and introduced himself as the owner of the place. I found it hard to make out what he was saying over the music, and his strong Irish accent didn't help, but he seemed friendly enough. It was all very lovely and uneventful. And for those specific reasons, I couldn't help feeling that it was all a bit odd.

In one of the other alcoves, Louise was deep in conversation with George Brandrick. She'd introduced Harry as the money man. George asked about her other friends from the previous evening, but she explained they were out working and couldn't be there. She made sure she was sitting close enough to him that occasionally they touched legs as she moved.

"So Louise has been telling me about the club," said George, turning to Harry. "It all sounds rather appealing, although some of the details could do with elaboration. Has she explained about me?"

"She has, my dear boy," said Harry. "Although I think I can only echo the message she has already conveyed. We appreciate your interest and look forward to your proposal, but I do fear it is rather late in proceedings to invite someone new to play."

"But can you tell me more about it?"

"I'm merely the accountant. You would need to speak to Adam, although I am sure Louise could appraise you, if she has his blessing."

"I spoke to him earlier," she added. "Apparently you do check out. No offence, but we had to make sure. So I've been given clearance to answer any question."

"That's excellent news."

"Although not tonight," she added quickly. "Obviously there is a limit to what I can say in public, and I did warn you this would have to be a fleeting visit. But I can come and see you first thing. Perhaps without him?" She nodded at Jason, who was sitting apart from them, but keeping a watchful eye.

George smiled, but Louise couldn't fail to notice a lascivious undertone. He leaned over and whispered so that Harry couldn't overhear.

"I think that could be arranged. I will tell him to make himself scarce so we can explore, shall we say, the more intimate details of the arrangement." As if the innuendo wasn't enough, she felt his hand on her thigh again.

"That sounds perfect." And again she removed the hand. "I'll be at your office at eight." She smiled back, with a subtle, suggestive raise of her eyebrows.

They spent a few minutes in discussion. George wanted a good look round the venue, but Louise explained that discretion was paramount. They couldn't be seen to be taking an interest. At one point he got a little carried away, making a suggestive comment to a waitress about how she might soon be working for him, but Louise quickly managed to retrieve the situation by apologising and blaming the drink. All the time, she was aware that Clare and the others were waiting for her, so at the earliest opportunity, she decided to wrap things up.

"I hate to be rude, but I am going to have to leave you now," she said, loud enough that Harry could hear. "I'm so sorry, but I did say I only had half an hour and I must be elsewhere."

"Don't worry, I can take over," said Harry. "That is, of course, with the tacit acknowledgement that I don't have quite the same charm. Another drink, George?"

Louise sensed George's disappointment, but he said he would have a brandy. She shook his hand and then made her way back to Clare and the others, trusting that Harry would make sure that neither George nor Jason would watch where she was going.

Louise rejoined us, and asked if she could squeeze in next to me and Danny. And again the conversation flowed. Nobody mentioned my boots, though, which was as annoying as it was predictable. I asked Louise to do a magic trick, and after much faux protest she managed to make a napkin disappear, even though it must have been in the palm of her hand and couldn't possibly have gone anywhere. I was transfixed. When she said it was on the next table I was tempted to believe her, even though I couldn't swear that there hadn't been one there all along. Her hand was empty as she unfurled it.

The old man Harry popped back at one point, to say farewell, and it had been a pleasure to meet us. Shortly after, Clare looked at her watch, and announced we should be leaving too, if she was going to keep her promise of having me in bed by midnight.

When the taxi dropped us off back at mine, Louise came in with me, but Clare and Danny said they would continue to homes of their own, even though I offered a nightcap. It was all tremendously civilised.

I should have seen the signs. I really should. But by the time I worked it out, it was far too late to do anything to avoid the carnage.

Chapter 29

Friday, January 24th, 1997

SHORTLY after 7am, Adam's tanzanite blue Mercedes E320 pulled up not far from Anna's flat in Camden. With a final glance over her shoulder, Louise pulled the front door closed, making as little noise as possible, and made her way to the car. Adam reached across and opened the door for her, then once she was seated, he guided the car to a quiet residential street close to Mornington Crescent.

He reached into the back seat and retrieved a small leather briefcase.

"I'm worried about this," he said. "I want to come in with you."

"I'll be fine," she said. "I've done my research."

"But that's the issue. We know his reputation. I don't think it's safe for you to go in there on your own. What if he attacks you?"

"There are laws against that kind of thing."

"There are laws against most of the things he does, but that's never stopped him. And I have a responsibility to keep you safe."

Louise turned in her seat to face him, aware that her already-short skirt had ridden even higher in the process.

"That's exactly my point," protested Adam, pointing to her legs with his outstretched hand, before she'd had a chance to speak. "And the law isn't going to protect you from the mental scars that could haunt you for a lifetime."

"Adam," she said, then stopped, waiting for him to look up to her eyes. "I will be careful. I can be tough when I need to be. Believe me, I've dealt with far more dangerous people than George Brandrick. Our entire strategy has been to play to his weaknesses. He wants me there on my own. And of course he's going to try it on, but I'm prepared for that and in the worst case I have pepper spray. I'll be fine."

But Adam was shaking his head. He reached into his bag and passed her a mobile phone.

"At the very least take this," he said. "I've got to go to a meeting, but I've got someone on standby very close by. It's got an emergency number programmed into every memory location. Press any number on the keypad and then the call button, and help will be with you in minutes."

Louise looked at the phone.

"Okay, if you insist."

"And this."

He passed her a second item, wrapped in a dark blue piece of fabric. It felt cold, hard and metallic.

"What the f ...?"

"Just take it."

"It's a gun, Adam. I don't want to take a gun."

"I insist that you take it."

"What am I supposed to do with it?"

"If necessary, shoot him. In the leg if you want, I don't care. But he'll listen to that more than he'll listen to you saying no."

"And if he sees it?"

"Then he knows you're not going to be messed with."

"Jesus."

She looked at the weapon. She didn't recognise the make, but it was tiny enough to fit in the palm of her hand.

"It's a Seecamp LWS-32," he said. "You've got six rounds if you need them, but hopefully you won't need any."

"I'm not taking a gun."

"Look, you don't need to shoot him, but it's there so he takes notice. And you are, or I'm coming with you."

"You just said you had to be at a meeting."

"I'd rather cancel it and lose a deal than see anything happen to you."

She sighed, and put the weapon in the outer pocket of her royal blue coat.

"Fine."

"Good. Thank you."

"Thank you for looking out for me, but really, you don't need to worry."

"Let's hope that's the case."

He restarted the ignition, and pulled out into the early morning traffic.

"What time are you meeting him?"

"Eight."

"Not for ages. Sorry, I thought it was earlier."

"Don't worry. If you can drop me off somewhere close I'll be able to amuse myself for half an hour."

"Are you sure?"

She nodded. And Adam set off in the direction of Shoreditch.

<hr>

At one minute before eight, Louise entered the lobby of George's building, and called him to make sure the coast was clear.

"I'm here," she said. "Just checking you're ready for me."

"I'm always ready for you," he said. "You know the way from the lift? Unfortunately Jason won't be there to meet you."

Again, the implication was clear.

"I know the way."

She ended the call. There was no mistaking the intent behind George's words. Well, she'd just have to be careful. Keep it business, and keep him on edge. Make him see that there were far greater riches just around the corner. But a bit of flirtation might help seal the deal.

She pressed the button for the lift, then gazed idly at the row of numbers above the car door. The four was lit. It would be down in a moment. She waited. But the lift didn't move. She looked at her watch. It had been three minutes already. Maybe it was broken. She could take the stairs, but climbing five floors was hardly the best preparation. She didn't want to arrive breathless.

But still the lift didn't come.

With a sigh of frustration, she walked to the staircase. On the fourth floor she stopped briefly to check the lift. Someone had left a heavy fire extinguisher propping open the door. It was so inconsiderate. Out of spite, she removed the extinguisher, and watched the doors close, and the car begin its descent, before returning to the stairs. At the top, she took a couple of deep breaths to regain her composure, and made her way to George's office.

The door was ajar. She knocked, and then reached for the handle to pull it open.

And then she stopped, panic shooting through her veins. She reached for the gun, suddenly grateful for Adam's foresight. George was there, behind his desk. But she no longer needed to worry about him trying anything on. Not if the blood was anything to go by, or the bullet-shaped hole in his chest. It took a moment for the full horror to register, as she moved closer to the body, to see it close-up, and make sure there was no mistake.

But then a chilling thought forced adrenaline through every synapse. She'd just spoken to him on the phone, and he'd been very much alive. The killer couldn't be too far away.

There was the noise of movement from the corridor outside.

Chapter 30

LOUISE cocked the pistol and started to move towards the door, just as Jason appeared. Time stopped.

"What the fuck?" he shouted, launching himself at her. But she was young and mobile, and she managed to evade him, diving to the right, and then clambering over the back of the sofa. But he wasn't going to give up that easily. He turned and threw himself at her again, fist raised. She avoided the punch, but the weight of his body crashed into her, knocking them both to the floor, the pistol spinning from her grasp. Her head cracked off the wall, shards of pain instantly exploding in her brain. He was huge and he had the advantage, but she had to fight. She tried to lash out, but he grabbed both her arms, pinning her to the floor. Until she managed to ram her knee into his groin.

His grip loosened as he reflexively flinched. But the hatred in his eyes was unmistakeable. He raised his fist to deliver a knockout blow, but Louise was fast, and her elbow crashed into his jaw.

That was the chance she needed. She scrambled away, reaching out for the pistol. It was so close. But not quite close enough. And Jason was coming again. She reached out for the coat stand and pulled it over. It wouldn't be heavy enough to stop him, but it might give her a vital extra second.

Jason swept away the stand as though it was made of matchsticks, sending it crashing into the middle of the room. But as he prepared to lunge again, a bullet flew from the end of Louise's tiny pistol, whistling past his ear, close enough to burn.

Louise sat back, and aimed the gun again.

"Get back," she shouted. Jason hesitated. "Now!"

At last the words seemed to register. He took a step back.

"Give me the key," she shouted. But it was clear he had no idea what she was referring to. "The key to the office."

"I haven't got a key," he spat back. She could see his brain working, calculating, planning his next attack.

"Somebody's got a key. Check the desk. There!"

She nodded in the direction of a keyring on the edge of George's desk.

"Throw it to me. And don't fuck about or I'll shoot."

He threw the key, but not hard enough. It fell to the floor a couple of feet away.

"Stand by the window."

But Jason had no intention of standing by the window. He launched himself forwards again.

The second bullet missed by an inch, but it was close enough to convey the message. Jason stopped, and stepped back. Louise reached out her foot and dragged the key towards her, then reached down to pick it up. She edged back towards the door and tried it in the lock, making sure it would turn, all the while keeping watch for any sudden movement from Jason.

The key worked. This wouldn't stop him for long, but it would give her a head start. Acting in one swift fluid movement, she stepped back into the corridor, shut the door, turned the lock, and fled to the staircase.

Her breath coming in ragged gasps, Louise sprinted away from the building as fast as she could in her heels, darting across a road and down a side street. She turned again, wanting to put as much distance and as many variables as she could between her and Jason.

What had just happened? Why was Jason there? George had confirmed that he was on his own. Had Jason killed his boss? It was the obvious conclusion, but why?

She grabbed the emergency phone and was about to dial the number, but stopped herself just in time. The last thing she needed was someone turning up to George's office. Instead she reached for her normal phone and dialled Adam.

"Louise," he said. "I'm in a meeting at the moment. What's up? Is it urgent?"

She took a moment to regain her breath.

"Yes. I need to see you."

"I need to see you too, actually. Are you okay?"

"Not really. But safe."

"I can't really talk now, but at the hotel in an hour? Can you be there?"

"Yes, that's fine. It'll keep till then."

An hour later, she entered the lobby of the hotel. Adam was talking to the concierge. He turned when he saw her approach. He didn't look happy.

"Everything okay?" he asked

"I'll tell you when we get upstairs."

He nodded in acknowledgement, and pressed the button for the lift.

As they walked towards their room, it soon became evident that something was wrong. The door was wide open. Adam broke into a run, with Louise close behind.

They were greeted by a scene of destruction. Furniture was upturned, pictures smashed. The sofa had been ripped apart.

They stood, silently, surveying the chaos. Then Adam slowly

stepped forward, walking through the debris, checking the damage. It was total.

"I don't know what to say," she said.

"I fucking knew it," said Adam.

"Knew what?"

"Knew this might happen. And knew who'd been put up to it."

"It wasn't George. George is dead."

Adam turned, sharply, his eyes laser focused.

"What?"

"That's what I need to see you about. I turned up, called him from downstairs, he was fine. The lift was broken, and by the time I got up there, someone had killed him."

"For fuck's sake."

"Jason turned up. I don't know whether he killed him, or he thinks I did, but either way I managed to get out, after a struggle."

But if she was expecting concern and sympathy, she was about to be disappointed.

"This is about last night," he said. "What the fuck were you playing at?"

"What do you mean?" asked Louise, instinctively taking a step back.

"You met George last night."

"Yes, with Harry. You knew that."

"But I didn't know *where* you were bloody taking them. What in God's name made you take them there?"

She couldn't say it was Clare's suggestion. She had no idea what was going on.

"It was a random choice? Why does it matter?"

"Do you have any idea who runs that place?"

"No, who?"

"Liam O'Callaghan."

She shrugged and held out her hands.

"I'm not from round here. Should that mean something?"

Adam closed the door, so they were alone among the chaos.

"He's Irish," he said. "Links to the IRA. Rumour has it he's raised funds and laundered proceeds. He's dangerous and walls have fucking ears in that place. If you or Harry mentioned anything about looking to take the place over, or he thought you were trying to muscle in on his territory, in any way whatsoever, it's no wonder he acted. He's not the sort of bloke to ask questions first."

"You think he killed George?"

"Christ knows. But it's a fucking big coincidence. First thing the morning after, George is dead and this place smashed to pieces. He knows people. He's got the means. And there'll be plenty who owe him favours, no questions asked."

"I'm sure George has plenty of other enemies."

"I'm sure we do, too. But the same morning?" He left the question hanging in the air.

"Where are the others?" asked Louise, once his temper outburst began to subside.

"They're not due till later. I'll call them and find somewhere new and we'll reconvene this afternoon."

But something else suddenly hit Louise.

"I suppose this puts an end to the project," she said.

"It's certainly going to make it difficult to screw a mark when he's dead."

"Which means you get to keep the fifty grand. I'm sorry."

"The what?"

"The deposit."

"Oh, that? Forget that. Seriously, that's the least of my worries."

"Really? Are you sure?"

"Look ..." His face softened and he came closer. "Last night was a fuck-up. No question. But I don't blame you. If anyone, I blame Harry. He should have been alert enough to stop you and suggest somewhere else. This has never been about the fifty grand. Yes, it helped me think you were serious. But I've seen how you work. I know you're serious. I'll rip up the draft, or give it back, or whatever you want. The bigger issue is finding out who we've upset and making sure we calm the waters before this gets out of hand."

"I don't know what to say." Louise was shocked by the sudden display of decency.

"You can thank me later. But for now, make yourself scarce. I've got calls to make. I'll speak to you later."

Louise picked her way through the splintered furniture to the door. When she reached the street, she took out her phone and called Clare.

"I need to see you," she said.

"Trouble?"

"Big trouble."

"Okay, my darling. I'll come to see you. In two hours, at Anna's?"

"You can't be any quicker?"

"I'll try. I'll be there as soon as I can."

Louise ended the call and set off back to Camden, grateful that she still had four bullets left in the gun.

Chapter 31

ETECTIVE Sergeant Amy Cranston was reviewing CCTV of the latest in a spate of armed robberies at petrol stations when the call came through.

"You'll want to take this, boss," said DC Akash Breakspeare, before waving her back to her desk.

That rarely signalled good news.

She listened to the voice, telling her about the sound of gunshots in an office building in Shoreditch. How first responders had discovered the body. And how the body belonged to a local gangster. George Brandrick.

She put down the phone and closed her eyes for a moment, wishing this wasn't happening. But it was. And she knew exactly where to start her enquiries.

"Oh, Clare," she said under her breath. "Do you ever, ever change?"

Louise opened the door of Anna's flat, and led Clare and Danny inside. Anna, thankfully, had already left for work.

"So what happened?" asked Clare, taking a seat on the large sofa. Danny joined her, with Louise taking the smaller one opposite.

She ran through the events of the morning, from the call from the lobby to the discovery of the body and her escape from Jason, and how close she'd come to shooting him.

"You're doing well to look so calm," said Clare.

"Believe me, I wasn't. What are we going to do?"

"First of all, we're not going to panic. Take me back a bit. When you called George from downstairs, are you absolutely sure it was him that you spoke to?"

"It definitely sounded like him. Or if not, it was a very good impression."

"And exactly how long did it take you to get to his office from the time you ended the call?"

"I don't know. It should have been less than a minute, but the lift was stuck. I waited for that for a couple of minutes then went up the stairs. So probably five, six in total."

"That gives us a very closely defined window. And you didn't pass anybody on the stairs?"

"No, of course not. I didn't see anybody. Until the bodyguard turned up."

Clare stood up, moved to the window, and looked out without speaking. After a moment she turned back to the others and re-took her space on the sofa.

"I'm going to run a few theories past you," she said, turning to Danny. "See if any of these make sense."

"Okay," he said. They both looked to Louise, who nodded.

"First, it was somebody random. Perhaps a business rival, somebody he'd ripped off. The timing was purely coincidental."

"Not keen on that one," said Danny.

"Me neither. Although it could be that he - if it was a man - turned up to have a meeting with George. He's taken a gun. Perhaps they're negotiating, or perhaps he's gone there with the express intention of killing him. And the timing is explained because when George speaks to you, our killer knows his time is running out. Any minute now they're going to have company. So he has to act and he pulls the trigger. Then all he has to do is escape, or hide until you make a run for it, and then let himself out in relative serenity."

"That's more likely," said Danny. "Still not convinced though."

"Me neither," added Louise. "George said he wanted to meet me at eight because he'd be on his own. I can't see he'd have arranged another meeting beforehand, especially so early."

"Unless it wasn't prearranged," said Clare. "The killer just turned up on spec. But I agree, it's not the most likely. So, second possibility, it was Jason. As you said, he wasn't supposed to be there, but did he know you were going?"

"I've got no idea. I got the impression it was a private meeting."

Clare nodded, warming to her theme.

"Okay. So Jason turned up. Why? If he's innocent, he might have prevented the murder if he'd arrived a few moments before. But equally, he could have been our killer."

"But why then attack me?"

"Either because he thinks you murdered his boss or because you're the only witness to him doing it and he wants to silence you. Or he wants to frame you. Make it look like you were guilty."

"But why would he do that? Or was I just a convenient passer-by?"

Clare looked to Danny, but he was devoid of theories at the moment.

"It's a good question," she continued. "Let's think about his motivation here. Perhaps he knew you were coming in at eight. He wasn't supposed to be there, but he knew you were going to be, so he thought it would be a great opportunity to do it, and pin it on you."

"But that doesn't make sense," said Danny. "If he wasn't supposed to be there, he'd have a reasonable chance of concocting a believable alibi elsewhere. But as soon as he showed himself, the alibi's gone. There's a witness."

"That's a good point."

"But that would mean he didn't do it," said Louise. "We're back to the start. *Why* was he there? And if he didn't kill George, somebody else did."

"Where were you this morning?" asked Danny, looking at Clare.

Her expression changed, her eyes narrowing.

"You know where I was. In a coffee shop, having a conversation with you."

"From about half past nine onwards, but before that?"

"Getting ready, travelling."

But Danny persisted.

"Okay, but at the time of the shooting, the specific few minutes between Louise ending the call, to arriving at the office, you were where?"

"I don't know. In the shower possibly. Getting dressed." Her expression had turned to ice. "Danny, if you don't trust me, you can go now."

"It's not about trust," he said. "What is it you've always told me? Never assume anything. I assume I can trust you. But I'm just covering all bases."

Clare turned back to Louise, ignoring Danny.

"Did he give you any indication that somebody was threatening him?" Clare continued.

"No. Nothing."

Clare's phone started ringing. She looked at the number and frowned.

"I have to get this," she said, then apologised as she made her way to the kitchen, closing the door behind her.

Danny and Louise sat in an awkward silence. Eventually Danny broke it.

"Have you settled in okay?" he asked, looking around.

"Uh-huh," she said.

"And how's Anna?"

"She's good."

The silence returned. Danny used Louise's reluctance to make eye contact as an opportunity to study her. There was something about her demeanour that unsettled him. Maybe it was the Polish upbringing and different frame of reference, but he recognised a steel core behind the outwardly youthful innocence. He wanted to trust her. He wanted to believe everything Clare had told him, and he wanted to take away the pain that must be consuming her every moment, the heartbreaking loss of her father. But there was something else that he couldn't quite pinpoint. A hint of danger, perhaps, or maybe simply a rebellious streak. But whatever it was, she couldn't be underestimated.

A couple of minutes later, his thoughts were interrupted by Clare's return.

"I'm going to have to leave you," she said. "There's something I need to do."

"Will you be coming back?" asked Louise.

"I'll call you, both of you."

Danny started to lever himself off the sofa.

"Stay where you are. I can see myself out." She paused. "And before you ask, that was Amy. She wants to meet me."

"Police Amy?" asked Danny. Clare nodded.

"About this morning. In the meantime, focus on Jason. Who is he? Where does he live? How long has he worked for George? What motivation would he have for killing his boss? Was he working for a rival? Where is he now?"

"How do we find all that out?" asked Louise.

"With difficulty, probably. We need to find some of George's contacts. Speak to them. Ask questions. But be aware that one of them could either have killed him, or have given the order to have him killed."

Danny stood up anyway.

"I'm not sure about this. I don't like it," he said.

"You're not losing your nerve, are you?" asked Clare.

"No, not in the slightest. I don't mean it like that. But I don't believe in coincidences. We've got three bodies. Your father," he nodded towards Louise, "the Polish girl in my room, and now George Brandrick. Before he died, Greg was framed to make it look like he'd committed a murder. The Polish girl was killed to implicate me, and now it looks like someone shot George to implicate Louise. Do you see the pattern?" Clare nodded, looking thoughtful. "I don't think we can pass off what happened this morning as something done by an unconnected business rival. It might be, and it might be something completely separate, but to me it follows the theme too closely."

"And don't forget, somebody broke into Adam's suite and smashed it up," added Louise. "The timing of that would have to be a coincidence too. Or was that separate as well? Somebody they'd ripped off, taking revenge?"

"Exactly," said Danny. "But in each of the murders, the key thing is this. Someone is doing it, but in such a way as to pin the blame firmly on someone else. One of us. And I don't want to scare anyone, but if you follow the pattern, and then look at what happened to Greg ..."

Clare fastened her coat.

"Okay. Lots to think about," she said. Danny thought she looked worried. Normally she was ice cool, ultra-calm and in charge. But now it was as though events were spinning out of control. The unfamiliar, pale expression he'd noticed after the balcony attack in Warsaw was back. "I'll go and talk to Amy and see what I can find out. Let's meet up again this afternoon and have a proper brainstorm."

"I've got to meet Adam and the others this afternoon," said

Louise. "I'm waiting on a call to tell me where. Can we do it after that?"

"Of course. Take care, the pair of you. We have a couple of ways forward here. We can stop now, because we're scared, or we can find out who is doing this. I think the latter but I'd understand if either of you want out."

She stepped forward to give Louise a hug.

"I'm with you," said Danny. Louise nodded agreement as well.

"Okay. Be vigilant. And I'll call you."

A man in a car watched as Clare left Anna's flat and started walking in the direction of Camden High Street.

"She's leaving now," he said into the mouthpiece of his mobile phone. "Do you want me to follow?"

"Yes."

"On foot?"

"Is she walking?"

"At the moment."

There was silence from the other end of the line.

"She's still walking," he said. "I can strike now if you want."

"Not yet. We need to see where she leads us. Get out, follow on foot."

"Understood."

But by the time he was out of the car and had started jogging to catch up, Clare had turned a corner, caught a cab, and was gone.

Chapter 32

LOUISE offered to make Danny a cup of tea, and then, once she'd returned with two mugs, she curled up on the sofa, her legs underneath her.

"I get the impression you don't fully trust Clare," she said in a tone more matter-of-fact than accusatory.

Danny put his mug on the coffee table while he thought how best to formulate a reply.

"I trust her with my life," he said.

"That's good."

"But ..." He stopped.

"But what?"

His eyes alighted on Anna's Wassily Kandinsky print. It reminded him of happier, simpler times, when it had hung on the wall of the front room they'd shared together. It seemed like a lifetime ago.

"But ..." He hesitated again, but this time Louise didn't interrupt. "Sometimes I wish we could wind back the clock," he said at last. "Go back to when we worked together. When Clare was the most feared investigator on Fleet Street and we dealt with scams and corruption, and politicians on the take. Not the world she inhabits now. Because, you know what? I think she's brilliant. I think she's the most amazing person in so many ways. But something happened back then, and everything changed. And I know we've discussed it all a million times and she says it was a temporary aberration. But ... " He reached for a metaphor. "If she was a car, she'd be a Lotus. Dynamic, fast, powerful, and desirable. But as the saying goes, Lots Of Trouble, Usually Serious."

"I understand." Louise's voice was soft, and now it was her turn to look reflective. "I wish I'd known her better back then. It's my biggest regret in some ways. I wonder if I could have done anything to stop her."

"We all wonder that, but we had no idea. I think it was in her. Could we have stopped it? I don't know. She was always under a lot of pressure. Maybe it was just a massive release. But it's a case of once bitten twice shy, I suppose. So yes, going back to your question, I trust her. But do I trust that at some point she won't go off the rails again? That's more difficult. If it's happened once, it could happen again. But she's never been anything other than brilliant with me, and with Anna. Even if she sometimes has a weird way of going about things."

They both paused to take a sip of tea, but it was still a bit hot for each of them.

"I'll go and find us a biscuit," said Louise.

"Ooh, you're brave. Anna is very protective of her biscuits."

Louise smiled, and in that moment the ice was broken.

Her phone rang while she was in the kitchen, so she came running back through to answer it. After a brief conversation, she ended the call.

"That was Toby," she said.

"Who's Toby?"

"He's one of Adam's crew. He's young but he's good. They want me to meet them in Regent's Park, out in the open, so nobody can overhear. Is that far from here?"

"It depends which bit, but no, just round the corner, really."

"He said near the zoo."

"I know it. I can walk you up there."

"Thank you," she said.

Danny reached for a Digestive and dunked it in the tea, then, judging by Louise's surprised expression, decided dunking probably wasn't the done thing in Poland.

"Clare told me your real name, by the way," he said.

"Agnieszka." He nodded. It sounded sexy when said by a native.

"If you'd rather I started calling you that, I'll try to learn how to pronounce it properly."

She laughed.

"No, Louise is fine. I'm getting used to it now."

"For what it's worth, I think you're being incredibly brave. Which I hope doesn't sound condescending. I genuinely think it's a phenomenal thing you're doing."

Warmth spread across her face.

"Thank you. And likewise. Thank you for your help."

"Anna said you wanted to go into acting."

"Hmmm."

The warmth was transforming into mischief.

"What?" asked Danny.

"That seemed like a good cover story. And I suppose it is acting in a way. I'm playing a role. But I'm not sure I'd want to do this long term. Although I suspect real acting is a bit less hazardous." She looked at her watch. "We ought to get going. Would you like to meet them?"

"Who?"

"The rest of the team."

Danny finished his tea and replaced the mug on the table.

"Would they be okay with that?"

"I don't know, but I can ask them. Come with me and hang around for a bit. And if they say yes, I'll call you over."

"Good plan. But yes, I think that could be a big help if they're okay with that."

Louise took the mugs to the kitchen, and then they set off in the direction of Regent's Park.

DS Amy Cranston pulled over in her Ford Mondeo pool car and opened the passenger door for Clare to get inside.

"So, you're back in the country and what do I know? The bodies start piling up," she said, as she piloted the car into a multistorey car park.

"And you think this is something to do with me? Really?" asked Clare. "I'm sure there are gangsters getting killed in feuds every day of the week. Just because I happened to mention one of them to you in a conversation on Monday doesn't mean it's anything to do with me."

Amy reversed the car into a space on a relatively deserted floor, then killed the engine and applied the handbrake.

"It's going to be like this, is it?" she said.

"What?" Clare's voice was full of protest. "If you recall, I was planning to expose him. It's not exactly going to help me if he's dead. But talking of which, do you have a time for when it happened?"

"Some time this morning."

"Early? Late?"

"Does it make a difference? Why are you so interested?"

"Because I was going to tell you where I was. I assume it would help if I could give you an alibi?"

Amy's expression was full of scepticism.

"It would help but I wouldn't necessarily believe it."

"I won't bother then."

"Have you actually got one?" she asked, turning round in her seat.

"For this morning? No."

"Heaven's sake. You really don't help yourself, do you know that?"

Clare frowned.

"You know as well as I do that I haven't killed anyone - "

"Not actually true."

"- recently. And certainly not George bloody Brandrick. We wouldn't be having this conversation if I had, because I'd be hiding somewhere. And if you really thought I had, you'd be slapping on the handcuffs."

"So who do you think did then?"

"More difficult."

Amy undid her seat belt, then reached across to the glove compartment in front of Clare's knees and removed a notepad and pen.

"If you'd asked, I'd have done that for you," said Clare.

"I'm not in the mood for this. Not today." She flicked to the first blank page, then made a couple of notes at the top. Clare strained to read the words, but the handwriting was too small to be legible. Probably deliberately.

"Is this a formal interview?" she asked.

"Evidently not, given that we're in a car rather than a room at the station, but I didn't think you'd be so keen on that." Amy finished writing. "Okay, so you don't have an alibi. What about your young protégé?"

"Louise?"

"Let's start by giving me her real name."

"Agnieszka Przezdzienkowski."

"*What?*"

"Agnieszka Przezdzienkowski."

"Are you taking the piss?"

"I'll write it down for you, but that's why I call her Louise."

"God's sake, Clare."

"What? It makes sense. I can't even promise that if I write it down I'll spell it right, but it'll be close enough. Kind of a phonetic approximation."

"Either way, does she have an alibi?"

"You know what? I really don't know. But I can promise you she wouldn't have had any involvement in stabbing him."

"But you know he was stabbed?"

"I don't know. I assume so. Was he?"

"No, he was shot."

"There you go then."

Amy sighed and shook her head.

"I wasn't born yesterday, Clare. Can you stop trying to be clever and be serious for a minute? Because I can slap the handcuffs on and do this officially if you prefer, but I couldn't then promise that some of my superiors wouldn't take the opportunity to also speak to you about a couple of unsolved dead art dealers."

"Technically only one of them was a dealer, but I take your point."

Amy started to respond but then stopped. And took a deep breath instead.

"I'd suggest looking for Brandrick's bodyguard, Jason Harrigan," said Clare.

"We are. God, hold on." She reached for her phone and answered an incoming call. "DS Cranston."

"I'll leave you to it and go for a walk around," mouthed Clare, but Amy snatched at her arm, forcefully grabbing a handful of coat sleeve, then shook her head as if to say *you're going nowhere*.

"Excellent work," she said. "And they're in the cells now? ... Okay, call me when they get there ... Yes, I'm on my way back soon. Make sure they're made to feel welcome ... Haha, my thoughts exactly." She ended the call. "Yes!"

"Good news?" asked Clare.

"Very. Although not in connection with this."

"Go on then, tell me."

Amy smirked. "You're unreal. You know that?"

"What do you mean? I'm happy for you if you're happy. Is that bad?"

"No. But expecting me to divulge information about a live case is. You know that."

"Oh, sorry to ask, then." She feigned offence, but Amy ignored her.

"Where is Louise now?" she asked instead.

"I don't know."

"That's not very helpful."

"I honestly don't. She's got legs and if you want to be particularly paranoid, I think she's still got a hire car parked up somewhere. But she's staying with Anna if that's any help. I can call her if you like."

"Please do."

Clare called up a saved number in her mobile phone, but it rang eight times and then went to voicemail.

"Is Anna still in Rochester Square?"

"No, but nearby. I'll give you the address. And Louise's number if you like. Pass me the pad."

"Do you seriously think I'm going to pass you my actual notepad?"

"Yes, if you want me to write something down in it. God, you don't trust me, do you?"

Amy raised her eyebrows.

"I'm not even going to answer that. What's the address and number?"

"Charming."

Clare read the number from her phone and then told her Anna's new address. When she was finished, Amy put away the pad and refastened her seat belt.

"Why do I get the feeling that you're trying to give the illusion of being helpful but you're still hiding something from me?" she asked.

Clare shrugged.

"I am being helpful. I don't know what more I can do."

Amy stared directly into Clare's eyes, and Clare returned the look in a battle of wills, determined not to be first to crack. Until she felt she was going to laugh.

"I'm going to sneeze in a minute with the scent of your air freshener," she said, "so let's say you've won that one, even though it wasn't a fair contest."

Amy turned the ignition and fired the engine.

"Stay in touch," she said. "I mean it."

"You're not going to give me a lift home?"

"I'm heading back to work, and you're more than welcome to come along if you'd like to sample our hospitality. Otherwise, I'm going to count to three ..."

"Amy, you're no fun any more."

The detective's patience finally snapped.

"Three," she said, and started pulling forward.

"Hold on, that's not fair."

"It's a cruel world, Clare. You know that." She picked up speed, and steered the car down the ramp to the floor below. "And if you're not careful, I'll do you for not wearing a seatbelt." The Mondeo was getting faster and faster as it spiralled down to the ground floor. Eventually, when she reached the exit, she slammed on the brakes by the barrier, then turned back to Clare.

"Enjoy your walk," she said. "I'll be speaking to you very soon."

Clare got out of the car, and watched it leave. And then went back to collect her own BMW 5 Series from the first floor.

Chapter 33

S HORTLY after 2pm, Louise and Danny passed through the wrought iron gates at the northern end of Regent's Park. After walking for a couple of minutes, Louise spotted Abby, Toby and Harry, standing on the grass, in between a pair of mature trees.

"Wait here," she said to Danny. "Let me speak to them first. Then if they're okay, I'll introduce you."

"Good plan."

She set off across the grass to join the others.

"Adam not here yet?" she said, when she was close.

"He was unavoidably delayed," said Harry. "I have been entrusted to convey his apologies, although he should be with us shortly."

"Who's he?" asked Toby, nodding in the direction she'd come from. She looked round to check he meant Danny.

"That's Danny," she said, turning back. "He's a good friend. He wants to meet everyone."

"Wooah," said Toby. "You can't do that. You can't just bring strangers along with you."

"It's fine, he's good. He's a journalist."

"Christ. That makes it worse." He looked furious. "Abby?"

"I'm with Tobes." She'd never seen Abby look quite so venomous before. "I mean, who the fuck even are you?"

Where had this come from?

"You know who I am."

"Really? You've been with us five minutes. Got a geezer killed and our place smashed up. I'm sorry, but I ain't sure I trust you, darlin'."

Louise looked to Toby, but his furious expression had only intensified.

"She's got a point," he said, in a voice cold with accusation.

"Harry? Are you siding with these two?"

"I'm sure your friendship with this man is well-founded," he said, amiably. "But we're a democratic body, and alas, my dear, I am outvoted. I suggest waiting till Adam appears, and we canvass his thoughts on the matter. And if he approves, then of course, we shall gladly welcome him into our little fold."

"So in the meantime I just leave him standing there?"

"You should go and keep him company, babes," said Abby.

"Fine. You know what? I'll do that. Tell Adam to call me when he gets here. We'll be in the pub."

She turned and set off back towards Danny, without a second glance. But she hadn't got far before Harry caught up with her.

"Please excuse the youngsters, my dear," he said. "I'm afraid they are somewhat in a state of shock after the events of this morning."

"I appreciate that," said Louise. "But I don't want to fall out with them, so I think it's better if I wait elsewhere."

"Yes, I do rather think that would be wise. I am sure everything will be resolved, once Adam arrives. I will ensure he calls you, with utmost haste."

"Thanks, Harry."

He gave a reassuring smile, and squeezed her shoulder. It was as though he had more to say, but something was stopping him.

Maybe it wasn't the time. He turned on his heel and set off to rejoin the others.

"Well, that was a disaster," said Louise, when she reached Danny.

"What happened?"

"Abby and Toby have freaked out, thinking I'm some kind of imposter after what happened this morning. Harry was all right, but Adam's not here yet. I think we need to let them cool off, and then, when he arrives, we can try again."

"So what now?"

"Back to Anna's, I suppose. We might as well wait there as anywhere. Harry's going to call me."

They started back along the path.

"Can I tell you what's bothering me?" said Danny.

Louise stopped.

"Not you as well?"

"What? No. Of course not. I just don't know where we go from here. Correct me if I'm wrong on any of this, but my understanding is that you were getting close to George because he was somehow going to lead us to whoever killed your father."

"So Clare seemed to think."

"But if he's dead, we're nowhere. I mean, where do we even start looking now?"

"You know what?" She looked down to the pathway, as though embarrassed. "I think that's the nicest thing anyone has ever said to me."

"In what way?" Danny was confused, replaying his last sentence in his mind.

"You said where do *we* even start looking now. We. You don't know me. I could be anyone. And yet you haven't given up on me. You sound willing to help me. I can't tell you how much that means." She looked up, and Danny noticed tears forming in her eyes. "Clare said you were the best. I don't think I'll ever be able to tell you how grateful I am."

"I don't know what to say," said Danny, suddenly feeling self-conscious. "Clare told me what happened in Poland, and my heart goes out to you. I got into this business, journalism, because I wanted to put right things that were obviously wrong. And yes, I know I don't know you, and I don't believe for one minute that you're Clare's niece ..." His face broke into a smile. "But I know you're hurting, and you've suffered a loss that nobody should have to go through. So yes, I'm there for you. And it will be a privilege to do anything I can to get justice. I can't bring your dad back, but I can do my absolute best to help you find out who was responsible."

They started walking again, slowly, towards the exit, their strides in synch with each other.

"No, I'm not Clare's niece," said Louise after a pause. "I think it's only right to be honest with you."

"I know," said Danny, walking back through the gate. "But don't worry. I'm not going to pry." His mind flashed back to the sight of Louise and Clare in Anna's front room. The way they'd been holding hands. The kiss.

"Thank you, but I think I should tell you the truth."

"If you want to, I'd feel honoured, but only if you're ready."

But she didn't say anything more. She'd stopped, motionless. Danny turned round, but her eyes were filled with panic. And then he saw what she was looking at. A man running towards them. Even from a distance, it was impossible to mistake his look of sheer, brutal aggression.

"It's Jason," she said, almost inaudible with shock.

Instinctively they started to run, but Jason was fast, and he was gaining.

Chapter 34

A HEAD of them, a car screeched to a halt. They were cornered.

But then they saw Clare behind the wheel. Just as Jason drew within grabbing distance, she opened the doors for them. Danny dived into the back, Louise the front, and as they slammed the doors shut, Clare floored the accelerator. Jason made a lurch for Louise's door and managed to prise it open, but it swung back with the forward momentum of the car, knocking him to the ground.

"Ouch," said Clare, then glanced left to Louise. "I can't leave you two alone for a minute."

"Where did you come from?" asked Danny, desperately trying to get his breath back, the adrenaline pumping hard.

"I was parked up along the road," she said, as though it was the most normal thing in the world.

"And I'm glad you were, but I still don't know how."

"It's not hard, Danny. I spoke to Amy, drove back to Anna's with the intention of taking you both for a nice lunch, but I passed you walking down the street. So I turned round, saw you go into the park, then thought I might as well wait for a bit.

Admittedly, when I noticed Jason park up, I thought you might be in a spot of bother."

"Thank you," said Louise.

"And likewise," added Danny.

"So what were you doing in there? Going for a lovely nature walk?"

Louise took over, explaining about the meeting and how it hadn't gone well.

"Do you believe in parallel universes?" asked Clare. "Danny?"

"Do you mean like in an infinite galaxy there's going to be another one, almost identical to this, but in which you're actually a nun?"

"Something like that. Because I sometimes do wonder. More about my own ability to teach, than anything else. On what planet was that meeting ever going to be a good idea?"

"I thought it might help," he said, knowing that it sounded feeble.

"God. That's the really scary part. And you –" she glanced at Louise "– in which part of my extensively detailed instructions did I say, *'wait until it's all turning to shit and then bring a journalist along to meet a bloody long con crew'*? Was there a bit where I said, *'once it's all gone hideously wrong, feel free to improvise'*? Was there?"

"No."

"No. Funny that. Because if you want to know the technical term for what you've both managed to achieve, it's 'fucked things completely up'. I don't want to appear churlish, but I do feel a churl coming on."

She pulled the car over and killed he engine.

"And sorry to elaborate, but the more I think about this, the more I have one question for the pair of you. What the fuck were you actually thinking?" She looked furious. Danny didn't know what to say, but doubted that anything would help diffuse her anger.

"I'm sorry," he said, looking down, finding it difficult to meet her eyes. "But don't blame Louise. It was my idea."

"I blame the pair of you. You, then, for the idiot idea, and her for not telling you to piss off out of it."

Clare turned back to the front, then closed her eyes and forcibly banged the back of her head on the headrest.

"But if I ..." Danny started.

"Shut up and give me a minute," she snarled. And that was the end of that.

Eventually, she calmed down enough to continue.

"I was going to take you out for a nice lunch, but as punishment it's going to be McDonald's. Do you have McDonald's in Poland yet?"

"Of course," said Louise.

"That's good. Because you'll appreciate this is not some kind of reward. And consider yourself bloody lucky that I'm a nice person, or it would be Burger King."

"I am grateful for small mercies," said Danny, daring the hint of a smile. "How was Amy, by the way?"

"Amy was Amy, what do you think? She's so annoyingly straight. She wouldn't even let me in on some top secret case that she was working on."

"She wanted to speak to you about George?"

"She did. I don't think she believes I'm responsible, though. You, on the other hand." She pointed at Louise.

"Me what? I hope you told her I had nothing to do with it."

"Obviously I tried. But I think she wants to speak to you."

"I can't speak to the police," said Louise, looking panicked.

"You might have to."

"And tell them what? Yes I was trying to target him? That I was there when he was killed? And then expect them to believe me when I say I'm innocent? I'm the token foreign girl. They'll throw away the key."

"Quite possibly, but we'll all come and visit." She softened.

"I'm joking. It'll be fine. I'll tell you what to say. Honestly, it's not as scary as you think. They're not going to do anything without evidence."

Clare started the engine.

"It's long past lunch time. Let's get food, have a brainstorm, and then I'll take you home, okay?"

She put the car into gear and headed north.

I'd had a decent morning at work, until I decided to test out my shiny new gym membership on an extended lunch break.

What the fuck is that about?

The Olympic athlete (I assume) who showed me round clearly thought I'd welcome him standing over me, making encouraging comments while I struggled to get to grips with the various machines. But I very much didn't, not least because every time it hurt (which was almost constantly) he told me to fight the pain, push my boundaries, feel the burn, and all sorts of other nonsensical platitudes, when I'd much rather he'd gone to the café and returned with a yummy slice of cake.

So by the time I arrived home, all I really wanted to do was curl up on the sofa with a nice cup of tea and quietly die, hoping that whenever Louise got home she'd at least arrange a decent burial. And I'd successfully managed the first two-thirds of that when there was a knock at the front door. I nearly didn't answer, assuming it would be for one of the other flats, until my doorbell started ringing. And even then I still nearly didn't answer, because I wasn't entirely sure that what was left of my leg muscles would manage the short journey from my front room to see what on earth they wanted. But then I thought, maybe somebody who was aware of my pain had done an amazing thing and ordered me a pizza. So I stood up, wincing, and hobbled to the door.

It wasn't the pizza boy. It was two scary-looking men in ill-fitting suits, asking if they could come in. And when I said no, because I didn't think they looked particularly friendly, they came in anyway. Even though I made it back to my own door and managed to close it, that didn't stop them either. Because a moment later, it came off its hinges, and shortly after that, I was in the back of a car, wearing a blindfold, wondering what the hell was going on.

Chapter 35

FOLLOWING a late lunch and then a couple of hours discussing all of the problems they now faced, Clare pulled up outside Anna's flat.

Louise undid her seatbelt.

"I'm going to pop in as well, actually, to say hello," said Danny.

"Good idea," said Clare. "I suppose it wouldn't do any harm." She moved the car further down the road until she found a proper parking space, and then all three set off for the flat.

Louise undid the outer door with her key. But a key wasn't required for the second. It was hanging open, with splinters on the floor, near where the lock had been forced.

"Anna," shouted Danny, running forward, with a rising sense of panic, checking from room to room.

But Anna wasn't at home.

"Maybe she's not back from work yet," said Louise.

Danny could hardly hear her. His eyes were focused on the jacket and shoes by the sofa, and steam still rising from the mug of tea.

He turned to Clare, fury rising above the immediate sensation of acute concern.

"You promised me," he said, in an ominously low voice.

But Clare looked almost as worried.

"Admittedly," she said, "this wasn't in the plan."

"So, we've got three dead bodies, and now Anna has disappeared," said Danny, as soon as Clare came off the phone to the emergency locksmith. "Let's assess how well you think this is going."

There was no point in trying to call Anna's mobile, because it was lying on the arm of the sofa.

"Just think for a minute, Danny," said Clare, leaning forward and putting her head in her hands.

"What the hell else do you think I'm doing? We've got to call the police."

"Let's not panic. I'm not sure that would help."

"Because that's not the thing you do when somebody gets abducted?"

"Because our only priority here is to get her home safely, and until we know where she is, we don't know what we're dealing with."

But Danny was agitated, fidgeting, feeling that every second that passed was a second that Anna was further away. And with every minute, the chances of her safe return decreased exponentially.

"I do not believe this," he said.

"Well, start believing, and then actually come up with some constructive ideas," said Clare. There was an unfamiliar sharpness in her voice.

"What links everyone?" asked Louise, from the other end of the sofa.

Danny sighed and tried to think.

"Let's go back to the beginning," he said. "Somebody killed Greg, and you thought George would be able to tell you who. But somebody didn't like us asking questions in Poland. And crucially, somebody then decided that they'd stop George from helping by killing him too. I get that. But why would they abduct Anna? It makes absolutely zero sense."

"Unless it was Jason again," said Louise. The other two both gave her their undivided attention. "I still think he was the most likely person to have killed George. He was there when he shouldn't have been. He came for us this afternoon. If he'd worked out where I was staying somehow, then maybe he was coming for me. But when I was out he took Anna instead."

"And she becomes a pawn," said Danny. "I don't like this. I don't like this at all."

"No," said Clare. "And actually ..."

But her words were interrupted by the ringing of the doorbell.

Chapter 36

"CAN I come in?" asked DS Amy Cranston.

Danny stood aside for her and her colleague to pass. A uniformed police officer stayed standing outside.

"Hello again," said Clare, who was propped up against the internal door frame, hiding the splinters.

But Amy ignored her, and continued through to the front room, where Louise was still on the sofa.

"I need you to come with me," she said.

Louise nodded, then silently stood up and retrieved her coat.

Half an hour later, they were on opposite sites of a desk in a bleak, grey police interview room. Amy had introduced herself and her colleague for the benefit of the tape, although Detective Constable Darren McQuade was sitting silently, taking notes.

"This is about George Brandrick, I assume," said Louise.

"It is."

"I heard. It's terrible." She took a sip from a small plastic cup of water.

"Where were you this morning?" asked Amy.

"All morning?"

"Yes."

Louise adopted an expression that she hoped came across as thoughtful.

"I started at home. I then had a meeting booked with George, but I turned up and there was no answer. It's terrible to think he was probably lying there."

Amy didn't seem impressed.

"What time was your meeting?"

"Eight. You don't think the killer was still there, do you? That's terrifying."

Unsurprisingly, her question wasn't answered.

"And then you did what?" Amy continued.

"I left, and went off to meet my friend, Adam."

"And he can vouch for you, can he?"

"Of course."

"And you had no idea anything had happened to Brandrick?"

"No." She shook her head, trying her best to look sincere and plausible.

"What were you wearing?"

"This morning?" She paused. "A brown leather jacket, dark grey skirt. Actually it's virtually black. Underneath the jacket, a white shirt. And underneath that ... How far do you want me to go?"

"Let me show you this," said Amy.

She turned the screen of the portable video player towards Louise, and held her finger over the *Play* button. DC McQuade wrote something in his notebook.

"For the benefit of the tape, I am showing the interviewee CCTV footage from outside an office building in Cygnet Street, Shoreditch, from 7.58am this morning," said Amy. After a minute or so, she paused the tape and pointed at the screen. "Is that you?"

"It looks like it," said Louise.

"Sure?"

"Yes."

"Good. So you're entering the building at almost precisely 8am. And how would you describe your walk."

"My walk?"

"Yes. Casual? Determined? Rushed?"

"Just normal."

"Okay. So now look at the next scene. This comes eighteen minutes later."

Amy let the tape roll and then stopped it, pointing to a frozen frame.

"Would you say this is also you?" she asked.

"Yes."

She pressed play. The screen showed Louise running from the building, looking back towards the door, and then darting between oncoming traffic before disappearing from the shot.

"Equally as normal, would you say? Because to me that looks like you're in a hurry."

"I was. I was late for the next meeting."

Amy made a show of exchanging glances with her colleague before turning back to Louise.

"So, let me get this right," she continued. "You turned up for a meeting at eight. The meeting was cancelled, but you waited around in the building for nineteen minutes, until you suddenly realised you were running late for the next one, even though you found yourself with maybe an hour or so to spare? Would you care to think about that for a moment?"

Louise took another sip of her water.

"When I got to the lobby, I phoned George, but he didn't answer. I didn't immediately think the meeting was cancelled. I thought perhaps he was running late and would be along in a moment. But eventually I gave up and I phoned Adam. But he was heading out, so I had to be quick to catch him. So that's why I was in a rush. Otherwise I'd have missed him."

"You called him on your mobile?"

"Yes."

"Can you please pass me your phone?"

Louise reached into her jacket pocket then handed the phone across. Amy flipped it open, and scrolled down to the list of outgoing calls.

"That's interesting. There's a call just before eight. But the next is twenty-two minutes past. Which is after the time stamp on the CCTV. So I'll ask you again. Why were you running?"

Louise paused, and rubbed the side of her nose, then clasped her hands together on the desk.

"Sorry, I don't think I explained it very well the first time," she said.

"That's perhaps the first true thing you've said."

She took a deep breath, then sighed.

"Okay. I remember the specifics. It's not quite how I said."

Amy sat back with her arms folded.

"Go on. Enlighten me."

"I already knew Adam was going out," started Louise. "I wasn't supposed to be meeting him. But when the appointment was cancelled I thought it would be a good opportunity to catch him. So I started to rush, then called him on the way, once I got on the bus, to make sure he was still there, and let him know I was coming."

"Right."

Amy sat in silence, but gestured for Louise to continue. Louise looked at the desk, and took another sip of water.

"Where did you meet him?"

"Who?"

"Adam."

"At the hotel. You know the one because you met me there the other day."

"The Vervain?"

"Yes. Although if you want to speak to him, I don't think he'll be there. Call him, though. I'm sure he'll vouch for me."

"And you're sure about that?"

"Of course."

"And you didn't see anyone else in Brandrick's building, perhaps acting suspiciously, holding a gun, covered in blood, that kind of thing?"

"No, although …" She stopped and frowned.

"Although what?"

"Well, now I think about it, I did hear someone."

Amy laughed derisively.

"Really. From where? In your head? Through the walls?"

"No, from the lift. Something about it being stuck on one of the floors and the doors not closing."

"Right. And you heard that on the ground floor?"

"The sound travels. It's like a hollow rectangular tube, isn't it?"

"And I suppose you're now going to tell me who it was?"

"No." Louise shook her head and finished the final dregs of the water. "I mean, it sounded like his bodyguard, Jason something. Sorry, I don't know his surname. But it couldn't have been. Not really. Because George specifically mentioned that he wouldn't be there." She paused. "Unless, of course, he was."

Chapter 37

WHEN they finally removed the blindfold, I discovered I was in a dank and dingy-looking storeroom, being stared at by a big bastard. Neither the room nor the man was particularly fragrant, but I sensed there was little point protesting, or trying to escape, given the overwhelming size of him. There was a low throb of music, coming from somewhere far off.

Normally I'm a fan of the strong, silent type. This wasn't normal. And neither was the way he was constantly looking at me, seated with his legs apart, arms folded, and close enough that I very much wished he'd fancy a stick of minty chewing gum.

Then he stood up and walked away, and his place was taken by somebody I recognised, although it took me a moment to place him.

"What, exactly, am I here for?" I asked, hoping I sounded much calmer than I felt. On the upside, at least events had conspired to take my mind off my self-induced gym pain.

"We want to know what you know," he replied, in a distinctive lilt. Normally I'm also quite partial to a man in a suit, and I love an Irish accent, but I wasn't feeling the love on this occasion. And how are you supposed to respond to a question like that? *I know you'd look a bit better if you had a shave?*

"I recognise you. From last night. At the club," I said, instead.

"That's a bad thing for you," he responded, which did little to make me think this was going to end well.

"You're what? The owner? The manager?" I said.

He didn't seem interested in answering my question.

"Why were you there? What's the story?"

"I was having a night out with my friends." I should have known. I really should. Nothing is ever straightforward when Clare is involved.

"Who were your friends?" he asked, crossing his legs, and pinching his upper lip between thumb and forefinger.

"Why do you want to know?"

"Because it would save me having to kill you."

"Fair enough."

I'd met scary men before, so I was familiar with the drill. He'd try to intimidate me, then it would get worse. I'd start to feel really quite terrified and then ... Well, I'd never gone beyond that stage before, without somehow managing to get away. But given that nobody knew where I was, I decided the best approach was to start buying time.

"What is it you think I know?" I asked.

"If I knew what you knew, I wouldn't have to ask you. So who were they?"

"Last night? My flatmate, my former flatmate and his former boss."

"Who was the feek?"

"The feek?"

"The girl. In the red dress."

"That was my flatmate."

"Name?"

What was I supposed to do now? I could hardly deny knowing my own flatmate's name. Although, I presumed Clare had factored something like this into the equation when she'd given her an alias. Because I was in no doubt that Clare had not been entirely honest with me, and I should have trusted my instincts there too.

"Louise."

"Louise what?"

Now there he had me. I'd never actually been told that.

"I know you're not going to believe me," I said. "But I don't actually know her surname. She only moved in on Sunday. I could make something up, but I'd rather be honest about it."

"We need to speak to her."

"Is that why you turned up at my flat? To speak to her?"

"I'll ask the questions."

"Well, if you like, you can let me go and then I'll pop home and ask her to give you a call. What do you want to speak to her about?"

"I said I'll ask the questions. Where is she?"

That one had me stumped as well. Normally she'd be home when I got in from work, but today there'd been no sign of her.

"I have no idea. I know she's been looking to arrange an acting class, so possibly out doing that."

"Acting?" He laughed. "Do you think I'm some sort of tool?"

"I don't think I know you well enough to have a conclusive opinion on that, but given that you've kidnapped me and I've got no idea why, I'm developing one." As soon as I'd said it, I wished that I hadn't. Because suddenly I was starting to feel very scared indeed.

"You'll wait here," he said, standing up and heading to the door. In truth, I didn't have much option.

"Can I just point out that whatever happens, I am furious with you, and always will be," said Danny.

"I know," said Clare. "And you've got every right to be that way, and I'm not going to try to stand here and defend myself, and make the point that not everything that goes wrong in life is my fault, because the most important thing is to work out what has happened to Anna."

"But you made the point anyway?"

"I specifically just said I'm not making a point, Danny. Same as how I'm not going to remind you that if it wasn't for me, you'd already be dead, several times over."

"You are something else. You know that?"

Danny felt like he wanted to hit something, but he wasn't normally the violent type.

"So what are we going to do? Sit around waiting for Louise to come home or actually go out and start looking? And where the hell do we even start?"

Clare sighed and looked to the ceiling.

"I don't know," she said, softly. "At the moment we're waiting for someone to come and fix the door."

"You don't know?"

"No, right at this minute, I don't." The softness hadn't lasted long. "Let's think about this. The only suggestion I've got at the moment is that Jason, for whatever reason, wasn't happy that Louise escaped, so he came here, found Anna, and took her instead, presumably as some sort of bargaining chip."

"Which isn't reassuring," said Danny. "So we need to find Jason. I don't suppose he'll be hanging round the office, waiting for us. What do you know about him?"

"Not a lot. Give me a minute and I'll make some calls."

For once, Clare didn't move to a different room when she picked up her phone. But Danny was assessing the connotation. Was it because she had nothing to hide, or because she was hiding it in plain sight?

Chapter 38

THE only bit of good news was that they hadn't strapped me to the chair. But then, the more I thought about it, the more I started to wish that they had. At least that would have been an acknowledgement that I might try to escape, or at least put up a fight. Since they left me unrestrained, the implication was that they didn't see me as a threat. And although I could now knock "going to a gym" off my eternal to-do list, I wasn't sure that my single visit would have built the muscle mass necessary to take on a bald-headed, malevolent freak.

I had a quick look round the room while the club owner was away. It was like a tiny, rectangular prison cell. The door was locked, obviously, but aside from the two chairs there wasn't much I could use as a weapon. One long wall was bare, painted in a faded cream. The other was dominated by industrial-style racking, although all the shelves I could reach were empty, aside from a thick coating of dust. Even standing on the chair, I couldn't reach the top shelf, but from my limited perspective, that one looked empty too. There was a window at the far end, opposite the door, but it was covered with iron bars, and the glass had been whitewashed.

So, that left the chairs. In theory I could use one to hit somebody over the head, but the room was too narrow to get a proper swing. I could try prodding them, but then they'd just grab the chair leg, and quite possibly punch me. So I decided it was best to wait, try to be as helpful as possible within the context of genuinely being clueless, and then hope that they weren't quite as psychopathic as they were pretending to be.

After perhaps twenty minutes, the club owner came back, followed by his bald-headed goon. I still didn't know his name, but this time I dared to ask.

"You can call me Liam," he said, taking his seat. I didn't know if that was progress or not, because it suddenly occurred to me that the less I knew, the better my chances of being let out alive.

"Who are you working for?" he asked.

"You want to know about my day job?" I said. "It's an American internet company."

"Try not to be a funny gobshite. It doesn't suit you." To be fair, I'd rarely met anyone quite so humourless. "Who were you working for at the club last night?"

I sighed, getting exasperated.

"I wasn't working for anyone. I told you. I was having a night out with friends. I don't know who you think I am, or what you think I've done, nor why my friends are of so much interest to you. But if you really, really want to know, it was my birthday on Tuesday, and they suggested going out for a belated birthday drink. Why your club, I have no idea, pleasant though it was."

"See, we've got a problem now," he said, after a moment of reflection. "Either you're lying to me, which would be very dangerous for you. Or you're telling the truth, in which case I should let you go. But that would be very dangerous for me, because you might decide to make a formal complaint to the police and then they'd want to talk to me, to ask me why I brought you here, and they'd want to know what I'd asked you and why. And really, that would not do."

"I can see why you say that. But it's one of those things. isn't it? Accidents happen. Let me go and we'll both promise we won't mention this to anyone."

He started to laugh, but again not in a particularly humorous way.

"You make me smile," he said. "You don't look as scared as you should be."

Appearances can clearly be deceptive.

"Believe me, if I had anything to hide I'd be terrified, but I don't, so I'm quite prepared to forgive and forget, with emphasis on the forget bit."

His expression changed. The life left his eyes. He said something to his colleague in a language I didn't recognise. Possibly Gaelic, if that's even a thing.

"You will wait here," he said again, and for the second time they left me on my own.

Clare put down the phone on the arm of the sofa.

"It's not looking good with Jason," she said, resignedly. "Nobody knows anything about him. The people I thought might know, put me onto places he's been known to go to, but no one there has seen him. Or at least, not as far as they're willing to tell me."

"So we go and find him ourselves," said Danny.

"We could do that." But Clare didn't look convinced. Danny was struck by her lack of urgency.

"What is it?" he asked.

He could have sworn there was the hint of redness in her eyes.

"The more I think about it, the less it makes any sense," she said, looking away. "I mean, what's his motivation? Yes, I could understand, if it was Louise. And then you're back to whether he's trying to take revenge or silence her. But I think we need to go back further. Something happened. Something changed. Up to the end of yesterday, everything was going to plan. But then we went out, and this morning it all turned to shit. Why?"

"So you think this is related to the club?"

"I don't know, but possibly."

"Okay." Danny thought for a moment. "You said you were interested in the bloke that ran it. That he was up to no good."

"Exactly. And we needed to take Brandrick to somewhere, and we couldn't take him to the real one."

"Because it doesn't exist?"

"Exactly."

"So somebody must have seen us, all four of us. And if they've got a problem with you or Louise, then they've seen Anna and thought she was with you. Involved somehow."

Clare nodded, slowly.

"That's what I'm thinking."

"But who and why? And why were we even there?"

They were questions that weren't going to get answered.

"What's the time?" asked Clare, as though emerging from a trance.

"Nearly seven."

"Where's the bloody locksmith then? As soon as he's fixed the door, I think we should go back to the club and start asking serious questions."

As if on cue, the doorbell chimed. Danny and Clare couldn't talk while the locksmith set to work, replacing part of the door frame and making sure everything was secure. He asked if they wanted the lock to be replaced, but after a moment's thought, Clare decided against it. If Anna arrived home unaided, it would add insult to injury if she found herself locked out.

As he was tidying his tools and preparing to leave, Clare's phone burst into life. She connected the call, then disappeared into the kitchen and closed the door.

A couple of minutes later, she reappeared, just as Danny was showing the locksmith out.

"News?" he asked.

"That was Louise," said Clare. "They've taken a DNA swab and fingerprints, but she's out. She's coming back to get changed and then we're all heading out."

Chapter 39

THEY asked for the same table as the previous evening. Danny was nervous.

"This is high risk," he'd said on the way. "We're putting ourselves in the spotlight here. If Brandrick's murder was related to last night, it stands to reason that whoever was responsible was there, watching us. We need to be vigilant."

"We do," said Clare. "But let's hope they're here again."

But there was no sign of anyone acting suspiciously. The club was busy, but the Friday night drinkers seemed intent on letting go after a hard week at work, and paid little attention to the three people at the back of the room.

"I'm going to go for a walk," said Louise, eventually. "I'm going to retrace the route from last night, when Harry turned up."

"I'll come with you," said Danny.

They set off, in the direction of the bar.

"We stood here, and had a drink," she said, once they'd arrived. Danny had to strain to hear over the music. It was louder than the night before, perhaps reflecting the onset of the weekend. "George was there. Harry was here, and I was standing next to him."

"Notice anything?"

She looked around.

"No." It was hopeless. "I don't recognise anyone. The bar staff, maybe, but none of the customers. We could be anywhere."

They waited for a moment, then Danny leaned in close to her.

"It's not just about what we can see," he whispered in her ear. "It's about who sees us."

She nodded in acknowledgement. But waiting around much longer seemed pointless. They made their way back to Clare, who was smoking a cigarette and talking to a young man in a pink shirt and navy suit. At the sight of Louise and Danny, he turned and walked away.

"Who was that?" asked Danny.

"Seemingly an admirer," she said. "I've been asked out on a date."

Danny shot Louise a look, to see how she reacted.

"Go you," she said. "Did you accept?"

Clare laughed.

"He wasn't my type," she said with a wink. Then Louise squeezed in alongside her on the sofa. Danny noticed the way their legs touched, under the table, but neither seemed to pull away.

He took the chair opposite, with his back to the rest of the room.

"Is there something you two aren't telling me?" he said.

Clare frowned.

"In terms of?"

But Danny turned his attention to Louise.

"You were about to tell me something when we were leaving the park. You said you thought I ought to know the truth."

Louise turned to Clare, but immediately looked embarrassed. Clare, on her part, was looking daggers.

But before anyone could say anything, there was a disturbance at the far side of the club, and then everything turned to chaos.

Liam and his big bald chum came back again. Again, the Irishman sat in the chair, while his mate hovered in the doorway.

"You present me with a very serious problem," he said.

But before I had a chance to respond, someone else came rushing to the door. It looked like one of the bar staff, which added weight to my suspicion that I was somewhere within the club.

"They're back," she shouted. "Table fourteen."

In an instant, I appeared to be forgotten. Liam and his mate went haring off, leaving the door wide open. I wasn't going to hang around waiting for a second chance. So with my heart pounding, and the adrenaline doing its best to anaesthetise the lactic acid burn in my legs, I set off after them.

They were ahead of me, but as I pushed through a fire door, I emerged into the crowded main room of the club. I could only just see a bald head among the throng, heading in the direction of the table we'd occupied last night. And then I saw Danny, Clare and Louise. They saw me. And all four of us went running in the direction of the exit.

I felt an arm around my waist as I battled to the front of the crowd. I turned, ready to strike out, to regain my freedom. But it was Danny. And suddenly, I felt the power of his arms as he swept me forward. Behind him there was carnage. Tables were overturned. People were shouting. And from the midst of it all, Louise and Clare emerged, running as though their lives depended on it.

Danny and I made it to the exit first. I thanked a God that I'm pretty sure doesn't exist that there was a taxi outside, dropping off a well-dressed couple heading for a big night out. We dived into the back. While Danny shouted something to the driver, I held the door open, urging Louise and Clare forward. The big bald bastard was close behind, pushing customers out of the way in his desperation to catch them. But they made it. Just. And as I closed the door behind them, the taxi driver floored the throttle in a way more akin to a racing driver than a London cabbie.

"What are you lot up to, then?" he shouted through the partition. He momentarily glanced in our direction, and seemed exceptionally pleased with himself.

"Long story," said Danny.

"Dispute over the bar bill," added Clare.

Louise put her arm around me. I couldn't remember when I'd ever been so pleased to see them.

Chapter 40

Saturday, January 25th, 1997

I WOKE up in Clare's spare room. I'd been there before, although I'd kind of assumed she'd have given up her Knightsbridge flat by now. Apparently not.

The others were waiting for me in the front room. I had no idea where they'd slept. Presumably Danny had the other spare room and Louise had gone in with Clare. But now wasn't the time to get to the bottom of that particular car crash. We'd had so much to discuss the previous night, but once Clare had given me the summary of what this was all about, she was insistent that we should try to sleep and address it all fresh in the morning. I wasn't going to argue.

"Are you all right?" asked Danny. "It looks like you're hobbling."

"I'm a bit stiff, if you want the truth," I said.

"Not the bed I hope," said Clare, looking concerned.

I decided I might as well confront the issue, head on.

"No, just the after-effects of a gym session," I said.

I'd known Danny since I was nineteen. But I'd never seen him looking quite so shocked.

"A what?" he said, his face going from incredulity to something approaching hilarity.

"I think she said gym session," said Clare. "What have we been smoking?"

"Get over it," I said, lowering myself onto one of the giant horseshoe-shaped sofas, with a wince and considerable effort. "Next question?"

"Would you like a cup of tea?" asked Louise, heading over from the open-plan kitchen.

"That, you see, is a woman with manners," I said. I didn't have the energy to get up to ensure it was made properly, so merely said yes, thank you, and decided I'd have to take my chances.

Once the tea was delivered, all eyes were back on me.

"So talk us through it. What exactly happened?" asked Clare.

I gave her the summary, from being captured, through to my fortuitous escape.

"And it was definitely Liam?"

"He said his name was Liam, and he was definitely the bloke who introduced himself the night before. The Irish one. So yes, if that's his name, it was Liam. He asked me who I was working for."

"And what did you say?" asked Clare.

"I said I wasn't working for anybody. I thought I was going for a nice night out."

"So, did the Irish people kill George Brandrick?" asked Danny, looking across to Clare.

"I wouldn't put it past them," she said.

"But why?"

She shook her head and sighed.

"I don't know."

"Does that mean we're back to square one?" I asked.

"Not exactly," said Danny. "At least we know who abducted you. We can report it to the police, and get them off the streets."

There was a sharp intake of breath from Clare.

"Bigger picture, Danny," she said. "We could, but what would that achieve? Do you think they're working in isolation? If they're working for the IRA, they're part of a huge network. We really don't want to make ourselves targets. You do know what happens to IRA informers?"

"But we can't just let them get away with it."

"We won't, but we need to know what they're so worried about. If we get them locked up, then we really are back to square one. Let's not forget what we're trying to do here. Ultimately we're trying to find out what happened to Greg."

"I kind of miss the old days when Graham March was the villain," I said. "At least we knew who we were dealing with."

A phone started ringing, making Louise jump. She answered the call and we all sat in silence until she disconnected.

"That was Adam," she said. "He's found new premises. He said he wants to have a meeting. They're all getting together this morning."

"There's nothing to have a meeting about, is there?" said Danny.

"Not in terms of the original project, but he wants to know if I'd still be interested in working with them."

"As a con artist?" I said, slightly shocked.

"I haven't said yes," she said, looking defensive. "Anyway, I said I'd talk to him."

"You do that," said Clare. "It can't do any harm. In the meantime, I'm going to arrange a meeting with our Irish friends."

I was pretty sure I'd misheard her. But then when I looked at Danny and Louise, I saw they were thinking the same.

"Didn't we just escape from them?" I said.

"We did," said Clare. "Which is all the more reason for going back."

Chapter 41

THE new hotel suite was less obviously opulent than the original one, but Harry was there with muffins, pastries and a warm welcome. Toby and Abby seemed less enthusiastic about Louise's arrival, but Adam greeted her with a handshake. Louise helped herself to coffee, noticing that Abby didn't offer, as she always had previously, and then they all took chairs around the much smaller meeting room table.

"We might as well confront the issue from the outset," said Adam, looking directly at Louise. "Your journalist friend."

"Yes," she said, maintaining her focus on Adam, but catching the hostility from Toby and Abby in her peripheral version. "Obviously, I apologise for any misunderstanding."

"You had your reasons for bringing him?"

"I did. And I understand why it came across badly. But there was nothing sinister."

"And the reasons were?"

"He's a good friend. He's been helping me enormously with some personal issues, and it doesn't get much more personal than discovering a dead body and being framed for murder. But rest assured, I have not told him about what we do here - " there was a snort of disbelief from Abby "- and I specifically told him to wait until I could come to talk to you, explain who he was, and see if it was okay to introduce him. But obviously, as we know, you weren't there."

"You can vouch for him?" Adam continued.

"Of course, I ..." She hesitated. "He's a good man."

"Okay." Adam looked at the others before continuing. "Well, I suggest once this meeting is over, we should definitely have a chat about it, one-to-one." Abby scoffed, and he shot her a glance. "It's not the biggest issue we face, but we can take it offline."

"What's bigger than knowing who you can trust?" asked Toby, who was also clearly still far from happy.

"In one sense, dear boy, there is nothing," said Harry, joining in. "But circumstances are far from optimal in other respects, and we are devoid of any evidence of a material breach of trust in this circumstance."

"Indeed," said Adam. "So, moving on, obviously you all know about the attack on our other room, and you all know about George Brandrick. Both of which present challenges, not least of which is the need for a new project."

"Do we know who smashed the room up?" asked Toby.

"No, not yet, but it will be investigated."

"Do you think they're related?"

"And do you really think that neither has anything to do with her?" added Abby, giving Louise an ice-cold stare.

"I think we should keep an open mind for now," said Adam. "Obviously, the murder is a police matter and our primary objective is to distance ourselves, for obvious reasons."

"Although in the interests of full disclosure, the police have spoken to me about it," said Louise.

"Oh, fuck off," said Abby. She turned to Adam. "Sorry, mate, I know you're the guv'nor, but this ain't right. Which bit of distancing ourselves from the geezer involves going running to the fucking Feds?"

"What could I do?" asked Louise, feeling the urge to defend herself. "I didn't go to them. They came to me, because they had me on CCTV."

"I'm not listening to any more of this shit." Abby stood up. "I suggest you two have your little one-to-one, then you let me know what's happening. In the meantime, I'm out of here. Tobes?"

"Yeah, I'll come with you," said Toby.

Adam didn't try to stop them. Louise kept looking at the desk, aware of movement behind her, and then eventually the slam of the door.

"You seem to have created quite a stir, my dear," said Harry, after a moment of silence.

"I know." She sounded exasperated. "But I think it's massively unfair. I'm the one who put my life on the line for us over this, and very nearly paid for it. I'm the one who's under police suspicion. I don't actually think I've done anything wrong. I don't know what I could have done differently. It's not my fault someone murdered him."

Adam nodded, looking thoughtful.

"It seems like a good time to adjourn," he said. "And yes, I take on board what you're saying, but they're both young and highly strung. I'll speak to them, and deal with it. Harry, I'll be in touch, okay?"

"As you wish," said Harry, rising from his chair. He collected his coat, and headed out of the room.

And then it was just the two of them. Adam moved to the sofa, crossed his legs and sighed.

"I know I gave you a hard time about going to that club," he said, "but I'm prepared to accept your explanation. What I'm finding harder to accept is that you appear to be acutely accident-prone, and that's not a good thing in this business."

Louise moved from the table to the armchair opposite.

"I appreciate that, but I'm really not," she said.

"And again, I'm inclined to believe you, but you can see my problem?"

"I can, if you only take things at face value."

Adam had more to say.

"We operate a team here. We work together, go into battle alongside each other. It's not a place for mavericks, and it's never going to work if there's animosity. Toby was right. The most important thing, above everything else, is trust. And it doesn't matter what I think, and what Harry thinks. If the other two don't have absolute faith and trust in you, it's going to come down to making a choice. And I'm afraid I'm a firm believer in the better the devil you know."

"But what can I do?" asked Louise. "I think they've got the complete wrong end of the stick. You very nearly came with me to that meeting. The irony is, if I'd refused to take the gun, which I was very nervous about, then you would have done."

"I know, and in hindsight I should have done. I take responsibility for you being in that situation in the first place, and it was an error. But the fact remains, if the others don't want you, and specifically don't trust you, there's no way you can continue working with us."

"Are you firing me?" She sat back, ran her hand through her hair, and then reached for her bag. Adam watched as she withdrew a pack of paper tissues, took one out, and dabbed the corners of her eyes. "I'm so sorry. I feel like I've let you down. But I appreciate you giving me the opportunity."

"No, I'm not firing you," said Adam, in a soft and reassuring voice. "I see potential in you. I think you could be a real asset. Harry speaks incredibly highly of you. And yet I'm struggling to see how you're going to fit in. Rebuilding bridges with those two will be difficult. I've seen this kind of thing before, and it's never led to a reconciliation. So there is my conundrum. "

"Can't live with me, can't live without me?"

"I don't think I'd go that far." He smiled. "But something along those lines. Incidentally, I worked out how you did the cufflink thing."

"Really?"

"Uh-huh."

"That's a shame." The corners of her mouth curled into a mischievous grin. "And does that mean you want your wallet back?"

"I know you haven't taken my wallet."

"How come?"

"Because I locked it in the drawer before you arrived."

"Touché." She paused. "I assume you've checked the drawer?"

For a moment, Adam's face was etched in concern, but Louise couldn't help laughing.

"Don't worry, I'm messing with you. I told you, I'm only a beginner."

"Mmmm." Adam looked at his watch. "And that is where *I* wonder if I can trust you, because I don't believe a word of it. What are your plans for this weekend?"

"I haven't really got any. I've not had a chance to think beyond the end of today. I should go looking for a permanent place to stay, though, so probably making a start on that."

Adam nodded, then reached for his jacket.

"Do that," he said, while standing up. "Keep a low profile, stay out of trouble and I'll speak to you on Monday. There's no point in talking to either of them today, but maybe tomorrow, when they've had a chance to think about things, they'll be more open to a sensible discussion."

"Thank you," said Louise, standing up and fastening her coat.

"Do you need a lift anywhere?"

"No, but thank you," she said. "I've got some shopping to do. I'll be fine."

"Okay." He led her to the door. "Try not to worry."

She nodded without saying another word, and headed to the lift.

Clare ended the call.

"Well, that's all sorted," she said. "At his club, in an hour."

"I'm coming with you," said Danny.

Clare thought about it for a moment, then nodded.

"Yes, that would be good," she said. "You can be all manly and protect me."

I thought I detected a hint of irony, but I could see why she wouldn't want to go alone. Liam and his friends were clearly psychopaths.

"Me too," I said. They both looked at me as though I'd gone mad, which in fairness I possibly had.

"You're not serious?" said Clare. "That would be stupid."

"What am I supposed to do? Wait here? Hide forever? If you two are negotiating a deal, I want to be in on it."

"But you've literally only just escaped."

"Yes. And I managed that all by myself. This time I'll have you two with me. What can possibly go wrong?"

"Lots can possibly go wrong," said Danny. "We're dealing with people who launder funds for Irish terrorists who quite possibly thought nothing of murdering George and Jason just for visiting their club, and nothing either of kidnapping you and holding you hostage."

"It's too dangerous," added Clare.

"Bollocks to the pair of you," I said.

Danny was about to say something, but I hadn't finished with Clare.

"Can I point out, I didn't ask to be involved in any of this. I thought I was doing you a favour, helping your *friend*, sorry, niece, with a place to stay. So from my perspective, which as far as I'm concerned is the only one that matters, you owe me, big time. And that means not treating me like some kind of a child. So with no further argument, get used to it. I'm coming with you."

"Fine," she said with a sigh. Danny looked like he was about to say something again, but she cut him off. "But be aware, as far as they're concerned, my name is Charlotte Sadler."

"Wow. I've not heard that one for a while. That was one of your old aliases from back in the day."

"It still comes in handy," she said.

"Let's hope he doesn't ask to see your passport," said Danny. Clare laughed. I have no idea why.

"Okay, Charlotte," I said, with a smirk. "And our approach is?"

"We have one objective," she said. "They're worried about something. We need to know what that is."

Chapter 42

THE club was empty, apart from Liam and his bald-headed thug of a friend. "Charlotte" introduced herself as Charlotte, and then Danny and myself as ourselves. I didn't know whether to be annoyed by that, but decided they probably knew my name anyway. We weren't offered drinks, but we were shown to a table, ominously far from the exit.

"We meet again," I said with what I hoped was an edge of menace.

"There's still one of you missing," said Liam, ignoring me. "The girl in the red dress."

"She's our insurance policy," said Danny, impressively, although I had no idea what he meant. But I could tell our host was disappointed. Maybe it was as simple as the fact he fancied her. Men are strange like that at times.

"So here's the deal," said Charlotte. "You kidnapped Anna. We could have you locked up for that if we wanted to. We could call the police and they'd close you down. But that's not why we're here, so let's cut the crap because we haven't got all day. We want to know what you're worried about. Why you killed George Brandrick."

"Who?" asked Liam.

"You know who."

"I really don't. Hand on heart, and I swear on my children's lives, I haven't killed anyone."

"But you know who he is. And if not you, then somebody who works for you then."

He appeared to be getting impatient, which was a worry.

"I don't know who the hell you think I am, but I don't do that. None of my employees do that. Nor any of my associates."

"Is that true?" said Danny. "I heard you have friends from Northern Ireland."

"Oh, stop acting the maggot."

"You threatened to kill me," I interjected, with no idea what maggots had to do with anything.

"Of course I did that. I'm not averse to a bit of intimidation when I need to get answers to something, but I was only codding ya. I'm not a violent man. I run a respectable business."

Charlotte looked about as convinced by that as I was.

"Right," she said. "I think we all know what you do. So why were you so worried about him?"

"I still have no idea who you're talking about."

There were blank stares all round. This was going nowhere.

"Okay, we'll try another tack," I said, in an attempt to break the deadlock. "Why were you so interested in me and who I might have been working for?"

"Why were you in my gaff?"

"This isn't going to get us anywhere if we keep going round in circles," said Danny.

We all looked at Charlotte. She frowned, as though lost in thought.

"Okay, Liam," she said at last. "I'm going to be honest with you. I will tell you why we were in your club. You might not believe me, but it will be true. And if you think we were up to anything else, I'd appreciate it if you could tell me, so I can try to get to the bottom of this. Deal?"

He nodded.

"First thing to know, Anna, here, and Danny are friends of mine. That's the extent of it. They aren't involved in anything, but it was Anna's birthday this week, so we took her out for a celebration."

"Go and bollox."

"Trust me, it's true. I'm not saying that's the only reason why *we* were here, but it was the only reason they were."

At least that backed up my story. I had an urge to raise two fingers at him, but resisted.

"Go on," he said.

"As for the girl in the red dress, she works with me. She's Polish, and I call her Louise because that's easier to pronounce than her real name. We were trying to do a bit of business with George Brandrick, so we took him out for a bit of old school corporate hospitality. Two birds, one stone."

"What kind of business?"

"Similar to what you run, but, I should point out, *not* in competition. We've been looking at clubs and bars. We have a business plan but one of our investors pulled out. Someone suggested George, so we had a couple of meetings, we were getting to know him, we thought it would be good to get to know him socially. And that was it."

"Really?"

"Yes, really."

He laughed.

"You look like an intelligent woman."

"Thank you."

"Which makes me wonder why you're telling me that. Because either you're lying, and that would be dangerous, or else you really were looking at going into business with George

Brandrick, and that raises all sorts of questions about you, your character, and frankly, your sanity."

"Because?"

"Because, as we both know, unless you've completely failed in your due diligence, George Brandrick was a bent, drug-dealing shitehawk."

"So you do know him then?"

"I know of him. His reputation."

The atmosphere was so frosty I began to wish I'd brought a hat and gloves.

"That's a fair point," Charlotte continued. "But you don't know the terms of the deal. And yes, I acknowledge, he wasn't the perfect business partner. But you assume that it was going to be a mutually beneficial arrangement. The fact was, George wasn't going to benefit as much as we were. If you catch my drift."

"I'm beginning to. But then I'd have to question your choice of enemy."

She shrugged, clearly on a roll.

"I'm fairly resourceful," she continued. "Let's put it this way: I knew his weaknesses. I knew some of the things he'd done. I knew his interests and the chinks in his armour. And we were confident that between us we could keep him in the place we needed, while benefitting from his considerable investment."

Liam exhaled, then reached for a packet of cigarettes and lit one. Belatedly he offered them round. Charlotte accepted, and then I did too, just to annoy her, and shock Danny. I gave him my best *I'm a grown-up* look.

"If you're telling the truth, I still maintain you're either brave or not the full shilling," Liam said.

"Let's settle on brave. But it's a moot point now, because somebody killed him before we had a chance to close the deal, and that means two things. We're pissed off because we've lost a good opportunity to make some serious money, and we're nervous because until we know who and why, we have to assume that we're also at risk. And given that you kidnapped Anna and threatened to kill her just for being out with us, I've got to say, I'm looking in your direction for answers."

A silence hung heavily over the room. It didn't look like answers were forthcoming.

"So now, your turn," said Charlotte. "What spooked you so badly?"

"What do you know about me, and my club?" he replied.

"I'll be honest with you. Not a lot. I'm sure I could find out a lot more if I wanted to, but – please don't take this the wrong way – you're not somebody I've ever thought about before yesterday. I know the club. I'm a member, although only since recently. And I heard rumours about your connections in Northern Ireland, but that could be just malicious gossip."

"Although your man already referred to it." He looked at Danny. His expression wasn't friendly.

"Can you blame him? You start kidnapping my friends, we're going to start thinking the worst. Which is where we still are, unless you stick to your end of the bargain and actually answer the question."

"All right, I'll tell you." He paused to take a drag on his cigarette. I followed suit and then fought hard not to cough. It wouldn't have accentuated my hard-woman image. Finally, he continued. "The club is good. It makes money. It's a tough business, sometimes, but that's London nightlife for you. Let's just say, I'm happy with what I do, and I'd like to continue doing it. And yeah, there are people who depend on me for that, and I really don't want to disappoint them."

"Understood," said Charlotte. "But?"

"But I have to keep my ear to the ground, if you know what I mean. I hear things. I remain alert to things. It's a competitive world. So recently, over the last few weeks, I've heard whispers about a group who think they could do a better job of running my club than I can. Who could be interested in what you'd call a hostile takeover, if you know what I'm saying."

"That's not us," said Clare. "I promise you. We've been looking at premises, but hand on heart, not any that aren't already open to offer, and certainly not yours."

"Although Brandrick told one of my bar staff that she would soon be working for him."

"Okay. Well, I can only apologise for that. Maybe he thought she was doing a good job, and he was going to try to poach her. But I promise you, that would be the extent of it. We have absolutely no interest in your club here, apart from thinking it would be a good place for a night out."

"All right. I take that on board."

"So?"

"What do you mean *so?*"

"I still don't know why you kidnapped Anna."

"Because I didn't know who you were, and who you were working for. This group isn't British. Or Polish. But I've also heard a whisper in the last week or so that maybe George Brandrick was involved in something. And yeah, I know about him and his reputation, even if you seem to be a bit naive regarding some of it. So when he turns up, acting the big man, with a girl with an accent, then I get to thinking that he's taking the piss. That they all are. So I wanted to find out about it and I want to put a stop to it."

"So you killed him?"

"No, I did not fucking kill him. And I don't know who the fuck did. The fella wasn't short of enemies of his own without me joining in."

"But somebody did."

"Evidently. Which rather fucks up your investment."

"Unless you'd be interested."

"Don't start taking the piss."

"Understood." She paused. "So where do we go from here?"

"I don't give a fuck where you go. I'm going back to work. Do yourselves a favour and forget about the last couple of days. We'll put it down to experience. And I wouldn't spend too long wondering about your mucker George. You've dodged a bullet there. Possibly literally."

"Okay." She regarded me and Danny in turn. "In that case we will leave you in peace."

Liam turned to his big bastard bodyguard.

"Show these people out, would you?" he said.

We stubbed out our cigarettes and then followed him to the door.

Chapter 43

DS Amy Cranston was crossing the open-plan office to her desk when Detective Inspector Guy Dowsett called her into his office.

"I'm getting pressure over Brandrick," he said. He was old school, and decent, but Amy knew he wouldn't take any nonsense. He had a reputation as a gentle giant, but could be ruthless when he needed to be.

"We're working on it, boss," said Amy.

"Any success in tracking down the bodyguard?"

"Not yet. Every way we turn, we hit a dead end. I can't help thinking Clare knows something."

"Clare Woodbrook?"

"Yeah." The atmosphere changed, and his eyes seemed to darken.

"Is she back?"

"I thought you knew."

The DI shook his head.

"Nobody tells me anything. But if she is, and she's keeping things from us, she's taking the piss."

"I'm inclined to agree."

There was a knock at the door.

"Sorry to interrupt, but can I borrow you?" asked Detective Constable Aarav Choudhary. He was one of the newest members of the team, but his youthful enthusiasm was making up for his lack of experience.

"What is it?" asked Amy.

The DC looked nervously from Amy to her boss.

"We've found something interesting," he said.

"You go," said the DI to Amy. "Bring me up to speed if it's anything important."

She nodded, then followed her young colleague to his desk.

"We've been going through the forensics from Brandrick's office," he said, gesturing at his computer screen. "And there are a couple of anomalies that don't fit the testimony from the Polish girl."

Amy was more disappointed than surprised. She wanted to believe the best of people, but it rarely came to fruition.

"First of all, we found an indentation on the wall," he continued. "It could have been caused by anything, but we found a hair sample alongside, which tends to indicate a struggle."

"Any DNA match?"

"Too early for that, but it's long and dark blonde, which fits. Obviously, we're waiting on confirmation, and should have that in a couple of days. But then we also found fingerprints on the door handle."

"From her?"

He nodded.

"So she lied, then. She didn't just phone from reception. She was in the room."

"A lawyer would argue they could have been left on a previous visit," said the DC.

"If nobody else had used the door handle in the interim, which seems unlikely."

"Exactly."

"No sign of the weapon?"

"Maybe."

"What do you mean maybe?

DC Choudhary consulted his notes.

"They found two bullets at the scene, aside from the one that killed Brandrick."

"So she was a lousy shot?"

"Possibly. We're still waiting on forensics from the body to know if they match the murder weapon."

Amy patted him on his shoulder.

"Good work. But it sounds like there's still a lot to do."

"There is, but there's a bit more," he continued. "A witness came forward. A passenger on a bus."

"And?"

"He reported a young woman jumping on the back, at the traffic lights, close to Brandrick's office, about twenty past eight. And she fitted our description."

"Okay, but we know she caught a bus. She admitted that."

"Indeed. But this was the guy she sat next to. And he said he nearly freaked, because when she went into her bag to get money for the fare, he saw what looked like the barrel of a gun."

"God." Amy sat down on the edge of the desk. "And he's reliable?"

"Works as a doctor, apparently. Juries like that kind of thing."

"They do." Amy thought for a moment, but really it was only to confirm what she'd already suspected. "So what do we know? She lied. She was in the room. She had the means, the motive. And we've got the evidence that links it all together, awaiting further confirmation on the DNA. We don't know that she pulled the trigger, but let's look at shot angles, to see if they can create a height profile. Either way, I think that's enough to charge. Let's go and bring her in."

I couldn't quite get used to the thought of Clare having a car. I knew she'd had one years ago, because it was found abandoned on the hard shoulder of the M25, around the time that she first disappeared. But I'd never known it since, and yet here I was, in the front of a BMW, with Clare behind the wheel. Did she even have a licence? What if she crashed it, and had to swap insurance details? That could be awkward. I imagine she'd considered the practicalities, but I didn't dare to ask. Perhaps it was Louise's hire car. Or had she taken that back by now? The last I heard, she was still looking for the keys.

Clare drove straight from the club to Mintern Street, on the edge of Shoreditch Park. A row of residential flats faced the park, but on our side of the road there was a fence bordering a big open space, with wide tree-lined walkways.

"Are we getting out?" I asked.

Clare scanned the street but was noncommittal.

"We can if you want, but it's a bit cold," she said. "Danny?"

"I'm easy," he said, from the back seat.

"We know that," I chipped in, and Clare sniggered. "I'm happy to stay in the car."

"Okay," she said, undoing her seat belt and turning to face me. Danny moved to the middle of the rear bench.

"So, first question first, do we believe him?" he asked.

"Possibly," she said. "It sounded plausible."

"What I don't understand is why we went to his club in the first place," I said. "I get that Louise had to meet someone, but why did the three of us have to go with her?"

Clare took a deep breath before replying. I hoped that wasn't purely to buy thinking time before spouting a fiction.

"Separate to George Brandrick, Liam is still a person of interest to me," she said at last. "He might be a respectable businessman on the surface, but I think you've seen a hint of his darker side. But more than that, I'm interested in who he works for."

"Which is?"

"Factions of the IRA. You heard the accent."

"He was definitely Irish," I said.

"Exactly. And I heard rumours that he was cleaning money for them, and providing all sorts of assistance."

"Which is what you alluded to?" I said, turning to Danny.

"Indeed, although he didn't seem keen to talk about it," he confirmed.

"So that was one part," Clare continued. "And aside from that, I wanted to see George in person, so I could try to get a measure of him. I wanted Danny to see him too. And then, if I'm perfectly honest, I really did want to take you out for a birthday drink, and it seemed like the perfect opportunity."

"But there was still an agenda?" I said.

"Call it multitasking more than an agenda." She looked genuine, as though she actually believed that.

"I'm really not happy about the impact of all of this on Anna," said Danny, suddenly leaping to my defence. "When you first mentioned it to me, you promised me nothing bad would happen."

"I know, and it shouldn't have done. I'm sorry." There was authentic remorse in her voice. "I don't know what to say. I haven't even started looking into Liam O'Callaghan yet, so there should have been zero risk. But you heard him. He was paranoid about something else altogether. I can't be expected to know everything."

"But you do know everything," I said.

"I don't. All I know is how to make it look like I know everything."

"But even so," said Danny. His voice drifted off. I wasn't sure what point he was trying to make, because I think we both understood that Clare's explanation seemed reasonable.

"I do appreciate the support, Danny," I said. "Thank you for looking out for me."

"My pleasure."

Clare started to chuckle. Neither of us knew why.

"What's funny?" I asked.

"Oh, the pair of you," she said. "You do frustrate me. You deserve to be together. I've known you for how long now? Best part of seven years for Danny, and nearly as long for you. And all the way through, you're both in a constant state of mamihlapinatapai."

"Constant state of what?" I said.

"Mamihlapinatapai."

I tried to pronounce it but failed.

"You'll have to write that down for me."

She reached into her door bin for a pen and paper, then wrote down the word, and handed it over. It didn't make it any better. If anything, worse. I passed it to Danny, but he was similarly clueless. God, I hate a show-off.

"So what on earth does that mean?" I asked.

"You don't know what mamihlapinatapai means?"

"Evidently not, or I wouldn't have needed to ask. I don't even know how to say it, but strongly suspect you just made it up."

"It means a look shared between two people who both hope the other will initiate something that both of them desire, yet neither of them is willing to go first. Sums you both up, in a word."

"Ha! You think you're clever," I said.

"It has been suggested, but that's not for me to say."

"Anyway, Danny's got a girlfriend."

"I am here," he interrupted. "Can we change the subject?"

"I'm merely pointing out the obvious," said Clare. "Ignore me if you want."

"So where to now?" he said, ignoring her.

"I need to get Louise, and I've got a few things to sort out. I can give you a lift back home first, though, if you like."

"That's okay," I said. "I'm sure there's a bus, and if not I'll get a cab."

"I'll come with you," said Danny, putting his hand on my arm. "Make sure you get back safely and that the flat's okay."

"And boom! There's another example," said Clare with another chuckle. "Inseparable." It's a bloody good job she didn't know about the illicit drunken kiss.

"It's the very least I can do," protested Danny. "Call it a duty of care."

But I quite liked the idea of Danny coming to my rescue, looking after me and being chivalrous, even if I could never say that in public, in the modern politically correct age.

We got out of the car and watched her drive away, and then he put his arm around me, and I didn't try to pull away.

Chapter 44

LOUISE was waiting, as agreed, by the pedestrian crossing next to the National Portrait Gallery on Charing Cross Road, just before Trafalgar Square. Clare slowed to a halt, long enough for her to climb into the passenger seat.

"Everything okay with Adam?" asked Clare, pulling back into the traffic, and then turning left on Duncannon Street, heading towards the Strand.

"I think so." Louise fastened her seatbelt, then reached across and gave Clare a peck on the cheek. "Where to now? Harry's?"

Clare nodded.

"How do you think it's all going?" Louise continued.

"How do *you* think it's going?"

Louise hesitated.

"Can I have a think about that and let you know?" She laughed. "Do you think it's time to tell him about us?"

"Harry?"

"Yes."

"Wow. We've got to think of his heart. He's not a young man."

"Good point."

Louise settled back into her seat, while Clare guided the car through the busy Saturday traffic. Clare glanced left to check that she was okay, but Louise's eyes were closed. She looked peaceful. They continued on in silence until finally Louise broke it, in a soft voice, full of tenderness.

"I'm so pleased we found each other."

Clare reached out to squeeze her hand.

"Me too," she said. "You make me very, very happy."

"That's good. And likewise." Louise paused, seemingly lost in thought, but finally continued. "I nearly told Danny. Would that have been bad?"

"About us? When?"

"When we were coming out of the park. I was saved by Jason, ironically."

"Did you want to tell him?"

"Hmmm." She paused again, as though trying to decide. "I want to tell him when we're ready. When we both want to. I think it would be lovely to not have to be your secret, but there's no rush."

"We will, once this is all resolved. I promise you."

"I know." She smiled. "Although I can imagine their faces. It's terrifying."

"I've got a suspicion Anna already knows," said Clare.

"Really?"

"Possibly. It was something she said. I can't remember exactly what it was now, but it made me think. Something about the way she called you my *friend*. She knows you're not my niece, anyway."

Louise laughed.

"I told you that was ridiculous from the outset. Anna's nice. I like her."

Clare nodded in agreement, and continued driving.

"Of course it might all be academic, really," Louise continued, as the car slowed down outside a row of terraced houses. "Once this is all over, you might run off and leave me."

Clare pulled to a stop, and switched off the engine.

"You really think I'd do that?" she asked, turning serious.

Louise shrugged.

"That's what tends to happen in my life. It wouldn't be the first time."

"Oh, darling," she said, undoing her seatbelt and reaching across for a hug. "I can't change what's happened in the past, but I promise you, I'll never leave you." She reached up to sweep hair away from Louise's eyes. "Believe me, since you came along, I've realised what's important in my life. You might leave me, go off and explore the world, but look into my eyes ..." She waited until Louise met her gaze. "You mean more to me than you will ever know. I don't know what'll happen in my future, but I do know that I want you to be part of it. For ever."

"Until death do us part?"

Clare laughed, grateful for the break in the tension.

"Something like that," she said, returning to her own seat. "And I'll make it my priority to ensure that doesn't happen to either of us, for a very long time to come."

"There's Harry."

Clare looked round. He was standing at his front door, holding it open for them.

"Come on," said Clare. "We can continue this later."

"Drinks, my dears?" asked Harry, once Clare and Louise were seated in the leather armchairs in his front room. They both asked only for water.

"It seems terribly remiss to enjoy a brandy when my houseguests are both on the aqua," he said. "But one feels a small measure wouldn't harm."

He joined them, sitting deep on the matching leather sofa. Clare was grateful he hadn't started playing background music this time, although the constant tick of the antique clock on the fireplace meant the room was never silent.

"So, how was your tête-à-tête with young Adam, my dear?" Harry asked, turning to Louise.

She glanced at Clare before replying.

"It was okay. He told me to leave it till Monday, and let the others calm down."

"Ah yes, the impetuous two. They will come round, when they have had time for contemplation."

"How do you think she's doing, Harry?" asked Clare.

"I think she's doing admirably," he said. "Obviously, it's unfortunate about dear George, but we knew that was one of the hazards."

"We did," said Clare. "But at least we know they're serious."

"Quite. It really is all going rather splendidly to plan."

From somewhere there was an electronic beep. Clare looked at her phone, then pressed the button to open her messages. She hoped she managed to hide her reaction from the others.

"I'm sorry, Harry," she said, looking across to the desk in the corner. "I couldn't just borrow your computer for a moment, could I? And the printer?"

"Of course, my dear."

He walked across to the desk, and pressed the power switch. A moment later the screen burst into life. They waited for the Windows 95 screen to load, and then he pointed out how to start the modem, if she needed to access the internet.

While Clare started tapping at the keyboard, Harry returned to the sofa, and then leaned forward and reached across to Louise, taking both of her hands in his.

"I have to ask you a tiny favour," he said. "A request, to humour an old man, if you would be so kind."

Louise smiled.

"Of course," she said, glancing at Clare. Clare was only partly listening, and seemed distracted, but she gave a wry smile back.

"I have been disturbed in my slumbers, trying to solve the intractable puzzle of the cufflink." He frowned. "It was in your hand and then you made it disappear. And a moment later, by gosh it's resplendent atop the mantelpiece. I simply must know how you did that."

Louise grinned, mischievously.

"I can't tell you all the secrets, can I?"

"No, my dear, but you must. It's been torturing me."

"Okay, just this once, all right?"

He nodded, looking deeply honoured to be taken into her confidence.

"When I came in I shook his hand, but it was a two-handed handshake, okay?" she started. "And then it was a double deception. I'd deliberately painted my nails bright red, so he was fixated on those, but just to be on the safe side, I also squeezed his hand really hard, and for longer than normal, all so he didn't notice me undoing the cufflink."

"Which explains how you took it, but not how you made it resurface, ten feet away."

"That was the easy bit." She was enjoying her moment. "As far as Adam was concerned, his cufflink had gone, and he expected me to have it. So when he saw a cufflink in my hand, his brain believed it was his. But I'd planned it long in advance, and had a gold cufflink in one pocket and a silver one in the other, because I didn't know which he'd have. The one you saw in my hand was one of those. It was face down, if you remember. He could only see the post and whatever the end bit's called."

"The toggle," said Clare, from the desk, taking a sheet of A4 paper from the printer.

"The toggle then. How do you know things like that?"

Clare shrugged.

"Basic English. I'll teach you."

"Anyway," Louise continued, turning back to Harry, "I'd already put the real cufflink on the fireplace when I was walking round the room. Making the fake one disappear was just practice and sleight of hand. The only thing that could have gone wrong was if he was wearing a shirt with button cuffs, but if that had happened I'd have given him a hug, like I did with Toby, so I could lift something from his inside pocket."

Harry was clearly impressed.

"You're dangerous," he said. "In more ways than one."

Amy was watching the daylight fade to darkness outside her office window, and getting increasingly impatient, waiting for DC Darren McQuade. She wanted to arrest Louise and have plenty of time for questions before it ended up being yet another shift that went through into the early hours of the morning. She had her coat on, and her car keys in her hand, and he should have been there. But he wasn't.

She pressed the preset on her mobile phone, but as it started to ring, she saw him running towards her, from the far end of the office.

"You're late," she said, coldly, putting the phone back in her pocket.

But instead of apologising, he told her to follow him.

"You've got to see this," he said.

"See what?"

"CCTV."

"Of what?"

"Jason Harrigan." He beckoned her to follow him. "Or what's left of him."

A minute later, she was pulling up a chair in a video viewing room, while a technician prepared to start rolling a tape.

"So, this is video just in from the crime scene," said DC

McQuade. "We're waiting on forensics for all of this, but they rushed this back because they thought you should see it."

"And this is CCTV?" she asked.

"No, the CCTV is in a minute. This was shot by us. The stills are being processed now. Press play, please."

The screen showed the dimly-lit, sparsely-populated floor of a car park. There was a shape on the ground. As the camera got closer, it became clear it was a body, and then as it got closer still, the horrific state of his injuries filled the screen.

"What you're looking at is the remains of Jason Harrigan, bodyguard of George Brandrick," said the DC. "Discovered this morning in a multistorey car park in Bell Wharf Lane, near Cannon Street."

Despite her years of experience, it was still uncomfortable viewing. He'd taken a beating, but the exact cause of death was hard to determine from the video. There was so much blood.

"Time of death, we don't know for sure," he continued, "but then there's this."

The technician switched tapes, and suddenly they were watching CCTV of a car entering the car park just before 2am. The same car left ten minutes later.

"And you think that's linked?" she asked.

The DC nodded enthusiastically.

"We've found the car already," he said. "In a car park in Camden. And there was blood all over the back seat. We've taken it in, and forensics are looking at that too. Obviously, we won't know until there's a DNA match, but for now it looks like the same blood group."

"So we're basically saying he was killed or at least attacked somewhere, and then taken to the car park to dump the body," said Amy.

"Exactly that."

"And do we know who the car belongs to?"

The DC started to smile.

"That's the actual CCTV I wanted to show you," he said. The technician cued up a third tape and pressed play again. "It's a rental, taken out under the name of Katherine Ashburn."

"Who the hell's she?"

"Watch."

The CCTV was from the office of the car rental company. It showed an employee, standing at a desk, while a customer read through a form. He pointed out some of the small print, and they had a discussion. There was no sound on the tape. But once the form was signed, the employee handed the keys over, and the customer turned to leave.

"Pause it there," said DC McQuade. "That's Ashburn."

Looking straight at the camera, with the keys in her hand, was Louise.

"Bingo," said Amy, feeling a rush of excitement. This was what made the job worthwhile. "Excellent work. Let's go and bring her in. But she's armed and unpredictable, so we're going to need to go in hard."

Chapter 45

"I HOPE you're not going to try to take advantage of me, now you've got me here alone," I said, opening my front door.

"Only if you want me to," said Danny.

"Hold on. Somebody's fixed the door." That stopped me. "It was smashed off its hinges."

"Clare got someone out to mend it."

"Good on her. She's got her faults but she's useful at times."

I took him through to the kitchen and filled the kettle. I didn't need to ask. My tea-making skills are legendary. According to me, anyway.

"Do you think we were like that?" I asked, as we waited for it to boil.

"Like what?"

"Whatever that word was? Don't ask me to repeat it."

"That word." He watched me pour the water into two mugs and start stirring the Yorkshire tea bags. "I'm in your good books if I'm getting a Yorkshire," he added.

The hierarchy of tea bags is this: Yorkshire for myself and people I like, PG Tips if I'm pretty sure I don't like them, and Typhoo if there's a deep and pathological loathing. Thankfully I've never met anyone I've hated enough to justify keeping a stock of Earl Grey.

"Let's just say, you're not in my bad books as much as you used to be. Anyway, answer the question."

He propped himself up against the counter while I fetched the milk from the fridge and gave it a sniff. It was still in date, but you can never be too careful.

"I think it was difficult from the outset," he said. "Remember when we met in the student bar. You were having a bad time because you'd just been arrested and you were with that bloke, Todd."

"God, don't remind me."

"Sorry, I didn't mean to."

"And you had Shelley," I countered. "Who I still think you were making up, despite the fact I met her."

"Exactly. So we never met as two single people. We became good friends instead. But I remember you sitting at a bus stop, when you were nineteen, I think, telling me that that was it, you were done with relationships. Couldn't see the point of them. You didn't want a one-night stand, but weren't prepared to risk anything longer because you thought it would inevitably end in tears."

"Which in fairness to myself, it always does."

I think that hit home, given what I sensed were domestic troubles with Detective Gorgeous. We took the tea to the front room, and he joined me on the large sofa. I kicked off my shoes, lifted my legs up, then hugged a cushion, perhaps as some kind of subconscious message to prove that I'm not short of hugs and I can have them whenever I want. Even if it's just a cushion.

"And I remember telling you it didn't have to be like that and sometimes you have to work at things," he continued.

"Mmmm," I said, unconvinced.

"And then you met that other one, what was he called?"

"Which other one? I have no idea who you're talking about."

"Yes you do. A couple of years back. What was he called? Mitch! Yes, Mitch. Whatever happened to him? That seemed to end quite abruptly. Are you still in touch with him?"

"No," I said. It was best to leave it there. Clare and I had sworn each other to secrecy over Mitch. And I had no intention of telling Danny, or anyone else, how she had killed him, or the reasons why. It wasn't my proudest moment. Thankfully he didn't pursue it.

"But there you go. You've always been averse to any kind of relationship. But never averse to pointing that out to me. So, yes, I thought the world of you. I was madly in love with you. Probably always will be. But you kept telling me you didn't want that and I wasn't going to mess things up by trying to change your mind."

Oh.

"You've got Lisa now," I said.

"Because I didn't want to grow old alone. I wanted a relationship. And you'd made it clear that you weren't interested in anything more than being friends. I wasn't going to push it. But anyway, I don't think I have got Lisa now."

"Really?"

"She's not very happy with me."

I was torn between wanting to give him a reassuring hug, because I hate to see people I care about in any kind of pain, and high-fiving myself. But as I've never high-fived anyone - because I'm not American - I did nothing. Which probably came across as uncaring, but these things are easily misconstrued.

"I'm sorry to hear that," I said. "Really, I am. But you know the sad thing? While you were in the hospital at the start of last year, and I spent months in the flat, on my own, I came to realise what was important. I had a complete change of heart about all of that. I was going to tell you the minute you arrived home. I even spoke to Clare about it on the very morning. That I *did* want a relationship, and I wanted it with you, even though I knew it was possible you didn't want the same. So I'd steeled myself for heartbreak, just in case, but just not quite in the way it came."

"Wow. Clare's never mentioned that."

"Good. But you know what she's like. She kept going on about helping me choose a wedding dress. Asking if she could be a bridesmaid. But anyway, it was all a moot point, wasn't it? Because you turned up hand-in-hand with Lisa and that was the end of that. And so, the one time I made myself vulnerable and let my guard down, and decided that maybe I should give things a go, I had my heart broken within seconds. Lesson learned."

"I had no idea."

I shrugged.

"We live and learn."

"Is that why you moved out of the flat?"

Even the thought of this was bringing me close to tears. It was nearly a year now. I'd thought I was over it, but in truth, never a day passed without some part of it crossing my mind. The scars were far from fully healed.

"Yeah," I said, with a sniff, then asked him to pass me a tissue from the box on the table. "I was devastated, Danny. It wasn't your fault. I see that now. You hadn't cheated on me. I don't blame you. I didn't deserve you. But you've got to remember, I was also having a stressful time at work. I'd just lost my studio, my career. All I ever wanted was to be a photographer, and I'd worked bloody hard to be good at it, but then lost the lot, all in the same week. So ask yourself, if you were me, would you want to live in the same flat, and be reminded of that every day? Or would you want to reset your life, start again, tell everyone and everything to fuck off, and just do your best to get through every day without collapsing in tears, in the depths of despair?"

He didn't answer immediately, but I could see the words had hit home.

"Do you still feel that way?" he asked eventually.

"Heartbroken and on the edge of a mental breakdown? If I'm

honest, less so. I still think about it every day. Think about you. And her. What you're doing. What'll happen to me. But I tell myself that time heals, so I try to focus on the positives."

"That's not what I meant. I meant do you still feel that way about me?"

"Wow, that's a deep question."

"I'm sorry. I didn't mean ..."

"You don't need to apologise," I said, waving his protests away.

"I do because I don't want to upset you," he continued. "I never wanted to upset you. I only ever wanted to be with you. We were brilliant together."

"We were." I smiled a rueful smile. "And we could have been. But time moves on, doesn't it? You've got Lisa now, because I'm sure you'll patch it up. And her daughter, who thinks you're brilliant. So it's irrelevant what I think, and it's irrelevant what I dream about in a parallel universe, because I learned my lesson."

"Don't you start talking about parallel universes as well."

"What?"

"Oh, nothing. Just Clare was talking about them. Sorry."

"That's okay." I was nearly finished, but I had to give him the punchline. "What it boils down to is this. I was always terrified of relationships because I was always terrified of a broken heart. And then, finally, my resolve weakened, and I was punished for that in the most brutal, broken-hearted way."

And that is when the tears came, and I couldn't stop them, and the sickening, hollow feeling that I'd been so proud about conquering, came rushing back to hit me as hard as ever.

"Oh, come here," he said.

I thought about it for a moment, then moved along the sofa, and fell into him. His arm around me felt so secure, so reassuring. Our faces were inches apart. He leaned towards me and I kissed his cheek.

I nearly kissed him on the lips for the first time sober. That would have been wrong.

But he seemed willing, and my mind was a mess and I nearly kissed him on the lips again, looking into his eyes as our noses touched.

There was a knock on the door. Whoever it was didn't wait for an answer. And not for the first time, armed police stormed into my flat.

"Police! Don't move!" they shouted. Talk about a passion killer. Once they'd checked all of the rooms, and scared the life out of me, because they really did seem quite scary close-up, Amy walked in looking very serious indeed.

"Where are they?" she shouted at us.

"Who?" I said, although I suspected I knew.

"Don't try to be funny. Louise and Clare. Where are they?"

"I don't know," I said, trying to remain calm. "I can make you all a cup of Typhoo, though."

"Should we charge her with wasting police time?" asked her sidekick, who I hadn't seen before.

She put up her hand to silence him.

"I'm going to ask you one last time," she said.

I looked at Danny. He came to my rescue.

"Sorry Amy, but we really haven't seen Louise all day," he said. "Not since first thing this morning, anyway. And we saw Clare a few hours ago, but that was in Shoreditch. I've got no idea where she went after that."

She didn't look impressed.

"Which is her room?" she asked, her voice lowering a notch, but no less serious.

"First on the left, the smaller of the two," I said.

"Wait here," she said to her colleague.

A few minutes later she came back, holding evidence bags full of clothing and other things she'd found in Louise's room. Even the book on Meisner technique.

"If she gets in touch, or you suddenly remember you know where either of them are, you call me, immediately," she said, handing us both a card.

"Okay," I said. "And the damage to the door?"

"Yellow Pages. Carpenter, locksmith, I don't give a fuck."

Amy never swore. Things must be serious.

And with that, they left as almost as abruptly as they arrived.

Luckily, Danny still had the business card of the man who'd fixed the door the first time, and he was in the area, so he was with us within the hour.

"You're making a habit of this," he said, clearly bemused.

"Long story," said Danny. "Different intruders this time, though."

"You should call the police," he said, which was ironic in the circumstances.

Once he'd fixed the frame, and we could safely leave the flat, I grabbed my coat and we went out to the street.

"I wouldn't trust her not to have left some sort of bug," I said. "Presumably thinking I was going to ring Clare."

"Which you are now about to do?"

"Of course."

I opened the special Clare phone and pressed her number. She answered on the third ring.

I told her what had happened.

"Oh shit," she said. "Is Danny with you?"

"He is."

There was a conversation in the background before she came back on the line.

"Okay, here's the plan," she said. "I've got someone to look after Louise. He's going to take her off to a secure place. We need to meet, but obviously they could be watching you. So can you do me a favour?"

"Of course, anything," I said.

"Get on the Underground, go anywhere, keep swapping lines, train to train, platform to platform, north, east, south, west and anywhere in between, for probably an hour or so."

It sounded like my absolute worst nightmare, second only, perhaps, to having to drink Earl Grey tea.

"Really?" I said. "You do know who you're talking to?"

"I do, and I know it's a sacrifice, but honestly, I'll love you forever. The important thing is, if they're following, you've got to lose them."

"What about CCTV?" I said. "Couldn't they follow us on that?"

"Shit. Yes. I'm not thinking."

I'd never known her sound quite so panicked. This was not like the Clare of old.

"Okay," she continued. "Do the Underground, get off, catch a bus, walk for a bit, get to Oxford Street if you can, then in the front of John Lewis and out the back. Whatever it takes. I don't really care. The important thing is not to be followed. Then call me or I'll call you, and we can arrange to meet somewhere. You okay with that?"

"Yup, it sounds fun," I said. It didn't sound fun. It sounded exhausting, and my legs were aching from the gym, even more than they had been the day before.

Clare ended the call, and I explained it all to Danny. It felt like we were going on a proper undercover mission. As we'd just been saying, before we were rudely interrupted, we were brilliant together. It would be just like the old days.

Harry took Louise to his car, and fired the engine.

"Where are we going?" she asked.

"To stay with a friend, my dear," he said.

She wanted to know more, but she knew there was no option other than to trust him.

The lights changed from red to green, and he pulled out to cross the junction. Just as a giant 4x4 went piling into them from the side.

Chapter 46

AFTER God knows how many trains, at least four buses, and even a taxi, just for the thrill of someone behind potentially saying "follow that cab", we were pretty sure that nobody could have followed us.

I called Clare and told her our location. She said she'd be with us within half an hour. Twenty minutes later, she called and told us to go out on the street. I recognised her BMW as it pulled up. I got in the back this time, giving Danny the front. Part of me thought it was only fair. But the self-preservation instinct also suggested it was safer in the back, lying across the bench seat, should the bullets start to fly.

But there were no bullets. Clare drove us out to the middle of nowhere. I couldn't see much in the dark, but the built-up areas of London were behind us. Eventually she stopped, in the car park of a country pub. Apparently it had rooms and we could all stay the night.

She took us through a rear entrance and up a dimly-lit staircase to one big room, with two single beds and a sofa. And at last we could all breathe out.

"I'm afraid we're all going to have to share tonight," she said.

"Not that I think we'll get much sleep anyway. I'll get some food sent up."

It sounded like a plan. I tested one of the single beds while she made a call to the kitchen. It made a change from her making Danny and me share a double. I was determined not to be the one to end up on the sofa, despite being the smallest.

"What is going on?" asked Danny, not unreasonably, as Clare returned from the bathroom, drying her hands on a towel. "Why are armed police smashing their way in, looking for Louise?" That seemed reasonable too.

"Because she's been framed for murder," said Clare. "You know that."

"But isn't that why they took her in for questioning? And they let her out."

"They did. But whoever did it has presumably done something else, and now it's become more urgent."

"This isn't good," he said. His expression turned awkward. "I hate to say this, but are you sure she *didn't* do it? Brandrick was responsible, in part, for the death of her father."

"Did you kill the girl in Poland?" she asked, rather sharply.

What girl in Poland?

"No, of course I didn't."

"Well then, believe me when I say that Louise didn't kill George."

That was the end of that. But alarm bells were ringing in my head. What were they keeping from me?

"There is something I need to tell you, though," Clare continued, before I had a chance to protest. She glanced up at me but then focused her attention on Danny. "I had a message from a contact in Poland this afternoon. It transpires we've been played."

"What do you mean, played?" he said.

"I mean duped, double-crossed, whatever you want to call it." This sounded serious. She looked serious. "Anatol Rudyk."

"The Polish guy?" said Danny. "The one we met in Warsaw, who worked with Greg?"

"The one we thought we met in Warsaw. He turned up dead, yesterday."

"Jesus, not another one." Danny looked shocked. I didn't really know who they were talking about, but I was feeling pretty shocked too.

Then his face changed. "What do you mean we *thought* we met?" he asked, as though a light had just been switched on.

"When I say he turned up dead yesterday, I mean that's when they discovered the body. Best estimate, he died a week ago."

It took a moment for that to sink in.

"But who did we meet then on Wednesday?" asked Danny.

"Somebody pretending to be Anatol Rudyk," she said. She reached into her coat pocket and withdrew a piece of A4 paper, unfolded it and handed it to Danny. It was a picture of a man. "Recognise him?"

Danny looked at the picture, but didn't hesitate.

"That's him."

Clare nodded.

"Ironically, his first name is Anatoly," she said. "Which is close enough. Surname Kalashnik. He's Russian mafia."

"Jesus."

"And he represents a gang who have interests in Warsaw, specifically around contracts for building projects, basically controlling large-scale development and buying permission to do so."

"There was a hell of a lot of construction going on."

"Exactly. You've seen the state of the place. The irony is, they were desperate to get rid of the Russians. But now Russians are back, feeding off corruption. That's what Greg was working on. Exposing the people who were taking bribes, and even more so those that were paying them. And that's why he was killed."

All of this was going over my head, but it sounded scary.

"But that also explains why they shot at me on the balcony on Thursday morning," she continued. "They knew we were investigating Greg. They knew we thought we were talking to one of his friends. And they knew that they had to silence us. And that's also why they sent the Polish girl to kill you."

I couldn't let this go on. I now had no idea what they were talking about, although Danny looked almost as confused as I was.

"What Polish girl?" I asked, feeling immensely uncomfortable.

Clare tried to put me out of my misery.

"We had a night out in Warsaw," she said. "And there were two Polish girls all over Danny. To be fair to him, he was very well behaved. But when I went in to wake him up the next morning, one of them was lying on the bed next to him."

I raised one eyebrow. Then the other.

"It's not how it sounds," said Danny. "She was fully clothed. And also dead. She'd been strangled."

"*What?*"

"Yes," said Clare. We all looked at her, awaiting an explanation. She sighed, then took a deep breath. "Okay. She wasn't Polish. She was Russian. And she wasn't the innocent young hooker she pretended to be. She was working as a honeytrap because the Russians were onto me and they were onto Danny. She was sent to seduce him and kill him."

"What the fuck?" said Danny. But Clare hadn't finished.

"But when Danny resisted her advances she followed us back to the hotel. She'd decided to skip the seduction part and then return early in the morning, once she knew where we were, to do the second part. I caught her breaking into the room and - well, let's just say I put a stop to it."

"*You* killed her?"

"Again, I'm not sure I'd exactly use those words," said Clare, looking bashful.

Danny looked like he'd had his mind blown.

"You killed her?" he said again, as though on autopilot, with a horrified expression on his face.

"I prefer to think I stopped her from killing you," she said.

"And you never thought to tell me?"

"And have you freak out on me? I didn't know what we were dealing with, Danny. All I know is that they got you drunk. They didn't manage to kill you that night so they came back for another try."

"But why leave the body there?" he asked. "If you didn't want to freak me out, you did a monumentally shit job of it."

"Oh come on. You woke up not too long after. What was I supposed to do? Hide her in the wardrobe? Throw her off the balcony? And in any case, I couldn't purely make her disappear. It was important that whoever she was working for got a message that we knew what they were up to."

"The poor girl," said Danny. But Clare shook her head.

"I wouldn't have much sympathy. She knew the game. She was a trained assassin. She had an awful lot of blood on her hands. Appearances can be deceptive."

"And you know all this because?"

"Because while you've been poncing around with Louise, trying to mess things up by meeting her friends in the park, I've continued working. Making calls, speaking to people."

That sounded almost like a telling-off to me.

"But you could have told me what had happened," Danny continued, almost pleading.

"And have you freaking out even more because you realised that a group of unknown Russians had sent someone to kill you?"

Put like that, she seemed to have a point.

"And so you didn't go back and clean up?"

"No. I went straight from dropping you at Okecie to another airport, to get my plane. They'd have discovered her body as soon as they realised we'd escaped. If I'd gone back they'd have killed me too."

"Notwithstanding the tragedy over the loss of life," I said, changing the subject, and trying to lighten what had become an intensely sombre atmosphere, "are you saying that Danny can only pull glamorous women these days if somebody is paying them? Because that's what it sounds like." I winked at him. "You're losing your touch, my man."

In retrospect, it wasn't the optimal time to make a joke, and nobody laughed.

"There's one other thing we have to remember," said Clare. There was something about the way she said it that made it sound like it wasn't going to be trivial. She had our undivided attention. "The same gang also has interests in London."

The silence in the room was so complete, I thought for a moment my ears had stopped. The implication was loud and clear.

"And George Brandrick was working for them?" said Danny.

"I'll come onto that," she said. "But that's why they're targeting Louise: because they've worked out she's onto them too."

"Where is she now?" I asked.

"She's safe. Harry is looking after her."

But the reality was that she was as far from safe as it is possible to be.

Chapter 47

WHEN Louise came round, she found she was strapped to a chair in the middle of a room. It had a concrete floor with ominous dark stains. Her arms and legs were tied, but the man removed the gag so at least she could speak. It took her a moment to process her surroundings. She'd been in the car with Harry and then ... It was like an explosion. Glass, metal, and the faintest recollection of being dragged away. People shouting, then a van, then blackness. None of it made sense. She looked down at her clothes and was shocked by the amount of blood. Was it hers?

"Where's Harry?" she said, her voice weak. It hurt to talk. It hurt just sitting there. She felt like she was going to be sick.

"I am afraid he succumbed to his injuries," said the man. That didn't make sense. What injuries? Harry was there. Sitting next to her. And then the world caved in. The dust, and ringing in her ears. Lights. Getting closer. Fear. Grinding of metal on metal. Then an almighty scream.

Was he saying Harry was dead? He couldn't be, surely? But she couldn't process that now.

"Who are you?" she gasped.

"My name is Anatoly," he said. "I can speak Polish, but we will continue in English for the benefit of my colleagues."

Which colleagues? The physical effort of turning her head sent shards of pain rushing through her neck. And there was nobody else there. Just a wall, with a mirror. Was there somebody behind it, watching her now? Where was she? She had a compelling urge to close her eyes, and drift off back to a painful sleep. Where was Harry?

"You are in a lot of trouble." The voice brought her back to consciousness. "The police want to speak to you for the murder of George Brandrick. The evidence is compelling. I can help you."

"I had nothing to do with that," she whispered.

"The police think you did. But I can make the evidence point in another direction. Or I can make sure it sticks to you. It's your choice."

She coughed, but the pain in her chest was excruciating. She couldn't feel her legs. Pins and needles were shooting up her arms.

"Where am I?" she asked.

"Don't worry about where you are. You're safe and we will look after you. As long as you give us what we need. What did you want from George Brandrick?"

"I ..." What had she wanted from him? Money? No. Just to get close. It was Clare's plan. She had to follow the instructions. *It's better that you don't know, so there's less chance of you improvising and messing things up.*

"I wanted to get close to George," she said, although every word was a huge effort. "I had a business proposition for him."

"Bullshit. Who are you working for?"

"A group. Friends."

"And again bullshit. So let me tell you who you were really working for. Clare Woodbrook. Are you going to deny that? Believe me, I have a very low tolerance for bullshit."

"No."

"No what?"

"No I'm not going to deny it."

"That's better."

Louise closed her eyes. What else could she have said?

"I need to speak to Clare Woodbrook," said Anatoly, rising from his chair and walking, slowly, behind her. "But she is tough. If I ask her questions she will refuse to answer. So I will ask them to you." He leaned in close to her ear, close enough that she could feel the rough bristles of his beard against her smooth skin. "And if you refuse to answer, it will be very painful. If you don't know the answers, maybe Clare will help you."

"Where is she?"

"That's one of the first questions," he said, leaning back, and then returning to the chair in front of her.

Slowly, Louise's brain was kicking into gear. She had to know what she was dealing with.

"Who's through the window?" she breathed. "Jason? Is this what this is all about?"

The man shook his head. His fake smile was sickening.

"No, I'm afraid Jason isn't working for us. He made trouble for us. But he's making bigger trouble for you."

Chapter 48

Sunday, January 26th, 1997

AS it happened, the sofa wasn't all that bad. In fairness to the others, I nodded off long before we had the conversation about who was sleeping where, shortly after we'd made headway with the pizza and sandwiches that had magically appeared from downstairs. Danny and Clare were still talking, but I couldn't fight my eyes, which were closing of their own accord. At some point, someone put a blanket over me.

"What time is it?" I asked. Clare was already awake, sitting at the desk, looking at her mobile phone.

"Still early," she said in a whisper.

"How early?"

She looked at her watch.

"Not quite six."

I groaned and closed my eyes. But there was no way I was going to get back to sleep. There were too many questions to answer. I raised myself into a sitting position, wiping the sleep from my eyes. Danny was asleep on the bed, still fully dressed.

"There's a toothbrush for you in the bathroom," she said. "And a few other things if you want to have a shower."

"Have I got time?"

"Yes," she said, with a reassuring smile. "But I'd get in quick before Sleeping Beauty."

By the time I returned, reasonably refreshed, and much more awake, Danny had woken and Clare had organised a breakfast tray with toast and pots of tea. It was some sort of Twinings affair, according to the labels which dangled out of the side, on little pieces of string, but I was prepared to give it the benefit of the doubt, in an emergency.

"Is everything all right?" I asked, sensing her tension.

"I don't know." That worried me from the outset. Normally Clare is keen to portray an image of calm control. "I can't get in touch with Louise."

"Wasn't she going to a friend's?" I said.

"She was."

"Maybe her phone's out of battery."

"Maybe," she said. "But there's no answer from Harry either."

"Have you tried the friend?" asked Danny.

"I have." But I could tell there was more to come. "She and Harry didn't ever arrive."

I didn't want to state the obvious, but that wasn't good.

"I'll get dressed," said Danny.

"You are dressed," I said.

He seemed to notice for the first time.

"Oh yeah."

"I can recommend the shower. That'll wake you up. As long as you don't mind a slightly damp towel."

He glanced across to Clare, as though seeking approval.

"You've got time," she said. "And I think we're going to need to be as wide awake as possible."

Clare announced she was going outside for a cigarette while Danny was in the shower.

"And you're not invited," she added.

"That's charming."

"I mean you can come down to keep me company, if you want, but I'm not going to give you one."

"I don't smoke," I said, despite recent evidence to the contrary. She raised her eyebrows. It was far too early and far too cold to think about going outside, so I declined the offer.

About five minutes later there was a knock at the door. That was quick, I thought.

I went across to open it, and found myself face to face with DS Amy Cranston.

Louise didn't know how long she'd been left for, but it seemed like hours. She'd drifted off into an uncomfortable sleep at times, but every time her head fell forward, shooting pains from the whiplash brought her back round. Eventually the man returned and took his seat, and despite the fatigue and discomfort, she felt much more ready to face him.

"I don't think much of this hotel. Can I at least have a shower?" she said.

He ignored her.

"Let me tell you about Jason," he said. "He's dead."

She didn't know whether to be shocked or relieved.

"You killed him," he continued, "the same as you killed George Brandrick. Or at least that's what the police think, and the evidence, in truth, is quite compelling. But I can save you, if you want me to."

"What evidence?"

"When did you last see your car keys?"

There was a dawning sense of panic. Not for a few days.

"Here they are," he continued, dangling them from his finger. "The terrible thing is, somebody borrowed your car to transport

Jason's body, and I'm rather afraid to report they made a bit of a mess on the back seat. That, and the CCTV, aren't going to do you any favours."

"What CCTV?"

"Of the car, entering and leaving a multistorey car park, either side of depositing his body."

"You bastards," she spat.

He laughed. She expected he'd heard worse.

"So here's the deal. Give me Clare and I will ensure you're set free, and that the police are informed that you had nothing to do with it."

"No."

"It's your choice. But believe me, a lifetime behind bars won't do you many favours. If they let you out at all, you'll be an old lady, having wasted your life for what? Because of some misplaced loyalty to someone who cares so little about you, she puts you in positions like this?"

"Still no."

"Okay. As you wish." He paused, looked towards the mirror, then returned to Louise and coughed to clear his throat.

"What would it take, then? Money? I could make you rich."

"I'm not interested in your money."

"It could come in handy. Start a new life. You could even go straight. You wouldn't need to worry about repercussions from Clare. She'd understand. You could even come and work for me if you wanted to. I could always find a place for somebody of your abilities."

"Still no," she said, with granite defiance.

"I don't understand why. Do you think she'd do the same for you? And anyway, I only want to talk to her. I just need you to tell me where she is."

This time she didn't respond, but instead looked away, despite the extreme physical pain of turning her head.

"You're good at magic, I hear," he continued. "It's amazing

what you can do with your hands. I mean, look at them now. They're even changing colour, although that might be the lack of circulation. I'd hate to think of such a pretty girl losing a finger. Or maybe all of her fingers. Wouldn't you?"

Again she ignored him. But her eyes were fixated on the wire cutters he'd removed from his pocket. The full hopeless horror of her situation was beginning to dawn.

"Should we start from the outside and work in?" he asked, standing up and moving towards her.

Chapter 49

"WHAT are you doing here?" I asked, although I already knew the answer. "And how did you know I was here?"

"I knew I couldn't trust you," said Amy. "I put a tracker on your coat. I would have been here last night, but I had things to do and I thought it could wait."

"Outstanding." I looked beyond her. "Where's your private army?"

"They're not far away, and they'll come if I need them, but I'm hoping it won't be necessary. Can I come in?"

I don't really know why she asked. Evidently she was coming in anyway, whatever I said.

"Of course. There's only me and Danny here, though."

I don't think she believed that either. She entered the room and started looking round, checking the wardrobes.

"Don't go in the bathroom," I said, but that only encouraged her. Danny hadn't locked the door, and by the sound of the shout above the running water, I suspect she got to see more of him than she'd been bargaining for. "Warned you," I added.

"So where are they?" she asked.

But before I had a chance to answer, Clare appeared in the open doorway. Which rather saved me a task.

"Amy," she said, with an apparent lack of surprise. "Lovely to see you, as ever." She didn't run. This was more like the old Clare, taking control. "I saw your car downstairs. To what do we owe the pleasure?"

"I need you to give me Louise," she said. "Simple as that. Do that and I'm out of your way. Don't do that, and I'll take you in, instead. Your choice."

"That's not much of a choice," said Clare. Danny emerged from the bathroom, wrapped in a towel, looking to see what the fuss was, then headed back, presumably to get dressed.

"There's a cup of tea, Amy, if you'd like one," I said. "Although it might be a bit cold."

"I don't have time for tea," she said. "So which is it, Clare? Make your mind up. I'll count to three."

Clare sighed and sat on the bed.

"Amy, look, listen to me. I don't know what you think you've got on Louise, but let me assure you, there'll be an explanation."

"One."

"I've told you before, she's got nothing to do with George Brandrick. I told you what the plan was, and I appreciate it's evolved, but Louise is not a killer."

"Two."

"Oh, come on, stop being a child. What's going to happen? You're going to get to three and then you're going to arrest me? And then what? It's still not going to help you find her."

"Three."

"As you wish." She offered her wrists so that Amy could attach an imaginary pair of handcuffs.

"To be fair to Clare, we don't know where Louise is," I interrupted.

"Right," said Amy. "Well, that's obviously nonsense."

"No, it is actually true." I hoped I hadn't spoken out of turn.

Danny reappeared and took the chair by the desk. His hair was still damp, bless him.

"You do know that you're only free because you help us out, yes?" said Amy, moving closer to Clare. "Hiding someone wanted for murder is a significant breach of that."

"And I've told you, she hasn't murdered anyone. What about the bodyguard. Jason. Have you found him?"

That stopped Amy. Her expression turned cold.

"And what do you mean by that?" she asked.

"I mean he probably killed George."

Amy sat down on the bed next to Clare, and rested her chin on her hand, looking thoughtful, but with a hint of menace.

"I can't work you out, Clare," she said. "Yes, we found Jason."

"Good," she said. "Have you questioned him?"

"No."

"Why not?"

"Because he's dead." That changed the mood. "Are you going to tell me where she is?"

"A journalist never reveals her sources," said Clare.

"You're not a journalist."

"Okay."

Clare reached up and stretched, groaning in the process. I think she'd had enough. Eventually you've got to know when it's no longer worth the fight.

"Louise was supposed to be going off with Harry," she said. "They were due at a friend's until this all blew over. But they didn't get there, and she isn't answering her phone. So no, I don't know where she is, and at this precise moment, I'm as keen as you are to find out."

"Harry Rushton?" said Amy.

"Yes. I told you about Harry. And before you ask, he's not answering his phone either."

"No, he wouldn't," said Amy. She had our undivided attention now. "I'm sorry to tell you, but he was pulled out of the wreckage of a car late last night. But Louise wasn't with him."

———

The jaws on the wire cutters had just broken the skin when Louise finally cracked.

"Okay," she said, her voice broken. "I'll do it."

Anatoly hesitated for a moment.

"You'll do what?"

"I'll give you Clare. I'll call her. Or I'll give you the number and you can call her. But stop now, please."

He opened the jaws and let go of her hand.

"Good girl," he said. "I'll get you a phone."

———

I don't think I've ever seen Clare looking quite so pale.

"What do you mean wreckage?" she said.

"Exactly what it sounds like. Another driver likely hit Harry's car, then left the scene. We'll know more when forensics start looking at it."

"How is he? Is he okay?"

Amy started to shake her head.

"It's not good. I'm sorry. He's alive but in intensive care. There was a lot of blood loss."

"But no sign of Louise?"

"No."

"And what time was this? Where was it?"

"About seven. Not far from his house."

"Shit."

Clare leant forward with her head in her hands. When she turned her face towards us, I could see the tears.

"She would definitely have been in that car," she said.

"Well, unless she got out and walked away ..." started Amy.

"Then whoever crashed into them has got her," Clare finished, with urgency. She stood up. "Right, we've got to find her. Get everything you can about the crash. Any CCTV. Check for paint samples. That'll give us a make and model."

"Clare, calm down," said Amy. "We're doing all of that, of course we are. And as soon as there's any news, I'll be the first to know."

"You've got to believe me," said Clare.

"For the first time that I can remember," said Amy, "I think I actually do."

"Call me the minute you get any news, and I *promise* you I'll do likewise. You know who you're looking for?"

"Of course," she said. "And yes, I do."

With that, she left in a heightened state of urgency. For her part, Clare was extremely agitated.

"What do you mean when you said *'you know who you're looking for'?*" I asked. "Do you mean the Russians?"

"It's bloody obvious," she said. "Do you really need me to tell you? It'll be Adam."

Chapter 50

WHAT Clare had said didn't make any sense to me at all. I looked across to Danny and could see he was thinking the same.

"Adam Kirwin?" he said. "Adam from the long con crew?"

"Yes," said Clare. "Shit, shit, shit."

I stood up and put my arm around her, trying to get her to calm down.

"Clare, please," I said. "Panicking isn't going to find her. We've got to think about this. But what do you mean Adam? I thought Adam was one of the good people? Albeit a con man."

"No," she said, looking exasperated. "Adam's the whole point of this."

"What does that mean?" said Danny, still as confused as me.

"He's the one working for the Russians," she said.

"I thought that was George Brandrick?"

"Oh, Danny." She sighed. "Okay, let me explain this from the beginning."

"Please do," he said.

She returned to the bed. I moved back to the other one.

"Right, so the Russians, as you know, are working in Warsaw

and over here. Greg was investigating, and got killed in the process."

"So far, I'm with you," said Danny. "And you said they were working with someone over here."

"Correct."

"George Brandrick."

"No. Adam."

"So what's all the George thing been about?" I said.

She looked like she pitied me for not being able to keep up.

"Let's go back a stage," she said. "Greg spoke to me before he died, and asked me what I knew about Adam Kirwin. I said I'd heard the name but I knew someone who knew him better. Harry was an old friend, and I knew he was working with Adam on the long con stuff. So I spoke to Harry and made enquiries. As far as he was concerned, Adam was the boss. They were working together with Abby and Toby, and they'd been successful. But he said there had been a few occasions when he'd had cause for concern."

"Such as?" asked Danny.

"Such as, some of the deals they were involved in. There were a few things that were out of character. There was one big scheme that they'd spent weeks preparing, on which Adam pulled the plug, with no real logic or explanation. But when I spoke to Harry, and suggested Russian involvement, he said that made sense, and bells started to ring."

"So you needed to get close to Adam?" said Danny.

"Exactly. I needed to get inside his operation, see the way he worked, and then start digging from there. But I couldn't do that, obviously. If he started investigating me, he'd soon know all about me. So we came up with a plan."

"Getting Louise to do it instead?"

"Kind of. But that would have been a bit too obvious too. Why would he let her in? We needed to stack the cards in her favour. So I had to set up a mark."

"George Brandrick."

"In one. I knew George as well. He wasn't a friend, far from it, but he was someone I could at least speak to, to see if he wanted to help."

"Hold on a minute. You mean George knew about this?" Danny appeared flummoxed.

"Yes. Although Louise didn't know any of this. As far as she was concerned, it was authentic. That was important so that her actions and reactions were as natural as possible. Don't get me wrong, she was a hugely willing participant in this. She knew it was dangerous, and I'd tried to talk her out of it a hundred times, but she was relentless. Call it pester power, if you like. Eventually I agreed, just to shut her up. But I was trying to scam the scammer. I had to make sure that she appeared genuine and that George would do what I needed him to do. Play hard to get, but ultimately go along with it. Some of the stuff was fairly basic. He wouldn't be gullible enough to be taken in by it normally, so I had to rely on him to play his part. Which was a risk, admittedly, because he was a crook."

"But why would he do that?" asked Danny.

"He didn't want to at first. But then he got himself into trouble. One of his dealers was in a relationship with the daughter of an old-time East End thug called Tony Devlin. The daughter was done for possession, had turned to the game to pay for her habit. George's boy was the pimp, and worse still, he'd got her pregnant. Devlin wanted revenge, but George didn't want to give up his boy. I offered to sort it out for him, in exchange for him helping me get close to Adam."

"What do you mean sort it out?" asked Danny.

"Let's not get sidetracked," she said.

I didn't know whether to be horrified or relieved at the return of old-school ruthless Clare. I couldn't tell which side Danny was on, either. But not for the first time I made a mental note not to fall out with her.

"Anyway, even then that wasn't enough," she continued. "So I met with Harry. He had to sell it to Adam. So we came up with a plan whereby we'd make it look like he could rip us off in the process. Obviously Adam didn't know it was me at the time. Just someone approaching them with a deal that they could exploit. So as far as Adam was concerned, Louise had a personal reason for wanting to get to Brandrick. He could go along with it, risk free. If it paid off, he'd be able to rip off Louise and keep her share. If it didn't, she'd given him a £50,000 bankers draft as security. We had to appeal to his sense of greed."

"But where did she get £50,000 from?" asked Danny.

"From me, obviously. But equally obviously he was never going to cash it, because we'd have uncovered him by then. Exposed the Russian links and taken him down. Or, worst case, if he did cash it, then I'd be out of pocket, but it was worth the risk."

"But Brandrick got killed?" I said.

"Yes."

We let that one sink in for a moment.

"Who killed him?" asked Danny.

"At first I thought it could have been anybody. He had plenty of enemies. And honestly, I don't know anyone who'll be grieving. But then a couple of things happened. Louise went to see Adam. Obviously the £50,000 was security on the deal, but now the deal wasn't happening, so we knew we were going to lose that. But Adam said he wouldn't cash it. And of course, the hotel suite was smashed up. That was when I knew he was onto us."

I was beginning to get lost.

"Because?" I said.

"Because I realised that he'd worked out that George Brandrick was in on it. And George had been punished in the process. Adam was the only person who knew about Louise's meeting. He knew exactly what time she was supposed to be there, and to his credit he timed it perfectly. He dropped her off early, giving himself time to get in position. He even gave her a gun. Then as soon as he knew she was in the building, he shot George. He delayed the lift so it would take her a few minutes to get upstairs, which gave him time to escape. Then he went back to his suite and smashed it up himself, to make it look like it was a vendetta, and that they were under attack."

"Jesus," said Danny.

"Quite." She was on a roll now. "So by that stage he'd worked out that George was effectively in on a plot to scam him, but even then I don't know if he'd worked out the details. But then you absolutely royally fucked up."

"Me?" Danny looked astonished.

"Yes you."

"What did I do?"

"You went with Louise to the park. And she told them you were a journalist. I mean, for fuck's sake. That was that, then. It didn't take him long to piece together the rest of it."

Danny was crestfallen.

"I'm so sorry," he said.

"Yeah, well, what's done is done. We can discuss it later. Obviously, Louise had to go back for one last meeting, just to be sure, but I'd made sure Harry was armed in case it got out of hand. Harry, bless him, doesn't know one end of a gun from the other, but we hoped it wouldn't come to that. Adam doesn't believe in direct action. And remember, he wasn't working for himself. He'd be taking instructions from the Russians. But by now, they knew I was onto them. The park thing was confirmation that Louise was working for me. By extension, he knew that Harry was part of it too. Which is why Harry's now in intensive care, and why they've got Louise."

"For punishment?" said Danny.

"Partly. But mainly because they know that that's their best way of getting to me. I think they killed Jason for the hell of it, to put extra pressure on her, but she'll be getting interrogated. And the longer it takes to find her, the worse it's going to get."

Neither Danny nor I knew what to say. We were both trying to process everything we'd heard. I felt sick with worry for Louise. She'd been so brave, and now, who knew what sort of torture she was enduring?

The cold silence in the room was punctuated by the ringing of Clare's phone.

Chapter 51

LOUISE ended the call and handed the phone back to Adam.

She hadn't been surprised to see him. That was when she knew the game was up and there was no point fighting any more.

"What now?" she asked, trying hard to stop the tears.

"We wait for her to arrive," he said, his voice cold and hard. "We find out what she knows. We find out who she's been speaking to. And then we put a stop to it."

From behind her, a man fixed a gag over her mouth, tied uncomfortably tight, making it difficult to breathe.

"Ready?" asked Adam.

The man nodded. And with that, both he and Anatoly left the room, leaving Louise tied and broken, awaiting her fate.

Behind the mirror, there were plans to make.

Anatoly checked that the weapons were ready and loaded, and then handed one to each of his five men.

"Remember not to kill her until she's told us everything," he said. "And not until my specific instruction. We don't know how much she's got to give. She may take some persuading and we don't want to do it too early. Understood?"

They all signalled their agreement.

"And she's coming alone?" asked one of the men.

"I think we have to be alert to the fact that she might not. That she might try something stupid. But that's why she's not coming here. We're going to send someone to meet her and then bring her here ourselves."

"And Louise?" said Adam.

"You can have the pleasure of that one," Anatoly said. "But let her watch the entertainment first."

Danny was adamant that he wanted to go with her, but Clare was equally as insistent that she had to do this on her own.

"It's me they want," she said. "If there's anyone with me, they'd kill them without a second thought. I've already saved your life once, and I don't want to go down thinking that was wasted."

"But we'd be stronger together."

"No, Danny. We wouldn't. There'd be one more body to bury. Stay here. Look after Anna for me. Mamihlapinatapai, remember?" She gave him a hug. "And don't feel guilty about the fuck-up. They'd have worked it out eventually."

He watched her pull out of the car park in her BMW, aware that he might never see her again.

Clare said goodbye to me in the room, insisting that only Danny could escort her to her car. I tried to protest but she was adamant. By the time she pulled out of the car park, I was already on the phone to Amy.

"But you don't know where she's going?" she asked.

"No, she said she couldn't tell us. But if you're still in the area, you could double back, and follow her."

"I can try, but I'm stuck on the dual carriageway. Hold on." She disappeared for a moment. "I think there's a roundabout in a couple of miles. But even then I'm half an hour away. It'll be like a needle in a haystack. I can call some people but I think they'll tell me the same. Shit."

"This is when you need your private army," I said.

"Indeed. Listen, thanks for the call. Let me get onto it, okay?"

I put down the phone. It was pointless. I knew it. By the time Amy made it back to us, Clare could already be dead.

***

Clare pulled into the car park of the sports ground as directed and killed the engine. It was deserted, as she'd expected it to be. She got out of the car and waited, leaning against the driver's door, taking deep lungfuls of the crisp morning air. The field was covered in dew. There was no sound apart from the tweeting of birds. Then came the steady approach of an engine.

Two men got out of the car. One pointed a gun at her, while the other patted her down. He removed her phone and threw it to his colleague, who managed to catch it in one hand, without ever losing his aim.

When they were sure she didn't have any concealed weapons, they tied her arms behind her back and fitted a blindfold, then bundled her into the boot of the car.

The journey took no longer than ten minutes. She could hear gravel under the wheels as the speed slowed, and then the car came to a halt. A moment later, the boot lid popped open, and the blindfold was removed. She squinted, dazzled by the light.

A man, dressed in black, grabbed her arm and roughly pulled her out of the car. She stumbled, but he dragged her back upright, and then pushed her in the direction of the barn.

It was dark inside, and musty. There was a dampness in the air. A door opened in front of her, and then she saw Louise, looking bruised and beaten, tied to a chair. Clare's heart was broken. She hated to think that she was the cause of this. Next time, she said to herself, no matter how much she insists, the answer will be no. But there could never be a next time.

Out of nowhere, some sort of bat or truncheon connected with the back of her knees, sending her collapsing to the floor. She screamed in pain. Louise was struggling, desperate to help, but there was no way to escape the chair. The bindings were far too tight.

On the opposite side of the room, a door opened and the familiar form of Anatoly appeared, followed by another man who fitted the description she'd been given of Adam. So this was it. Time to let them have their fun.

Chapter 52

"WE meet again," said the big Russian. "I'd say it was a pleasure, but I suspect it's less so for you than me."

Clare was still on the ground, unsure if her legs could support her weight. She didn't think they were broken, but there was a stabbing pain on each where the truncheon had connected.

"You got what you wanted," she spat. "You can let Louise go now."

He laughed.

"And have her miss the fun? She's got to learn that there are consequences to her deception. Although obviously, how much opportunity she'll have to make use of that education is the subject of some debate."

Louise looked terrible. Her beautiful face was covered in bruises. Was it the result of the car crash, or had they been abusing her? Clare felt sick at the thought, horrific images of torture running through her mind. She knew Louise wouldn't have given her up lightly. They meant far too much to each other for that.

She watched while Louise struggled again, trying to break

free, trying to come to her rescue. Then again as one of the armed thugs slapped her hard across the face, her neck snapping back. Clare hated to see that, more than she'd hated anything in her life before, but she was powerless to stop it.

The man who'd hit Louise returned to his position in the group encircling Clare, all pointing their weapons down in her direction.

"What do you want from me?" she asked, trying to keep the fear from her voice. Trying to be brave for Louise.

"I think we both want different things," said Anatoly. "I want to know what you know. What Grzegorz told you. What you have done with that information. How many copies there are, and where they're kept. My colleague here is more interested in making you pay for trying to deceive him." He nodded in the direction of Adam.

"And if I don't tell you?"

"Then we make you watch while your young friend suffers. And believe me, I don't think you'd want that."

Clare tried to assess her options. But there were none. There was no way to escape. She'd never get out alive. And there was no point even trying, unless she could take Louise with her. But to manage that, she'd have to overcome Anatoly, Adam, their five armed accomplices, and who-knew-how-many behind the scenes. It was a pointless waste of energy even thinking about it. All she could do was try to prolong the moment, and hope for some miracle like a lightning strike or an earthquake. But, in truth, that was even less likely than disarming five gun-wielding Russians.

"You assume that Greg told me things," she said. "I told you, we were in Warsaw to pay our respects and to find out what had happened to him. What makes you think he told me anything?"

From behind, the truncheon cracked across her ankles. She screamed in pain.

"I'm not here to play games, I'm a busy man," Anatoly continued. "So cut the bullshit and tell me what I want to know."

It took a moment for Clare to get her breath back, and the gasps of pain to subside.

"Okay," she said, her voice strained, "but what happens if I tell you?"

"For you the outcome will be the same, either way. It's a matter of how much pain you both have to endure to get there."

"I'm sorry," she said, then swallowed. "I will tell you. But how will you know I'm telling the truth? What if I've made other copies that I haven't told you about? As an insurance against exactly this kind of situation?"

"Then the people who have the copies will discover the downside of looking after them for you." He came closer then crouched down in front of her. "So let's start at the beginning with what he told you."

So this was it. There was no way to prolong it any longer.

"I knew he was looking into corruption in Warsaw," she started. "The city is being rebuilt. We all know that. But the planning laws seem to be applied at random. He was interested in why that was. Did anyone actually have a vision for what the city would become? And why were buildings popping up all over. Who owned the land? Who gave the permission? Who was bribing who?"

"That's an encouraging start," he said, standing back up, his knees creaking in the process. "And what conclusions had he come to?"

From the corner of her eye, Clare could see a man holding a baseball bat. So that was what had hit her. He was in addition to the five with guns. She was even more outnumbered than she'd thought, although in reality it wasn't going to make any difference.

"He'd discovered names of corrupt officials within local government," she continued. "He'd traced the shell companies of the developers back to their ultimate owners. And where there seemed to be unusual decisions, he linked the two together. He'd linked specific members of the Russian mafia with particular people in Poland, and had bank records of the payments that had been exchanged between them. Of course, it was going to be a scandal. The Russians would go back to Russia, but the Poles would be exposed, and left to face the consequences. And yet he couldn't go to the police with it all, because he knew there was corruption there as well."

"But he felt he wanted to interfere? I have to ask why, when it was all working in such harmony?"

"Because it was wrong. Because it wasn't just planning. That was the start. Then there was the drugs trade. The supply of girls from Russia and Ukraine for prostitution. It was becoming a lawless city at a time when there should have been great hope for everyone."

"And you're saying none of these changes are for the better?"

Clare was tired of this. Tired of fighting. Aware that she was one person against huge, ruthless criminal organisations, and that her own track record was hardly flawless.

"Obviously some of the things happening in Warsaw are wonderful," she said. "He didn't have a problem with those. The freedom of movement. The influx of products in the shops. All of the social and political changes that led to improvements for everybody. They're fantastic. But not everyone is playing by the rules."

"And where do I come into this?" asked Adam. It was the first time she'd heard him speak. She turned slightly to address him directly.

"You were the point man over here. Nothing to do with the planning, but with extensive contacts in the underworld, so that the Russians could expand their other areas of interest with a local person to help them. Although don't get too comfortable. I've seen first hand that this kind of relationship doesn't last long once you stop being useful to them." Divide and conquer. It was a desperate last attempt.

"Good try," he said. "But why do you think they came to me? My mother is Russian. She has family connections that ensure nothing will ever happen to me."

"Good for you."

"And where is this information now?" asked Anatoly, taking the conversation back to Warsaw.

Clare swept her hands through her hair, and took a deep breath. This was the final piece of the jigsaw. Once she told them this, it would all be over.

"He made copies," she said. "He never gave one to me. But I know there were some hidden in his apartment. I went to find them, but the whole place had been cleared. I think if you pull the sofas apart, or look inside the mattresses, you'll probably find them. I'm not aware of any others. I've got one question for you, though, if you don't mind me asking."

He thought for a moment, then nodded.

"Go on."

"The person he was supposed to have killed, in his apartment. Who was that?"

Anatoly chuckled.

"That was one of his informers. He double-crossed our organisation, and he paid the price."

"I thought as much."

She watched as he took a step back. Adam did the same. All around her, she could hear the sound of guns being cocked.

"Any more questions?" she asked.

Anatoly looked to Adam, who shook his head.

"No," he said. "I think we're very nearly done."

And that was when the doors caved in.

Chapter 53

"WE can't just sit around doing nothing," I said. Danny was as agitated as I was. "Although we haven't got a car. I have no idea where we even are."

"Let's go down to the bar," he said. "See if we can speak to someone. Then, I don't know, call a cab, do something. Anything."

It wasn't much, but it was a start.

I tied the laces of my DMs, while Danny fastened his coat.

"Pass me mine, will you," I said.

He crossed to the coat rack, on the wall by the door.

"That's weird," he said.

"Are you looking in a mirror again?" I said, although I don't know why.

"Is this yours?" he asked, ignoring me, but holding up a navy blue jacket.

"No, it looks like Clare's. Mine was black."

He checked the pockets, and took out a packet of Silk Cut and a lighter.

"Looks like it," he said. "Why did she leave her coat? I'm sure she was wearing one when she set off."

And then I started to smile like I'd never smiled before.

"Did it look a bit on the small side?" I asked.

"Actually, yes, now you mention it. I thought it was a bit odd."

Danny clearly didn't know why I was beaming from ear to ear.

"Oh Clare," I said. "You clever, clever woman."

The gunfire was deafening. Clare rolled herself into a ball, as tightly as she could. Her eyes were burning where the tear gas was taking hold. All around was chaos. Men running, shouting, falling to the floor.

And then gradually it all subsided.

Her first instinct was to run to Louise, to check she was okay. There was blood all over her clothes.

Surely not. No.

Somebody big shoved her forcefully out of the way, while someone else started cutting the bindings and removing the gag. Between them, Clare was looking for signs of life. Any sign. Even just a glimmer. But the paramedics were blocking her view, and her eyes stung too much to see anything clearly.

And then, miraculously, she saw Louise stand. She stumbled, her legs clearly weak. They laid her on the floor. Clare could just make out the shapes. And then Louise's arm moved, with her thumb aloft, and Clare knew that everything was going to be okay.

"You took your time," said Clare. But she'd never been so pleased to see Amy. The detective was leaning on the bonnet of her car, while all around, others in uniforms set to work.

"Sorry about that," Amy said, in a tone laced with faux castigation. "But hopefully that'll teach you a lesson to behave yourself in future."

"I'm a bloody angel, me," said Clare. "It's everybody else you want to worry about."

"I'm not a hundred percent convinced by that. Well done for taking Anna's coat, though."

"I heard you say you'd put a tracker in it. I just had to hope it had a decent battery, and you'd actually think to check it."

"It's constantly monitored back at the station."

Clare shuddered.

"I'd better give it back then."

Just then, Louise emerged on a stretcher, heading to the waiting ambulance. Clare went running over. She looked in a bad way, but her eyes were open and she was smiling as much as the pain would allow.

"I thought that was it," Louise whispered. "I was convinced we were both going to die."

"I told you. Until death do us part, and I'm not going to let that happen any time soon," said Clare, warmly. She reached across and squeezed the only hand that was visible above the blankets. "The hospital will take care of you now. I've got to sort things with Amy, but I'll come to get you soon."

"Love you," said Louise.

"Love you too."

Clare watched the ambulance depart, then took a deep breath, aware of just how close that had been. She turned back to Amy.

"Anatoly? Adam?"

"Dead. And three of their men. The others are injured but under arrest."

Clare nodded.

"You've done well. I'm going to be a marked woman, but at least that'll put the brakes on them for now."

"It will. But I can't protect you for ever. You're playing a very, very dangerous game."

Clare sighed.

"But that's the thing. It's not a game. It's what I've always done. Fight corruption, expose it."

She stopped, her mind drifting off, thinking of all the battles yet to be faced, and then looking around at all of the activity. A covered body was being removed on a stretcher. Reflexively she fished in her coat pocket, then turned back to Amy.

"I'm aware you're going to have lots of questions," she said. "But most important of all, has anyone got a cigarette?"

Chapter 54

Monday, January 27th, 1997

HAVING never had a proper job until recently, I'd never taken a sickie. But there was no way I felt up to going in to the office, given the events of the weekend. I spoke to Nathan, remembering to sound croaky, and cough at regular intervals, and said I thought I'd feel much better by the morning.

In any case, Clare had invited Danny and me to lunch at her flat in Knightsbridge. She was collecting Louise from the hospital in the morning, and apparently they wanted to tell us something important.

"All credit to them both," I said to Danny as we walked from the bus stop. "I'm very open-minded about these things, but when you think of the age difference ..."

"Are you saying it won't last?" he asked.

"Notwithstanding my opinion on relationships generally, I don't know. It's like ..." But I didn't really know what I thought. Good luck to them both, I suppose. "I can't help wanting to ask, to paraphrase Mrs Merton, 'So what first attracted you to the millionaire Clare Woodbrook?'"

"You are terrible."

"I'm not. But she's nearly forty."

"She's thirty-four."

"Precisely my point."

Danny pressed the doorbell, and once we were buzzed in, we began the long climb to the top floor.

"You'd think with the price of these, they'd at least install a lift," I said.

"Shhh," said Danny. "Anyway, now you're a gym bunny, I thought you'd be glad of the exercise."

"Never, ever, say that phrase again."

"Exercise?"

"No. The other one. I can't believe you even said it, and I'm certainly not going to repeat it. But if you do, my offer of a room will be rescinded."

"You're offering me a room?"

But I didn't have time to answer. The door swung open and there was Clare. I handed her the bottle of wine I'd brought, and she gave us both a peck on the cheek. Louise was lying under a blanket on one of the leather horseshoe sofas. She looked tired and bruised but it was wonderful to see her. She sat up when she saw us.

"Drink?" asked Clare.

"Rude not to," I said.

"Make yourselves comfortable and I'll be straight through."

Louise made space for us to join her on the sofa.

"How you feeling?" asked Danny. "You look like you've been in the wars."

"But very good considering," I added, giving him a nudge. First rule of life: never suggest to a woman that she looks a bit on the rough side, even if she has an excuse. Actually, that's the second. The first is to never use phrases like *gym bunny*. Ewww.

"I'm okay," she said. "Slightly sore, and I was a bit dehydrated, but there won't be any lasting scars. At least, not physical ones."

The first shock was that she said all of that without a Polish accent.

"Sorry?" I said.

"What?"

"I completely missed what you said. I was sidetracked by the way you said it."

"I said I was fine, no damage done."

I turned to Danny.

"Did you hear that?" I asked. "She just did it again."

They both looked at me as though I was the odd one.

"Your voice," I said. "The accent."

"Ah."

Clare came through and handed us each a glass of cold white wine.

"I told you," said Louise. "I wanted to be an actress. I thought it'd be fun to try an accent."

"Hold on." This was all a bit much to take in. "You mean you're not Polish?"

"Never even been to Poland," she said with a grin. Then winced with the effort.

"What do you mean you've never even been to Poland?" I persisted. Danny had started to giggle.

"I was playing a role. So I thought, if I was going to do that, I might as well go the full distance. It could be a laugh. And it had a practical benefit too. If anything ever got awkward, I could play the foreigner-not-knowing-the-language card."

I turned to Clare.

"Did you know this?" Of course she knew this. She'd organised the whole thing. I turned back to Louise. "So who even are you? You're obviously not Clare's niece."

"No." Louise looked at Clare. "And I'm actually only eighteen rather than nineteen, not that it makes much difference. Do you want to tell them or should I?"

"I'll do it," said Clare, then paused, as though to give us time to prepare for the big announcement. But what she said next floored me. "She's my daughter."

"What?" said Danny, choking on his drink.

I couldn't think of anything to say that wasn't unladylike.

"You don't have a daughter," he continued, in disbelief.

"I do." She reached out an arm, and wrapped it round Louise. And then I could see it. It was in the eyes.

"But you're not old enough," Danny persisted.

"I know," said Clare. "I was sixteen. Which was why I wasn't able to keep her. And it broke my heart."

"Bloody hell," was all I could manage.

"But I had no idea," said Danny. "In all the years I've known you."

"No."

She looked close to tears. I couldn't imagine how that must have felt. The immediate, overwhelming love a mother feels for a newborn child, and then having the child taken away. That must be an incredible burden to carry. A deep, unimaginable loss. It didn't give Clare an excuse for everything she'd done, but I suspected it was a factor. There were so many questions to ask, but I wasn't sure that now was the time.

"But when we had our long conversation in Venice," I said at last, "we told each other everything, and you never said anything about being a mother."

"You didn't ask," said Clare, with a smile. "I promised you I'd give you an honest answer to any question you could think of. You asked about boyfriends and where I lived, but you didn't ask if I had any children. Anyway, you weren't supposed to ever mention that again."

Danny didn't know about our conversation in Venice. That would take some explaining.

"I don't know if you can imagine how painful it is to lose a child," Clare continued. "So no, it wasn't something I ever wanted to talk about. I threw myself into work, relentlessly pursuing injustice, because deep down, I bore the scars of the greatest injustice of all. I wasn't even allowed to visit."

I could see the hurt and fury in her eyes.

"It was unbearable," she continued. "I cracked eventually. I'm not proud of what I did. And I know that I'm a terrible role model. But when she turned eighteen I managed to track her down."

"I wouldn't have ever had a chance of finding Mum," said Louise.

"Exactly," said Clare. "I made it my primary focus, and here we are."

"You called her 'Mum'," I said, fighting hard to keep the incredulity from my voice.

She laughed.

"I only did that for effect. I've kind of got used to calling her Clare, now."

"So you're not actually called Agnieszka, then?" said Danny. "With whatever the surname was."

She shook her head.

"That was my little joke," said Clare. "I thought if we were going for the Polish thing then we might as well choose the most ridiculously complicated Polish name, mainly for the fun of seeing people try to spell it."

"And Greg wasn't your father?"

Louise shook her head.

"But you are called Louise?" I asked.

Again she shook her head.

"Actually Lucy," she said. And a knowing look passed between Clare and Danny that I didn't really understand.

"Okay, so I messed up and nearly let it slip," said Clare. "It won't happen again."

"She referred to Louise as Lucy when we were in Warsaw," Danny explained. "She said she sometimes called her that for short. Despite it having the same number of syllables."

"Hang on – sorry," I said, feeling indignant all of a sudden, and not giving a stuff for protocol. "You sent your own daughter into a bloody long con crew and nearly got her killed."

But Clare was shaking her head.

"That was totally my fault," said Louise. "I insisted."

"What do you mean you insisted?" I asked.

"When we met up, and once we got to know each other, she told me about all the things she'd done. And I thought it was amazing and exciting and I wanted to be part of it. So I asked if I could help."

"I said no, obviously," said Clare.

"But I kept on and on about it. And she still said no. So I kept on and on and on until she finally said yes."

"I told you," said Clare. "Pester power. It's what children do." She winked at Louise. "So in the end I agreed, but with the strictest of conditions."

"That's why she wanted me to stay with you. She trusts you. She thought you'd be able to keep an eye on me."

"Oh, so it's my fault now?" I said.

Clare laughed.

"No, anything but. I think she has a genetic disposition to get into trouble. Which again is my fault. Anyway, she's grounded now, which admittedly is a bit late in the process, and I'm not sure it applies when you're eighteen."

"And I don't listen to you anyway," said Louise with a grin. And then I could see it again. The same spirit of independence, the same spark of mischief, and the same steely determination.

"So what now?" I asked. There were so many more questions. Who was Lucy's father? Was I still going to have a lodger? If not, where was she going to live? What was she going to do? Was this the end of Clare's relentless mysteriousness?

"First things first, we've got to get her better," said Clare. "And we're going to get Harry better too. That might take a bit longer, but I spoke to him this morning. He's conscious and the prognosis is good."

"That's great news," I said. "And then?

"And then we're taking a little trip to Frankfurt," said Clare.

I hardly dared think what that meant, nor dared look at Danny. We were going to have to have a long talk about lots of things, but now wasn't really the time.

"Well," I said, draining my glass. "I think this calls for a drink."

The end.

SPECIAL THANKS...

Illusions Of Warsaw was as much fun to write as ever - not least because of a fascinating week spent exploring the Polish capital.

Special thanks to the amazing Darren McQuade - magician, actor, comedian, and good friend - for technical advice when it came to making things disappear.

As ever, there were candles and background music to help set the mood. Massive Ego's amazing Beautiful Suicide album was the most played, with a nod to Blume and Kirlian Camera.

Of course I am forever grateful to my editor, Carrie O'Grady, for vision and encouragement - and to Carol Lewis for proof reading beyond the call of duty.

Many thanks, as ever, to the advance readers and everyone who has left a review of one of the books on Amazon, Kobo, Nook, Apple, Goodreads or elsewhere. Your feedback and encouragement are a massive help and motivation. It is hugely, hugely appreciated.

FEEL FREE TO SAY HELLO... :-)

If you enjoyed the book, have any queries, or just want to say hello, I'd love to hear from you via www.davidbradwell.com. While you're there, you can download a **FREE copy of the series prequel** - In The Frame:

You can also follow me on Twitter: @dbshq - or see what Anna is up to: @AnnaBurginNW1

If you enjoyed Illusions Of Warsaw, you should read **Cold Press** - the first full-length book in the Anna Burgin series.

London. 1993. Investigative journalist Clare Woodbrook goes missing on the brink of unveiling her biggest-ever story. Is it kidnap? Murder?

Worse still, the police investigation into her disappearance is being headed up by a corrupt DCI - himself the subject of one of Clare's current investigations.

Clare's researcher Danny Churchill sets out to find her, and enlists the help of his flatmate - feisty fashion photographer Anna Burgin. But they soon realise that nobody can be trusted. And as the search becomes ever more desperate, suddenly their own lives are very much on the line.

Packed with intrigue, twists, conspiracies, and dark humour, Cold Press is a hugely entertaining British thriller, with a sting in the tail.

Order Cold Press NOW in print or ebook format at Amazon, Kobo, Barnes & Noble, Apple and more.

After Cold Press, the story continues in **Out Of the Red** - book 2
in the Anna Burgin series.

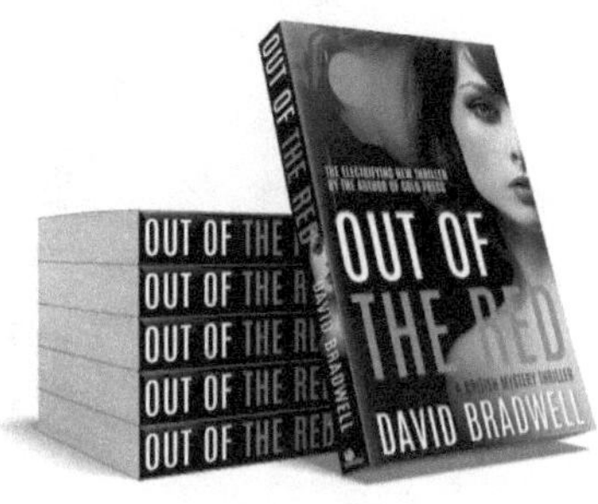

The gripping, twist-filled sequel to Cold Press.

Investigative journalist Danny Churchill is hot on the trail of
Graham March - the disgraced former police DCI. The
investigation takes him to Germany where he soon starts to
uncover dark secrets and new depths of depravity.

Back in London, and aided by his flatmate - fashion photographer
Anna Burgin - Danny's investigation intensifies, but as he gets
closer to the truth, the body count starts to rise.

*Help is offered from the most unlikely of sources, but if Danny
accepts, is he doing a deal with the devil herself?*

Order Out Of The Red NOW in print or ebook format at
Amazon, Kobo, Barnes & Noble, Apple and more.

Book 3 - **In The Frame,** the series prequel novella, is available as a FREE ebook at www.davidbradwell.com.

In The Frame takes us back to Anna and Danny's student years and explains how they became friends in the first place.

Photography student Anna Burgin didn't expect to be arrested, but she's the only suspect for a series of crimes, and the Police have found damning evidence in her room.

But Anna has no recollection of doing anything wrong. Was it a moment of madness? Or is somebody setting out to destroy her?

And is the stranger in the bar really trying to help, or just part of an evil conspiracy?

The sequel to Out Of The Red is book 4: **Fade To Silence.**

You know you've got problems when being hunted by a Serbian hitman is the least of your worries...

Balkan gangsters, corporate spies and a fugitive killer are all on the loose in London, but when a body shows up, all of the evidence points to the victim's wife.

Journalist Danny Churchill wants to find the truth. But when reports emerge of a huge shipment of weapons heading to the UK, it soon becomes the most dangerous and action-packed investigation so far.

Packed with twists, intrigue and dark humour, Fade To Silence is book 4 in the bestselling Anna Burgin series.

Order Fade To Silence NOW in print or ebook format at Amazon, Kobo, Barnes & Noble, Apple and more.

The sequel to Fade To Silence is **Court Me Kill Me.**

What if the only person you can trust is secretly plotting to kill you?

Fashion photographer Anna Burgin faces a career in ruins after her studio is destroyed, but when armed police burst into her home, she realises it's the least of her worries.

Murders in Seattle, Frankfurt, Venice and London all point to one common killer - and the chief suspect has just been in her house. The evidence is compelling, the body count is rising, but as news emerges of a corrupt business network that reaches into the heart of the police, nothing can be taken for granted - especially the promises of the person who offers to protect her.

Packed with twists, intrigue and dark humour, Court Me Kill Me is book 5 in the bestselling Anna Burgin series.

Order Court Me Kill Me NOW in print or ebook formats at Amazon, Kobo, Barnes & Noble, Apple and more

I had one last page, so all that remains to say is:

THANK YOU!

There will be more… but in the meantime, see www.davidbradwell.com for news, updates, and behind the scenes photography.